Beetlebrow
The Thief

Ben Parker

Beetlebrow The Thief
Published by The Conrad Press in the United Kingdom 2018

Tel: +44(0)1227 472 874
www.theconradpress.com
info@theconradpress.com

ISBN 978-1-911546-31-3

Copyright © Ben Parker, 2018

The moral right of Ben Parker to be identified as author of this work has been asserted in accordance with the Copyright, Designs and Patents Act 1988.

All rights reserved.

Typesetting and Cover Design by:
Charlotte Mouncey, www.bookstyle.co.uk

The Conrad Press logo was designed by Maria Priestley.

Printed and bound in Great Britain by Clays Ltd, St Ives plc

For Mum and Dad

With thanks to my publisher and editor, James Essinger, and to Penny Tobin and Kevin Jones

1
Lana

Beetlebrow woke up.

She heard footsteps outside the door.

Sixteen and skinny, with coppery skin and a threadbare grey robe, she felt hunger gnawing inside her. She pushed away her thin brown blanket. As she got to her feet, she heard carts clattering through the streets four storeys below.

She saw the light of the winter morning seeping through the single grimy window on her left. She heard her two half-brothers, Alder and Joe, snoring by the beige plaster wall to her right. Flies were settling on the empty wine-jars beside their crumpled grey blankets.

Beetlebrow knew which floorboards were prone to creaking. Her cold toes threaded a narrow path across the room's quiet planks. She passed the sleeping bodies of Alder and Joe with silent steps.

The door swung inwards. Her mother stumbled into the room. Beetlebrow saw the exhaustion in Lana's downcast gaze, and caught the scent of pomegranate perfume.

Her mother's left hand was clasping her mud-spattered, high-heeled shoes against her tight black robe. Beetlebrow noticed that the night had worn through the rose-pink make-up on Lana's lips, through the blue tint on her eyelids and the rouge on her cheeks.

Beetlebrow's hands reached out and held her shoulders. 'Mum, you need to sleep.'

Alder and Joe were getting up from their blankets. Beetlebrow glanced right. She saw the two stocky, black-bearded figures coming across the room.

Alder's face loomed above her. She felt his shadow on her body. Beetlebrow glared up into his heavy-lidded, bloodshot eyes.

Alder shoved her with his beefy right hand, and pushed her down onto the floor.

Joe started scooping copper coins from the pockets of Lana's robe.

'Mum needs to eat too, Joe!' Beetlebrow snapped, hurrying to her feet.

She darted left around Alder, and headed towards her mother. Lana glanced at her. Their gazes met.

Alder stepped in front of his sister. He leant downwards, his lip curling. 'Stay out of it, Beetlebrow.'

'Don't call your sister "Beetlebrow",' Lana said, her voice sounding tired and low. 'Call her Emma. That's her name.'

'What else could she be called,' Alder said, 'with those eyebrows of hers?'

'Don't be rude,' Lana replied. 'Her eyebrows are lovely. They remind me of her father's. But... of course, hers aren't as bushy.'

Lana dropped her blue, high-heeled shoes onto the floor, and began to lie down slowly on her blanket on the floorboards.

'Now, Joe,' Lana said, 'you give your sister a coin for some bread.'

Beetlebrow saw Joe glance at Alder and roll his eyes.

'Yes, Mum, whatever you say, Mum,' Joe replied.

Alder stepped away from Beetlebrow.

She watched Joe approaching. He avoided his sister's gaze as he doled out a single copper coin into her open palm. Beetlebrow grasped the small, flattened piece of circular metal within her left fist. She looked at her mother, and saw Lana's eyes were closed.

Alder and Joe hurried out of the doorway. Beetlebrow heard her brothers' footsteps rattling away down the wooden staircase. She knelt down beside her mother's blanket.

Lana's eyes slowly opened. Her left hand stretched out towards her daughter's hair. Beetlebrow felt her mother's fingers running through its long, black strands. She remembered being a child, and her mother combing through its knots with a stiff wooden brush.

Lana winced. Beetlebrow saw her remaining gaudy make-up starting to crack, and the tiredness in her face, etched in the lines across her forehead, and the bags under her eyes.

Every evening, when the light of day failed, she would watch Lana put on those high-heeled shoes and walk down the stairs. She knew where her mother was heading; down to the darkness of a street corner, to wait for men to come past and buy her for a few copper coins.

'Mum, you know I could work for a stall-keeper or something,' Beetlebrow said. 'There's always someone needs errands run. Tanners need people to pick up after dogs and horses. I could earn good money doing that. You wouldn't need to go out so much.'

Lana slowly shook her head. 'They wouldn't hire you, darling. There's only one job round here for a girl... that's why I want you to stay at home, with me.'

'There's got to be something I can do.'

'Just take the coin,' Lana whispered. 'Go and get yourself some bread.'

Beetlebrow stared.

'Please, my love,' Lana went on, 'you must feed yourself. You have to eat.'

'I'll bring back bread for us,' Beetlebrow said. 'For both of us.'

Lana, still lying on the floor, slowly nodded. Her eyes were closed. Beetlebrow touched her left shoulder. Lana did not move.

Beetlebrow opened her mouth to speak. She saw the stillness of her mother's body.

Sleep will help her, Beetlebrow thought. *Talking won't.*

She felt her eyes pricking. She looked at the door. 'I'll be quick getting the bread, Mum.'

2
Pook

Beetlebrow ran down four flights of dim, steep staircases and across the second-floor landing.

She spotted a sallow, short-bearded man rocking a dozing baby in his arms beside an open window. Beetlebrow nodded to him as she went by, before speeding down the last pair of staircases and stepping out the front door onto the bare earth of the narrow street outside.

She saw the light of the new day coursing through the thin river of a lane between the surrounding grey buildings. She smelt the sweating reek of liquid garbage spilling through the smoky air of the neighbourhood.

She glanced back over her left shoulder and looked beyond the tangled miles of streets to the north. Her gaze turned towards the white tower of the palace looming above the distant Capitat district.

She imagined breaking through one of its slender windows. She imagined her feet gliding along marble tiles set between the golden walls of an endless corridor.

Her route towards the palace felt infused with years of memories, as her steps had traced its path across her days and her thoughts had marked its turns and alterations across her nights.

She heard the snapping bark of a dog overhead. She glimpsed two teenage gangsters posing in their crisp silken robes on a flat rooftop above the street.

The two glared down at her. Beetlebrow lowered her eyes.

She became aware of her bare soles, rooted down in the dusty earth, and the copper coin in her hand.

She ran south down the street, leaping over the piles of fish-heads and pottery shards, and stepped into the market square.

She glanced around at the patch of dusty earth, its boundaries hemmed in on all four sides by flat-faced buildings, and saw women and men drifting between the salesmen sitting cross-legged in the dirt bearing bowls of sparse grains and stunted vegetables. The customers' feet were slow and their eyes drifting; their pockets were as empty as their stomachs.

Beetlebrow headed towards the flat-roofed, mud-brick bakery on the right of the market. She saw the short, spry, grey-haired figure of Elisa darting a tray of doughy loaves into the domed clay oven at the rear of the three-walled building.

Two policemen were leaning against the back wall of the square. Their tunics were red. Slats of brown leather armour covered their shoulders and arms. Their black-gloved hands were gripping the clubs strapped to their belts.

Elisa handed a loaf to the tall man at the front of the line and then took his copper coin. The tall man trudged away from the bakery. The remaining queue of three men took a step closer towards the counter.

Beetlebrow's stomach felt hollow as she joined the back of the line. She glanced right, and noticed a thin man sitting between a patch of leafy weeds below the cracked plaster of a beige-coloured wall. His head was slumped down against the chest of his blackened rags.

Beetlebrow looked at the three people standing ahead of her in the queue. Two were shaven-headed young men; the first was shifting his feet in the dirt – his lean face glancing around the market square – while the chubby second man was staring at Elisa.

Beetlebrow recognised the white-bearded widower reaching up towards the counter, his back hunched over in front of his shaky hands. She saw Elisa take Dessen's copper coin and hand him a small, round loaf in return.

She recalled a morning, nine years ago, when Lana had taken her by the hand through the streets and up the stairs to Dessen's third-floor flat. His wife had died the day before, killed in the market by a kick from a mule. Beetlebrow remembered seeing the square pinewood table standing at the centre of Dessen's single room. There had been two white-painted wickerwork chairs set underneath it. Dessen had been perched on a three-legged wooden stool by the whitewashed wall at the back of the room. A dusty crib had stood in a corner to his left. Beetlebrow remembered thinking how small Dessen had looked, staring down at the floor while Lana had offered her condolences.

She watched him shambling away from the bakery, his shuffling step barely disturbing the earth beneath his feet.

The line moved forwards a pace. Beetlebrow stepped with them. The two shaven-headed men slapped their copper coins down onto the counter.

Beetlebrow caught the yeasty scent of the loaves. Her empty stomach twinged.

Her gaze drifted left, to a grey building standing roughly twenty paces away from the bakery.

Beetlebrow noticed a skinny girl sitting at the foot of its mud-brick wall. Her skin had a rich cinnamon hue, her cheekbones were high, her tunic made from an old grain sack and her long, coal-black curly hair was tied up behind her head with a rag of sky-blue cloth. Beetlebrow guessed her to be around seventeen.

The girl was cupping her empty hands in front of her lap. Beetlebrow watched a grizzled, middle-aged man walking past the mud-brick wall, the crutch under his right arm striking the dry earth beside his sandaled feet. The girl looked up at his face. The man walked by. The girl lowered her eyes.

'What do you call this?' a man shouted from beside the bakery.

Beetlebrow faced towards the voice.

The thin shaven-headed man was holding up a grey-brown loaf towards Elisa while he cast his gaze around at the market.

'This bread's half the size it was last week!' he shouted.

'I'm sorry it's not as much,' Elisa replied, 'but the taxes -'

'...and still King Ancissus rules,' the thin man cried, 'with the golden hands of the House of Rashem around our necks! Holed up in Capitat, the monarchs in their palace behind the wall are draining us dry!'

'And they give us nothing!' the chubby man shouted.

Beetlebrow noticed his right hand sliding underneath his robe and slipping out a round wooden baton. She felt her body tensing.

'... while they live in luxury!' the chubby man went on.

'That's right...!' a man on the left shouted.

Beetlebrow saw his clean-shaven face scowling at Elisa. He was holding the hand of a toddler girl.

'And our rulers don't care!' the thin, shaven-headed man shouted. 'The city can be ours again, as it was centuries ago! Our comrades in the north of the Capitat district have kept the siege around the palace for over a year, refusing the royals entry into Stellingkorr. We can stop money getting back to them too, by refusing to buy anything the royals have taxed! Citizens, join me in taking the bread from this corrupt baker! Seize whatever you can!'

Women and men started surging towards the bakery. Elisa scrambled out its back door. The crowd leapt over the counter. They rushed towards the shelves.

Beetlebrow watched the frenzied hands tearing the loaves into white plumes. She gripped her single coin within her fist.

'May the House of Rashem fall to ashes!' a voice screamed out.

Beetlebrow saw a line of ten uniformed police advancing into the market from a street to the left. Seven men in black robes were running towards them from the right.

Beetlebrow noticed Dessen walking away from the square. He was holding his single loaf under his arm. A stout man rushed past him. His right shoulder struck the old widower's body. Dessen's thin frame crumpled down onto the ground. The bread spilled from his hands while the stout man ran deeper into the market square.

Beetlebrow hurried over towards Dessen. She knelt down by his side. She felt dust filling her throat.

Dessen looked up at her face. His sepia eyes widened. He grabbed the little loaf from the ground and clutched it against his chest.

'No,' Beetlebrow said, 'I wasn't going to...'

She heard batons cracking and voices screaming. Red and brown uniforms were charging into the broiling clouds of dust.

A hobnailed boot stepped on Beetlebrow's right ankle. Pain streaked up her leg. Her teeth clenched together.

'Death to the king!' a voice shrieked.

Beetlebrow noticed a pile of wooden crates stacked close to a grey plaster wall on the left side of the market. She hurried to her feet and started running across the swelling beige clouds of dust in the square.

A black-bearded man staggered past her. Syrupy blood was soaking through his hair.

Beetlebrow spotted a thin, rusted little fruit knife and two fat little figs in a discarded bowl on the ground. She bent down and grabbed them as she sped onwards. She slipped the knife into the pocket of her ragged robe.

She was breathing fast as she looked ahead. She noticed the skinny girl was sitting behind the shelter of the crates. Her back was against the wall. Her knees were huddled up around her sackcloth tunic.

A man's scream tore across the market.

Beetlebrow hurried behind the crates. She felt their shadow covering her body as she sat down by the wall. She glimpsed the girl sitting to her right.

The girl looked at her. Beetlebrow shared her gaze. She saw the black centres of the girl's brown eyes were wide and full.

Beetlebrow glanced downwards. She felt sweat itching against her armpits and emptiness pressing against her stomach. She heard the melee storming through the market, and noticed the two figs in her left palm.

She looked at the girl again, and held out her hand.

She saw a smile of even, white teeth spreading out across the girl's face. Beetlebrow glanced away.

'Are you staring at my eyebrows?' she asked. 'They are kind of big I guess. My brothers call me Beetlebrow.'

She looked at the girl again. She saw her smiling. Beetlebrow thought the coarseness of her sackcloth robe appeared rougher still below her grin.

The girl took one of the figs. 'I'm Pook.'

3
A single copper coin

'You, girls, come out of there!' a man's hoarse voice called.

Beetlebrow kept her back against the wall as she peered round the crates.

Dead bodies of women and men and children were lying in the settling dust of the market square, their hands open and their clothes torn and bloodied.

Beetlebrow saw police pulling the dusty bodies of people away from the square as casually as if they were sweeping crinkled leaves from an autumn path.

She noticed a thin-limbed teenage boy staring up through the drab morning light with sightless eyes. A toddler girl lay face down beside him.

A policeman was walking alone across the market. His hair was white and his cheeks saggy. The sun was reflecting the morning light across the silvery iron armour on his chest.

He glanced around at the square. His gaze settled on Beetlebrow and Pook.

'You don't need to hide any longer, girls...' the policeman said, the lines on his forehead sharpening.

Beetlebrow faced Pook, and saw her brown eyes looking back at her.

'Come on, girls...' the policeman said. 'Everything's back to normal. Order's been restored. Come out of there!'

'Pook!' a deep voice called from the right of the market.

Beetlebrow noticed the portly figure of Gozher emerging from the white arched doorway of his pillar-fronted house. She remembered hearing Alder and Joe talking about Gozher's house, hearing their voices discussing at night the girls there who would lay with men for a few coins.

'Pook, come to my house, girl, where it's safe,' Gozher called out across the market.

He peered out from his doorway, his purple-robed bulk hiding behind his black, chest-length beard and thinning tangle of stringy hair. 'Come and have a sit down, for an hour or two, where's it's warm.'

Pook stood up.

Beetlebrow watched her slim frame stepping away from the crates, walking across the dust of the square and entering Gozher's house.

The door closed behind her.

The sun passed behind clouds. Beetlebrow felt the glow of morning light dimming on her face. She noticed the broken baskets and cracked jars scattered across the dirt.

She looked at the bakery. Elisa was standing alone between the broken shelves, her arms folded as she stared down at the ground.

Beetlebrow slowly rose to her feet. She glanced at Gozher's door, and then headed towards the bakery.

She reached her left hand up to the dusty counter. She placed her copper coin onto its wooden surface.

Elisa glanced up. Her eyes met Beetlebrow's. Elisa's face crumpled into a smile. She stepped towards the counter, clasped Beetlebrow's hand within her own hard fingers and then headed away towards the remains of the shelves.

Beetlebrow noticed several women and men slowly walking back into the square from the nearby streets.

She saw Elisa returning to the counter holding two intact golden-brown loaves.

Beetlebrow lowered her hand.

She looked downwards. The single copper coin, its thin edges bumpy and misshapen, appeared small in the centre of her palm. Beetlebrow remembered it being all Lana could save from Alder and Joe.

She looked up at Elisa again. 'I've only the one copper...'

Elisa glanced across the market, and then faced her again.

'Keep it,' Elisa whispered. 'The extra loaf's for your mum. You get back to her quickly now.'

Beetlebrow nodded.

She wrapped the round loaves inside her ragged robe and looked north. Beyond the towering buildings was the white tower in the distant Capitat. To Beetlebrow it looked like a bulb of a plant rising from the earth.

4
Two loaves

Beetlebrow reached up, turned the handle and stepped back into the room. Alder and Joe were still out. Lana was lying on her blanket by the rear wall. Beetlebrow started walking towards her.

'Elisa gave me two loaves, Mum,' Beetlebrow said. 'She didn't even charge –'

She noticed the stiffness of her mother's skinny frame. Beetlebrow hurried across the floorboards. The loaves fell from her arms. She knelt down by Lana's side. She was trembling as she placed her hand on her mother's forehead. Lana's skin felt hard and still.

Beetlebrow stayed sitting on the floor. She tried to imagine being in this room without her mother; without hearing her voice, without seeing her opening the door.

The morning passed by. The slit of light from the single window slid between the walls. The two loaves of bread hardened in the middle of the frigid room.

Beetlebrow heard footsteps on the staircase. She flinched, looked up, and glanced around at the stillness of the room.

The door swung inwards. Alder and Joe swayed onto the floorboards.

'Please, Joe, Alder,' Beetlebrow said. 'Help me with Mum.'

Alder stopped in the doorway.

Joe slowly walked towards Beetlebrow, the staring gaze of his mahogany eyes set on the blanket where Lana lay.

He knelt down and placed two fingers against his mother's neck. He held his trembling hand against her throat for a few moments, and then took it away again.

'She's gone,' Joe said.

Beetlebrow looked down at her mother again. Lana's eyes were closed, her body still and her fingers rigid. Beetlebrow stared. Her mother, who used to walk with her through the city and tell her the name of every street they passed, was now a body on the floor.

Beetlebrow's arms started shaking. Her mouth was dry. She could not breathe.

Joe began feeling a corner of Lana's frayed grey blanket between his fingertips.

'We'll take her to the town grave,' Alder said.

Joe sniffed, hurriedly wiped his eyes and then started wrapping the blanket around Lana's lifeless body.

'Come on, Joe,' Alder said.

Joe heaved the bundled figure of Lana over his right shoulder and headed back across the floorboards.

Beetlebrow leapt to her feet, her gaze following her mother's body.

Joe carried Lana out of the doorway. Beetlebrow heard his steps creaking on the staircase outside.

She approached the doorway. Alder stepped into its frame. He stared down into his sister's eyes.

'You stay here,' he said.

He walked out the room and pulled the door closed behind himself. Beetlebrow heard the key turning in the lock.

She listened to her brothers walking away down the wooden staircase. Her breaths were fast and rough. She felt sweat covering her body. She wiped her forehead with her left sleeve.

She turned around, and saw her mother's high-heeled shoes lying together at the back of the room.

A fly landed on Alder's wrinkled blanket. Beetlebrow noticed fleas hopping in the folds of its woollen fabric. She scratched at the stomach of her grey robe, and felt the emptiness of her belly.

She thought of all the nights she had spent lying down in the darkness over the past few years, all the nights she had to ignore her growling stomach as she tried to grab hold of a few hours of sleep.

She glanced at the pair of round loaves on the centre of the floorboards. She walked over and sat down beside them. She picked one up. She felt the hard surface of the bread between her fingers.

She tore a piece away from its brown crust and slid it into her mouth. She wanted the bread to fill the hunger she could feel aching in her bones. Beetlebrow ate mouthful after mouthful until she had swallowed the first loaf. Where its taste would have been, she felt numb.

Hours drifted by. The afternoon rose, and the room became colder still.

Beetlebrow heard the door being unlocked. Alder and Joe sidled back into the room. Alder locked the door.

'Did you take Mum's body to the grave?' Beetlebrow slowly asked.

'That's right,' Alder said.

'Chucked some lime over it too,' Joe said.

Alder picked up the remaining loaf of bread and sat down against the wall on the right. He looked at Beetlebrow, and then pointed at a space on the floorboards in front of himself.

Beetlebrow glanced at Joe. He was leaning against the door, holding his hands behind his back. He was looking down at the floor.

Beetlebrow walked slowly over towards Alder and sat down cross-legged in front of him.

Alder rubbed the back of his right hand across his black beard.

'Now, girl, things are going to be different,' he said, staring down at his sister's face. 'Mum looked after us and now you'll look after us. You listening to me? I need your full attention here.'

He started tearing the loaf apart between his hands. Beetlebrow watched him wolfing down the bread, crumbs spilling from between his lips and catching in the furls of his beard.

'Right, Beetlebrow,' Alder said, 'from now on you'll be begging for us. We'll be taking you out at dawn, and you'll stay out until it's dark or until one of us collects you. During the day you'll sit in the streets we've chosen and look sad and hold out your hands. You can't spend any of the coins you get, but me and Joe'll bring you some bread now and then. Right?'

Beetlebrow glimpsed the key shining in his left hand.

'Say something, Beetlebrow,' Joe snapped.

She glanced at him.

'Don't look at Joe, look at me,' Alder said.

Beetlebrow faced Alder again. She saw his staring eyes searching across her face.

'I can do more than beg,' she replied. 'Perhaps I could be an apprentice somewhere, or do some sweeping –'

'You'll get used to begging, and you'll stop arguing,' Alder interrupted. 'You're just a girl; you've got no skills. You can't work like a man would, like me and Joe would, if those tradesmen'd give us a chance. Me and Joe'd work hard if those shopkeepers and merchants would give us a break, instead of hiring pretty boys to share their filthy beds.'

Beetlebrow noticed a white fleck of spittle forming in the right corner of his mouth.

'Yes, you'll beg for us,' Alder said. 'You'll work for our family, and appeal to men; what else is there for a girl?'

'I could steal things, then,' Beetlebrow replied.

'We're not thieves, Beetlebrow,' Alder stated, his heavy-lidded eyes scowling down at her.

His right hand reached out. He grabbed her left wrist. She felt his fingers clenching against its veins.

'We work for our money we do,' Alder went on. 'Working was good enough for Mum, and if you care about your family at all you'll look after us, like Mum did all these years.'

Beetlebrow felt Alder squeezing her wrist under his clasp.

'How old are you now?' he slowly asked. 'Fourteen?'

'Sixteen.'

'Sixteen! You look younger. Sixteen years old and you know nothing.'

'You're lazy, you're selfish and you're stupid!' Joe shouted at his sister.

She heard his footsteps stalking across the floorboards. Joe stopped beside Alder and glared down at Beetlebrow's face.

She glanced at Joe, and then looked at Alder again. The brass key in his hand briefly caught the light. In the gleam of the metal, Beetlebrow thought of the endless corridor set between golden walls.

She looked into Alder's eyes. She imagined slowly unfolding his fingers and taking the key from his grasp. She saw Alder staring back at her, and knew she could not open his hand by force.

'Yes, you're right,' she said, her shoulders softening. 'You're right about everything.'

Alder frowned.

'All right, I'll beg, for us,' Beetlebrow went on.

Alder scratched at his beard, glanced at Joe, and then looked down into her eyes again.

'Starting tomorrow, then?' Alder asked.

'Yes,' said Beetlebrow.

Alder let go of her wrist. He pushed another lump of bread into his mouth, staring at her as he chewed. 'Tomorrow it is, then. I'll wake you up before first light.'

Beetlebrow nodded. She looked over at her blanket. The small brown woollen sheet lay under the slant in the wall on the left of the room.

Beetlebrow heard Alder chewing. She looked at him again. He was gulping down the last morsels of the second loaf.

Beetlebrow glanced at Joe. 'Did you want some bread?'

Joe faced Alder for a moment and then looked at her again. 'What if I did?'

'I've still got a copper left over,' Beetlebrow said, 'if you're hungry.'

Joe stepped towards her. He held his right hand out, palm up. 'Give it me then.'

'I'll go,' Beetlebrow said. 'I'll get the bread. I'll go back to the bakery.'

Joe's dark-brown eyes peered down at her. 'You will, will you?'

Beetlebrow nodded.

Joe glanced at Alder.

'I don't trust her,' Joe said, his staring eyes turning towards his sister.

Alder chuckled and shook his head. 'Her? Beetlebrow? What's she going to do? Where's she going to go? Who's she going to go to? Unlock the door, Joe, and let the girl get us some bread.'

Beetlebrow watched Alder handing the key over to his brother. Joe walked over to the door. Beetlebrow stood up. She began stepping towards him.

Joe stared into her eyes as he turned the lock. Beetlebrow heard it click.

'Get the bread, then come right back, yes?' Joe asked.

'Of course.'

Joe opened the door. Beetlebrow stepped out onto the staircase and walked down its steps one at a time.

She opened the door four flights down and stepped out into the dimming light of the narrow street outside. She drew the brown wooden door back against its frame without a sound.

She felt hard dirt beneath her feet. She heard people in the nearby streets calling to one another. They sounded the same as they had in the morning.

She focused on the quietness in the street around herself. Where once there had been her mother's voice, now there would be this silence.

She looked south, and glimpsed seagulls perching on rooftops. She glanced at the alleys and lanes branching out to either side of the street. To Beetlebrow they appeared aimless.

She looked at the grey surrounding walls; their paint had been degraded by the sun and no-one had being willing to colour them again.

She thought of all the mornings she had walked down this street with a single copper coin in her hand. She thought of all the afternoons she had scurried through the corners and alleyways of the district, her eyes hunting for any spilled fruit or unattended bread, hoping to gather enough food throughout the day to keep her mother home for the night; she thought of all the evenings she had stepped back through the doorway with scraps in her hands, and had seen Lana shaking her head and slowly walking down the stairs.

Beetlebrow glanced back at the building. She saw the slit of a window four storeys up its grey surface. She did not know where her mother was. She knew she was not here.

She thought of walking back up the steps, opening the door and begging every day in the places Alder and Joe chose for her. She imagined women and men walking past her without a glance.

She remembered being in the market. She thought of the smile she had seen.

Beetlebrow's left hand drifted into the inside pocket of her robe. Against her fingers, she felt the spongy surface of a fig. She slipped her hand further down into the pocket to pull out the little fruit, and she touched the wooden handle of the thin, rusted knife she had found.

She let go of the fig, and looked towards the white palace in the north as she drew the knife from her pocket. She saw its metal edge gleaming in her hand. She squeezed her fingers around its wooden handle as she stared at the distant glow. She felt like she had an ember of her mother's fire inside herself, pushing her beyond the streets, urging her towards the palace. As Beetlebrow looked towards the Capitat, she knew she had to kindle the ember into flames.

She imagined walking across the city without Lana to return to at the end of the day. She glanced down at her knife, and remembered the fig.

Pook, she thought. *Pook deserves a place beyond these streets.*

From the hush between the towering grey buildings, Beetlebrow turned around and started hurrying south towards the market.

5
Gozher

Beetlebrow watched the evening arrive and blackness cover the streets. She stood in the narrow darkness by a brown mud-brick wall and looked out across the market square. She thought of Pook's smile. She thought of seeing it again. Beetlebrow had nothing else, and she knew it.

She saw the square being separated from the gloom in the rest of the Floodcross district by the orange light of two torches mounted outside Gozher's house. The wooden staffs, wrapped in linen and dipped in pitch and tallow, held flickering fires curling around their tops.

Beetlebrow watched clusters of middle-aged men and teenage girls huddling together around the patches of light in the market. The orange glow splashed their shadows across the surrounding grey walls. Beetlebrow heard the men's laughter, and saw their lingering hands giving the girls money and wine.

She remembered being woken up, two nights ago, by drunken singing in the street outside. The voices had volleyed up and down the nearby alleys and passageways. The noise had taken her away from the escape of sleep and sent her back to the frozen floorboards, where her stomach was empty and her toes were cold. She had heard the women and men nearing the building and their shouts growing louder. Her body had become still in the blackness. She had not breathed. She had heard the footsteps getting closer. She had grasped a corner of her thin woollen blanket between her white-knuckled fingers and had heard the drunken women and men passing beyond the nearby streets with laughter. She had lain awake in the silent darkness and stared upwards. In the morning, walking out of the building, she had found shards of broken pottery and glass scattered across the dirt of the street between pieces of fried food and puddles of gleaming urine.

She noticed Gozher walking out of his house and standing on his doorstep. He rocked on his heels, his long purple velvet robe swishing around his bulbous stomach. He lifted up his right hand and ruffled out his bushy, black beard.

Beetlebrow spotted the shadowed figure of thin girl walking across the gloom of the market. The girl was leading a short, middle-aged man by the hand. Beetlebrow watched her slim frame stepping across the darkness and approaching the pillars outside Gozher's house.

Gozher grabbed the girl by her right forearm.

'Hold on,' he said.

The girl entered the light of the torches. Beetlebrow saw her short, straight hair, and glanced away.

She spotted the flat-roofed bakery steeped in shadows on the right side of the square. A man's baying laughter echoed across the market. Beetlebrow felt the edges of her tattered robe between her frozen fingertips. She noticed scattered leaves in the dirt drifting away with the wind.

The middle-aged man handed several copper coins to Gozher. Gozher let go of the girl's arm. He began counting the money between his palms as the girl and the middle-aged man hurried inside the pillar-fronted house.

Beetlebrow glimpsed a burly, bald-headed figure swaying backwards across the market square. A wine-jar fell from his hand and cracked on the ground. His black shadow swept left across a mud-brick wall and exposed its grey surface to the light of the torches.

Beetlebrow saw Pook sitting down cross-legged in the dirt by the foot of the wall. Her fearful eyes were looking out at the market.

Beetlebrow started hurrying across the square. She felt the warm glow of the torches flashing across her face. She smelt sweat and wine. Men's hands reached down towards her. She dodged left and right away from their drunken grasps. The ground felt sticky against the soles of her bare feet.

She left the light behind and stepped into the gloom a few paces away from the mud-brick wall.

She saw Pook glance up at her. Beetlebrow looked into her large brown eyes. She felt her heart beating against her chest like a bailiff at the door.

'I know a place where we can work, where we won't go hungry,' Beetlebrow said. 'Do you want to come with me?'

'It's not up to you, Eyebrows,' a deep voice growled.

Beetlebrow glanced right.

Gozher was strutting towards her across the dirt of the market, his bulky frame silhouetted against the glow of the torches.

He placed his sandaled feet down squarely in the earth in front of Beetlebrow. His beady eyes stared down at her face. She saw Gozher's bulky frame bristling with the well-fed days and uninterrupted nights provided by the money from his brothel.

'The Floodcross district is my patch,' Gozher said, tapping his right index finger twice against his burly chest and then pointing the digit down towards Pook. 'I allow this one to beg here, at the back, until she's old enough for other employment; under my care of course. She's not going anywhere with you, or with anyone. She does what I say, all right?'

Beetlebrow scowled.

'You know who I am, don't you?' Gozher said. 'I know who you are. You're Alder and Joe's little sister. They're good lads, those brothers of yours; not too bright, but bright enough to know they couldn't afford the rates in my house of pleasure. They're getting what they want from life, your brothers, like men should do, but I've seen you, girl, queuing for bread every day with your single little copper coin. My boys on the rooftops, the boys in the fine silk robes, they've noticed you coming down from your little room most days, but some days you're not there are you though, 'cos your mum couldn't earn enough during the night. Is that correct?'

'And I know who you are,' Beetlebrow replied. 'They call you Gozher the Jaw, "cos you talk too much.'

Gozher grinned. 'That's right, and people listen to me when I speak.'

He extended his hairy right hand towards her. The light of the torches glinted across the blocky gold rings along his fingers. 'See this. Who else has got expensive things like these?'

Gozher held out his left hand towards Beetlebrow, opening his fingers to show the silver and copper coins held within his meaty palm.

'Or these?' he went on. 'That's all you need to know about me. I don't have to prove anything to someone like you.'

Beetlebrow glowered up at his face.

Gozher frowned down at her. 'Didn't you understand, you little gutter-rat? Nobody does anything in Floodcross without my say-so. Now clear off, back to your mother, unless you want your legs broken.'

Beetlebrow glanced at Pook. Pook's brown eyes rose to meet her gaze.

'Do you want to come with me?' Beetlebrow asked.

'Yes,' Pook said.

Beetlebrow felt a shiver striking down her back.

She looked up at Gozher again. She smacked her right fist against the underside of his outstretched left palm. His mouth opened. The silver and copper coins flew above his hand like sparks.

'You little bitch!' Gozher screamed.

Beetlebrow faced towards the gloom of the market. 'Money here! Money!'

She heard a thunder of footsteps approaching. The coins were clattering down into the dirt.

A group of drunken people started charging towards Gozher from the shadowed depths of the market square.

Beetlebrow glanced at his face. Gozher's eyes were wide as he stared at the mass of hungry faces.

'Get back!' he yelped.

Pook hurried to her feet. Beetlebrow grabbed her right hand. She and Pook ran around the corner.

Beetlebrow heard men and girls scrambling around in the shadows for the coins by Gozher's feet.

'Back!' he yelped.

Beetlebrow and Pook headed into a dark, wide road bordered by blackened shells of burnt-out, single-storey houses. Beetlebrow heard Gozher's panicked shouts echoing out across the market square. She felt thin grass under her toes. She slowed down to a walk. She let go of Pook's hand.

'He's not going to forget that, is he?' Pook said.

Beetlebrow glimpsed her face in the gloom. She saw Pook smiling.

She's at least four inches taller than me, Beetlebrow thought. *Like everyone but little kids.*

She looked away from Pook, and started walking through the shadows. She felt her steps becoming steadier as she sighted the distant palace.

She headed towards a wall between two houses, got down onto her hands and knees and crawled into the half-circle hole at the bottom of its mud-bricks.

'In here,' she said, her voice echoing.

She scrambled deeper inside the darkness of the hole, feeling dry earth and stiff weeds brushing against her palms and bricks scraping against her shoulders.

'Wait!' Pook said.

Beetlebrow stopped, and glanced back along the gloom. Pook's skinny legs were silhouetted beyond the southern entrance of the hole.

'What?' Beetlebrow hissed.

'I can't fit down there...' Pook said.

'You can,' Beetlebrow said. 'I can.'

She stretched out her left hand towards Pook.

Pook knelt down. Beetlebrow glimpsed her own shadowed hand reaching out towards her. The gesture appeared so confident and sure.

She saw Pook entering the hole. Beetlebrow looked forwards again, and started crawling further along its blackness, her hands pressing through the dirt and the grime.

She felt bare earth under her feet, and nothing against her shoulders. She realised she had reached the northern end of the hole. She slowly stood up.

She held out her hands and stepped through the darkness. She touched a plaster wall. She stopped, and fumbled across its coarse, bumpy surface until she found the wooden ladder leaning against it. The familiar rungs felt hard against her fingers.

Beetlebrow glanced back over her shoulder into the gloom. She listened. She heard Pook walking towards her.

'Up here,' Beetlebrow whispered.

Her right foot stepped onto the first rung of the ladder and she began darting upwards hand over hand. She felt the thin wooden frame rattling underneath her body. She glanced at the faint stars in the dark blue sky.

She felt the ladder becoming firmer under her grasp. She heard Pook climbing up behind her. Beetlebrow ascended the rungs with trembling hands, stepped out onto the flat rooftop and walked out alone across its gloom.

She stood at the precipice. Her toes gripped around the cracked tiles at its northern edge. She felt a breeze swishing up against her face. She heard the snuckling snores of a man sleeping in the room below.

Beetlebrow looked north. She saw the light of torches thinning out towards the black flint-stone wall bordering the Capitat district.

She heard Pook walking towards her across the rooftop. Beetlebrow listened to her coming nearer, step after careful step.

She heard Pook stopping to her left. Beetlebrow stared at the glowing light of the palace in the north. She looked across the black lines of slender windows embedded across the white tower. Her hands, down by her waist, flexed in the darkness. She knew she was slim enough to slip through these narrow frames.

'I know a way into the palace,' Beetlebrow said. 'If we can get inside we can find work…'

She glanced left, and glimpsed Pook's brown eyes gazing at her.

Beetlebrow looked towards the distant light of the palace again. 'Everyone who's got a job there, my… my mum told me, gets to eat three times a day. Mum used to work there, cleaning and washing clothes, but the siege stopped her from going. If we can get in, and get jobs, you and me, we won't go hungry again.'

She stared down into the darkness of the street two storeys below the rooftop. Her chest grew tight. She felt as if she had been talking for hours, the words spilling out of her.

'And you want to be there with me?' Pook said.

Beetlebrow slowly turned her head. She saw Pook grinning, her eyes narrowing out to give her smile more space to bloom.

Beetlebrow blinked. 'Yes.'

6
The barricade

Beetlebrow and Pook scurried across the brown earth of a shadowed lane between the blank outer walls of single-storey, whitewashed buildings.

Beetlebrow looked at the three men in black robes standing roughly twenty yards ahead of her path. She saw the torches they held in their gloved hands. The flickering flames were shimmering along the shallow black puddles dotted across the ground.

Beetlebrow glanced at the wall to her left. A mural of a red and brown man held on a lead by a figure in black robes was painted across its white surface.

'The Capitat district starts at the end of this lane,' she whispered to Pook. 'I don't know any other route, so we have to go past these men.'

She glanced to her left, and saw Pook stepping beside her through the gloom of the lane.

'Don't look at the men as we pass,' Beetlebrow whispered. 'Don't say anything. They'll think we're suspicious if we talk.'

'All right.'

Beetlebrow's left foot struck a policeman's dented metal helmet. She heard it clattering alone into the darkness to her right. She winced as the metallic sound echoed out across the walls of the nearby streets.

Beetlebrow and Pook neared the light of the torches. Beetlebrow stepped forwards with lowered eyes. She listened to the men's muttered conversations dying away. She glimpsed their gazes turning towards her.

'Evening, girls,' one man said.

'Evening,' Pook replied.

Beetlebrow heard a smile in her voice.

The three men stepped away from the centre of the street. Two leant against the shadowed wall on the right while the third man stood against the whitewashed wall on the left.

Beetlebrow kept her head down as she walked between the black-clad figures. She felt the heat of the torches stroking against her face. She smelt the stinging scent of tobacco. She noticed the knives on the men's belts.

'Watch out north of here, girls,' a man said. 'Red and browns have been busy these last few nights.'

'Thank you,' Pook said.

Beetlebrow headed through the glow of the torches and into the shadows at the end of the street. She heard Pook walking behind her steps.

Beetlebrow stopped at the neck of an alley. She looked up at the line of dirt scored along its mud-bricks walls. She remembered flood-water drowning this district the year before last.

She heard Pook stopping beside her.

'I thought it'd be better to speak to them,' Pook whispered. 'So they wouldn't suspect anything.'

'Right,' said Beetlebrow.

She started forwards, walking alone between the broken crates and jars scattered across the dirt of the alley. She peered up at a two-up, two-down mud-brick house in the street beyond. She saw the man standing on the rooftop above, his head and shoulders a black shape set against the dark blue sky.

Beetlebrow halted. Pook stood beside her.

Beetlebrow looked up at the house. Its four windows were empty black squares. Fingers of smoke had smeared their trails along the surrounding walls. Beetlebrow's gaze levelled. Weeds had raised their livid green stalks across the front-yard of the house between patches of muted purple and pale-yellow flowers. Two ropes were hanging below the outstretched limb of a thick-trunked yew tree, where a swing had once swayed.

She remembered Lana getting the job in the palace four years ago, and her mother escorting her through the dark mornings to this district. She recalled Lana leaving her with the family who lived in this house, and picking her up again when her work had finished in the evening. Beetlebrow remembered watching her mother walking away from the yard through the growing dawn, heading north through the Capitat district.

She thought of the family who had lived here. She remembered the father having grey hair and grim, wrinkled expressions, and the mother having a slight, youthful frame. She remembered the two being wary and polite. She could not remember their names.

She thought of their son, seven at the time. Beetlebrow remembered Sarren's shy smile and gangly limbs. She recalled sitting on the swing, Sarren's tentative hands pushing against her back while her tight fingers grasped around the coarse ropes.

She remembered swinging higher and higher, feeling a surge of speed as she had flown beyond the ground. Her legs had stretched outwards as the swing had reached the peak of its sway. The ropes had strained underneath the clasp of her hands, and the bough of the yew had creaked behind her. She had felt her body becoming weightless.

She thought of the moment when the swing had slowed in the air, before it began hauling her back down towards the dirt of the yard again.

She remembered seeing black-robed men on the streets of the Capitat in the following months, peering into streets and knocking on doors. She remembered Lana leaving her back in Floodcross afterwards, telling her to stay inside. Alder and Joe would go out with their friends, breaking windows and fighting with the local gangs, and Beetlebrow would escape out into the streets as soon as her mother had left the building. She remembered heading towards the Capitat, her bare feet beginning to build a route to the palace, while black-robed men were making a tourniquet of burnt-out houses around the royal buildings which no-one could pass.

'What are we doing about the man on the roof?' Pook whispered.

'We're waiting,' Beetlebrow replied, keeping her eyes focused on the rooftop.

She noticed Pook glancing at her. Beetlebrow heard a dog barking in a street far away to her right.

She saw the man's shape melting away from the top of the house. Beetlebrow started stepping forwards. She heard Pook following closely behind her heels. Beetlebrow felt the rutted tracks cut by cart-wheels under her feet.

'Watch out for the holes,' Beetlebrow said.

'What did you say?'

'Quiet.'

Beetlebrow headed alone the empty doorway of the house, slowing her steps as she entered its dark central corridor. She smelt stale air and flat beer. She heard rats scuttling away from her path.

She noticed doorways either side of the corridor. To her left was a slender, shutter-less window at the back of a square room roughly six-feet square.

She stopped. She glanced into the room to her right. Three black-clad men were sleeping on the bare wooden floorboards between stacks of wooden crates. Spider-web layers of graffiti coursed up the walls above their slumbering bodies. Beetlebrow noticed a thin, shaven-headed teenage boy sitting up against the side of an iron barrel. His eyes were closed. There was a knife in his right hand.

Beetlebrow peered out the open door at the back of the house. She glimpsed blades glimmering through the darkness of the street beyond. Dozens of men were standing behind the barricade of paving stones and broken furniture. Beyond the blackness of the mile of streets north of their blockade was the flint wall separating the royal palace from the Capitat district.

Beetlebrow glanced back over her shoulder. She saw only darkness.

'This way,' she whispered to Pook.

Beetlebrow turned left and stepped across the rough wooden floorboards until she reached the open window.

She turned around. She glimpsed Pook's slim shape walking towards her across the darkness. Beetlebrow heard the floorboards humming under her bare feet. She sensed the sweet smell of Pook's hair.

'Through here,' Beetlebrow whispered.

She turned towards the window, grabbed the sill, climbed out through the frame and dropped down onto the hard earth five feet below. She smelt the sharp reek of tomato-plants, and heard Pook landing behind her.

Beetlebrow stood up. She noticed a flat-roofed, rectangular building to the north. Far beyond its dark outline she saw the distant glow of the white tower of the palace; it appeared to Beetlebrow as large and as bright as the moon.

Pook bumped into her back.

'Sorry,' Pook whispered.

Beetlebrow kept looking north. She lowered her gaze from the tower and stared at the flat-roofed building in the street ahead. She saw two men squatting in the dirt in front of its open doorway. They were holding shivering palms over the embers of a fire.

Beetlebrow pulled out the rusted knife from inside her robe.

'We'll rush by these two,' she whispered to Pook. 'If they try to chase us, I'll lead them away and lose them in the backstreets. But you keep heading north, and I'll meet you by the base of the wall.'

'How about... instead,' Pook whispered, 'I tell them something, something they'd need to investigate...?'

Beetlebrow turned around.

Pook was standing in the shadows. Beetlebrow looked down at the blade gripped in her own cold fingers. She turned over its wooden handle in her palm. She looked at Pook again, and remembered the figs she had offered her in the market.

'But if you do that... what do I do?' Beetlebrow asked.

'Just wait here,' Pook said.

She smiled. She walked past Beetlebrow. Beetlebrow watched her running out through the darkness of the street ahead. She heard the tread of Pook's feet pattering across the dirt.

Beetlebrow saw the two men standing up beside their fire, facing towards the sound of approaching footsteps. Beetlebrow's hands squeezed into tight little fists.

The men reached for the knives in their belts. Beetlebrow's nails dug into her palms. She watched Pook step out into the shallow light of the dying flames. The men looked Pook up and down, and then lowered their blades.

'Red and browns, a few streets to the east,' Pook said. 'Seemed like they were checking houses for weak spots.'

'They didn't see you, did they?' one man asked.

Pook shook her head.

'Good work, girl. But you'd best get inside somewhere. It might get violent.'

'Thank you,' Pook said. 'I will. Thank you.'

The men hurried away to the right.

Beetlebrow slipped her knife back inside her ragged robes and walked out into the light of the street. She saw Pook smiling at her approach. Beetlebrow glanced at her face, lit by the embers of the fire, and then looked towards the open doorway ahead.

'Here,' Beetlebrow said.

She hurried into the house, ran through its rooms and out its back door. She heard Pook's steps behind her own. Beetlebrow felt the wind grabbing at her thin robe as she walked down through two dark, silent streets and towards the smell of salt and rotting seaweed.

She felt cold sand against the soles of her feet. She saw the horizon splitting the black sky from the dark blue sea to the west. The crescent moon was shining a rippled white reflection across the shallows.

'This is the way is it?' Pook asked.

'Yes,' Beetlebrow said.

'Have you been this way before?'

'No.'

'How do you know we can do it?' Pook asked.

'Seen it.'

'Why didn't you go before?'

'I... couldn't,' Beetlebrow said. She glanced back towards the vague glow of lights in the city. Her hands began trembling 'My mum, she needed me. She needed my help. And then she...'

Beetlebrow looked towards the distant light from the white palace in the north.

She walked away from the shadowed sand. She felt her feet treading into the steps her thoughts had carefully placed in these last four years. She imagined these rocks to be carved by the months she had stared at their surfaces, hoping that someday her hands could grasp their coarse shapes and be guided through into the palace beyond.

Beetlebrow began clambering upwards, heading towards the cliff-top looming over the water. She felt the wind pushing against her body. She heard Pook following behind her heels.

7
The cliff top

Beetlebrow glanced downwards. Between the glittering waves, the black shapes of fishing boats were tugging at the ropes binding their restless hulls to the shore. Beetlebrow's hands began feeling around at the rocks by her feet.

'There's a lip of stone around the edge of the cliff here,' she said to Pook. 'It's too narrow for anyone pretty much anyone else to get across.'

'Are you sure it's safe...?' Pook asked.

'For us it will be. And it was only last week the rocks broke. Soon it'll crumble too.'

She looked back at Pook. She saw only blackness and the distant lights of the city.

'Turn sideways,' Beetlebrow whispered. 'We'll walk along together.'

She faced out towards the sea. She saw the moon as a curved blade of white metal between the stars.

Beetlebrow started side-stepping right along the lip of rock, her toes gripping its edge. She felt the jagged surface of the cliff-face pressing against her back. She heard Pook side-stepping towards her.

Beetlebrow felt the wet breath of the sea sweeping across her feet. Her toes were sticking out over the black water. She kept her feet moving along the knife-edge line below the cliffs. She felt relieved to have darkness cloaking her trembling body.

'It's so narrow,' Pook said.

'That's why no-one else can go this way.'

Beetlebrow felt a seagull flying towards her face, its wings cutting across the air. The bird banked away again, heading back out west over the water. Beetlebrow took another side-step right, and then another. She felt cramp gripping against her thighs. She heard the distant waves clashing together far below.

She took another side-step right and felt the lip of rock widening out underneath her toes. 'The cliff-top's here.'

'I feel like I'm going to fall,' Pook said.

'Don't let yourself feel that,' Beetlebrow replied, 'or you will fall.'

She stepped away from the narrow shelf of stone and walked out onto the flat outcrop of stone beyond. She remembered the last time she had touched Lana's hand in the morning.

Beetlebrow stopped. Her chapped lips felt raw. Her face felt rigid with cold. Her mother's eyes had been closed, her lips slightly parted, and her arms had been lying on the floorboards with no more motion to ever lift them upwards again.

She heard approaching footsteps. She knew Pook was walking towards her.

'Why've you stopped?' Pook whispered, glancing around at the clifftop.

Beetlebrow started heading through the darkness towards the glow of the white tower. 'It's nothing.'

She felt slick grass slithering against her ankles; she heard a breeze hissing through its blades.

She watched the tower remaining distant while a silhouetted group of square buildings emerged from the blackness by its feet. She saw a torch mounted on an ivy-covered, red-brick wall. It illuminated a wrought-iron gate.

Beetlebrow stepped into the light. She pushed at the metal gate. It swung open without a sound.

She glanced across the lawn of neatly-trimmed, bright-green grass ahead of herself. Oil-lamps were hanging on hooks across the surrounding walls.

Beetlebrow looked upwards. A rectangular seven-storey building to the north of lawn was cutting out a vertical black shape from the sky of dull white stars.

She saw four-storey buildings standing to the west and east of the square of grass; between their dark shapes the bright lawn looked to her like an emerald set amid a black crown. She heard a peacock's mew echoing out far away to her left.

She glanced back over her shoulder. She glimpsed Pook standing outside the gate.

'No-one here,' Beetlebrow whispered.

She looked forwards again. She noticed an empty, grey marble birdbath standing underneath a balcony to her right. She started creeping towards it across the grass.

Her feet felt wet. She looked downwards. She brushed her right foot with her cold left hand. She noticed green paint smeared across its callused sole. She looked back at the lawn. Her steps had made a line of brown footprints across the painted grass.

She stepped forwards and climbed up onto the bowl of the marble birdbath. She reached out her hands towards the spindly stone columns of the balcony hanging above. She felt her hands missing its base by several inches.

She heard Pook walking towards, her feet swishing across the grass.

'I can do it,' Pook whispered. 'I can reach.'

Beetlebrow found herself clambering down from the birdbath. She stepped back across the grass and watched Pook climbing up into its bowl.

Pook grabbed the base of the balcony and hauled herself up the spindly stone columns.

Beetlebrow saw her bare feet leaving the birdbath behind.

Pook's slim figure disappeared over the balcony.

Beetlebrow saw blackness across the towering surface of the building.

Pook's grinning face appeared over the columns. She reached her hands down towards Beetlebrow.

'Easy,' Pook said. 'Come on.'

Beetlebrow climbed back up into the birdbath and stretched her arms out towards the balcony. She felt Pook grasping onto her wrists and pulling her upwards into the darkness.

Beetlebrow glimpsed the columns in front of her face. She reached out. Her hands gripped against their smooth stone surfaces. She felt Pook letting go of wrists.

She clambered over the balustrade in the darkness and stepped down onto the icy tiles of the balcony.

She saw the shadowed wall in front of herself.

'There're double-doors here,' Pook whispered. 'I found the handles.'

Beetlebrow reached her hands out towards the darkness of the wall. Her fingers touched a brass handle. It felt as cold as bone.

'Wait,' Pook said, 'what's our plan?'

'This is it, isn't it?'

Beetlebrow heard Pook chuckling.

'We turn one handle each?' Beetlebrow asked.

'Yes,' Pook said.

They pushed the double-doors inwards. Beetlebrow heard the hinges discreetly whine.

She and Pook stepped onto the carpeted floor of the pitch-black room inside and shut the double-doors behind themselves. Beetlebrow smelt beeswax and dust. She felt warmth surrounding her body.

8
The palace

Beetlebrow felt her toes sinking down inches deep into the carpet. She glimpsed Pook standing to her left.

She felt her eyes adjusting to the blackness. She watched the entrenched darkness of the room fading away and its outlines emerging into view.

She glimpsed two over-stuffed armchairs standing on the right of the room, and they looked to her like tensed bulldogs ready to the pounce.

Her body became rigid. Her hands were down by her waist, her fingers splayed, afraid to touch anything she did not know. She felt the rich fibres in the carpet clinging onto the soles of her feet.

She knew the remaining darkness in the room was beyond what her sight could pierce. She felt like a chained prisoner awaiting a public shaming in a street, getting ready to be struck with stones.

'There,' Pook said. 'The door.'

Beetlebrow heard her softly stepping away across the carpet. A metal handle turned. A door opened in the wall and a rectangle of white light burst into the room from the corridor outside.

Beetlebrow glanced around. Bookcases flanked the mahogany doorway of the room. On the left of its carpeted floor was an olive-wood desk. At its centre was a small white plate crossed with a greasy butter-knife.

She looked back at the armchairs. Their frames were slumped and their red leather hides were patched with brown squares.

She saw Pook standing in the yellow corridor beyond the doorway. Her face was lit by the white light of the whale-oil lamps mounted on the walls. Beetlebrow started walking towards her. The black floorboards felt smooth underneath her feet.

She noticed a dark-brown mole on the left of Pook's upper lip. Her cinnamon-shaded skin looked soft. Beetlebrow wondered if it felt soft to touch.

Pook faced her.

Beetlebrow quickly glanced up at the cobwebbed wooden arches of the ceiling. 'We need to be somewhere with lots of people, so that we can fit in, and then we start working.'

'So... if anyone asks, we just pretend we have jobs here already?' Pook asked.

Beetlebrow nodded.

Pook smiled. Beside her wide grin Beetlebrow saw a line of pink inside her dark purple lips.

Beetlebrow glanced left and right along the corridor. She saw no doors along the walls.

She noticed Pook looking at her.

'What?' Beetlebrow asked.

'Ain't you scared?'

Beetlebrow's expression softened. 'Yes.'

'You don't look scared.'

'That's just the way my face is, I guess.'

Pook shrugged. She glanced right. Beetlebrow followed her gaze. She noticed a black staircase ascending away from the corridor.

'Not that way,' Pook said. 'Servants don't go upwards.'

She started walking left.

Beetlebrow watched her heading towards the descending staircase. She noticed the sway of Pook's narrow hips.

Pook glanced back over her shoulder. Her eyes met Beetlebrow's. Pook smirked. Beetlebrow felt her cheeks becoming warm. She lowered her gaze. Her steps were light as she hurried after Pook.

Together they walked side-by-side down the cold, tiled staircase. Beetlebrow felt Pook's right hand bump against her left. They entered into the pallid gloom of the white corridor below.

Beetlebrow noticed a brightly-lit ballroom ahead. She saw ebony arches supporting its domed white ceiling, and gold-framed portraits of wrinkled, white-haired men glaring down from the walls of the ballroom towards the gleaming parquet floor.

She noticed two men in the ballroom staring at her. The pair wore plain oatmeal-coloured tunics and their wrists were bound with iron slave-cuffs. Beetlebrow spotted silver cutlery in their hands. The glimmering knives and spoons were poised above a gleaming wooden table surrounded by dozens of white chairs.

Beetlebrow looked left along the corridor. She glimpsed an outline of a door in the span of the white wall. She glanced at Pook and nodded towards the shape.

'You two, where are you going?' a male voice barked.

Beetlebrow saw a lanky, youthful-looking man marching towards her from the ballroom, his white robes flowing behind his long, loping steps.

His buck teeth were firmly clenched together and his thick black hair was swept back over his forehead.

Pook began stepping back towards the darkness of the stairs, her hands fidgeting with the sleeves of her sackcloth robe.

The man stopped in front of Beetlebrow.

'What exactly do you think you are doing?' he said.

Beetlebrow dipped her head. 'We got lost. Sir.'

She noticed the man glancing at Pook. Beetlebrow took a step closer towards him and looked up at his face. The man's glaring eyes turned towards her again.

'Sorry, sir,' Beetlebrow said. 'We'll return to the kitchens.'

She grabbed Pook by the right arm and started striding away to the left.

'The kitchen's the other way...' the man drawled.

Beetlebrow gripped Pook's arm tighter as they walked further down into the darkness of the white corridor. 'Keep going.'

'You do know where you're headed, don't you?' the man asked.

'Run!' Pook hissed.

Beetlebrow and Pook began sprinting along corridor, their bare feet slapping down together against the cold tiles.

Beetlebrow noticed a spiral-stairwell on the right of the corridor, its iron lattice frame lit by oil-lamps.

'Up here,' she whispered.

They ran up the corkscrewing steps two at a time, entered into the yellow-walled corridor at the top of the staircase and hurried past its rows of wooden benches and six-foot-tall terracotta urns. They turned left at an intersection of hallways and headed between scarlet walls lined with empty-shelved, glass-fronted cabinets.

Beetlebrow heard a clanking of metal. She saw a line of seven men in silver plate armour marching towards her from down the corridor ahead. Their sharp helmets and black-bearded faces were lit by the flaming torches in their hands. She saw their armoured frames as a silver barricade surging between the width of the walls.

She turned around. A second line of torch-bearing soldiers was sweeping towards her from down the other end of the corridor. Beetlebrow smelt pitch and tallow. She felt the soldiers' stamping steps vibrating the floorboards underneath her feet.

She glanced back at the first line of armoured men. Beetlebrow ran her fingers across the belly of her ragged robes. She felt the sharp edge of her thin knife inside its pocket.

She thought of charging towards the soldiers, urging them away with her knife, and then scuttling back along the corridor until she could find some place to hide in an overlooked room, dark and narrow, in which she could remain until morning brought more chances.

She heard Pook breathing fast beside her. Beetlebrow glanced at her. She saw Pook's empty hands.

Beetlebrow looked at the soldiers again, and then removed her fingers from her blade.

Beetlebrow heard their heavy bootsteps halting. She guessed their two lines were roughly five feet away on either side of her. The second line parted left and right.

Beetlebrow saw a plump man sidling towards her from between their ranks.

His broad, beige head was bald and a black and grey striped beard plumed around the bottom half of his face. His brown-belted robe was cream-coloured and a thin blue scarf was tied around his neck. Beetlebrow noticed the criss-cross wrinkles embedded against the far corners of his dark-brown eyes. She guessed him to be in his early fifties.

'Your first mistake, my friends,' the plump man said, his dry voice enunciating every syllable, 'was thinking anyone who dwells within these halls might get lost. We've been cooped up in here too long for that to happen. I long for any such ignorance, or surprise, within these thousands of rooms and corridors.'

Beetlebrow felt a droplet of sweat sliding down from her forehead. She saw the plump man picking dirt from under the nail of his left index finger with his right thumbnail as he looked at Pook.

'Your second mistake was thinking that a servant who works within these august walls might want to leave the part of the palace where they work,' he went on. 'Everyone here sticks to their jobs and works hard. People under siege are like that. It consoles them. They have nothing else, after all.'

Beetlebrow was staring into his eyes as she reached her left hand into her robe for her knife.

The plump man glanced at her.

'Would you like something to eat?' he asked.

9
Ray Rez

Beetlebrow heard the soldiers marching away from the corridor. She saw the orange glow of their torches fading from its scarlet walls.

She listened to the stillness sweeping across the carpeted floors. She had imagined all the corridors of the royal grounds to be wide and smooth; instead they appeared to twist and throttle through the building like the streets of the city outside.

She looked at the plump man. His grinning face was illuminated by the white light of the wall-mounted whale-oil lamps.

'What are your names, girls?' he asked.

'I'm Pook.'

'Beetlebrow.'

The plump man frowned.

'Beetle-brow?' he asked.

"Cos of my eyebrows,' Beetlebrow replied.

The plump man lifted up his chin and looked down at her.

'Well, you are evidently not part of those anarchist factions outside the walls, that at least is obvious,' he said, his gaze levelling. 'But why is it that you have – successfully, I might add – broken into our palace?'

'For work,' Pook replied. 'We can clean floors, sir, light fires, clean privies, muck out horses, anything you want.'

The plump man sniffed. 'We have plenty of people doing that already. We don't need any more.'

Beetlebrow saw the light of the whale-oil lamps flickering.

'But… you have found your way here, and you are obviously talented girls,' the plump man said. 'We value talent here, at this time most of all. You have told me your names; mine is Magell.'

He looked at Pook, and then at Beetlebrow.

'Do you fully appreciate what you have done, girls?' Magell went on. 'For over a year we've been trapped in this palace by this siege. We've sent squadrons of soldiers out to destroy the barricade and they were killed; we sent out spies, trained in the greatest techniques of stealth available to our scholars, but they too were killed. And those anarchists outside the wall sent their thugs, and their devious infiltrators, but our spearmen and archers held them back. On both sides neither has been able to get past the other, but you – you two girls – have broken in. You obviously have something we lack.'

He turned around. 'Please, if you'd like to follow me?'

Pook's brown eyes caught Beetlebrow's gaze. Beetlebrow shrugged. They started walking together behind Magell's smooth, brisk steps towards the end of the corridor.

Beetlebrow saw Magell opening an oak door set within the pointed hood of a limestone archway.

The room beyond was illuminated by the light of dozens of white candles placed upon shining silver candelabras. Magell stepped through. Beetlebrow and Pook followed.

Beetlebrow felt thick carpeting underneath her toes. She smelt sandalwood and woodsmoke. She saw faded tapestries, their colours bleached pale by decades of sunlight, hanging from the walls.

'Please sit,' Magell said.

Beetlebrow saw him standing in the middle of the room beside a short-legged ebony-wood table flanked by two divans. The pair of long, backless seats were upholstered in yellow and pink silk. Against the wall to Magell's right was a granite fireplace. Beetlebrow saw the flames gnashing at the stacked logs burning in its mouth.

Magell was holding open his right palm towards the divans. Beetlebrow and Pook walked towards him.

Beetlebrow felt the heat of the fire warming the right side of her body while her left remained cold.

Through the bay windows at the back of the room she saw miles of torch-lit towers and lawns shining out across the darkness of the palace grounds. She glimpsed the other buildings in the royal complex outside; black rectangles and squares cresting like waves between flat gardens and marble fountains.

Pook perched on the divan facing away from the windows. Beetlebrow sat down on her left. Her feet dangled inches above the floor.

Magell lowered himself down onto the opposing divan and flattened out his cream-coloured robe across his chubby thighs. Beetlebrow spotted an olive-wood bowl of walnuts and dates in the centre of the ebony table.

Magell glanced up at her. 'So, you are hungry?'

Beetlebrow stared at him.

'Yes,' Pook slowly said, glancing at Beetlebrow. 'We're very hungry.'

Magell smiled, and clapped his hands together.

Beetlebrow heard the fire crackle. She noticed lines of orange fire coursing through its smouldering logs. She shuffled back a few inches on the divan. She heard its springs creaking underneath her body. She looked at Magell. She saw him smiling towards her.

A stream of short-haired, white-robed servants swept into the room, carrying silver platters of golden-brown chicken legs, plump pink hams, pungent cheeses, piles of crispy bacon rashers, dishes of steaming whitebait, mounds of rice, stacks of oysters in their half-shells and piles of cylindrical pies and currant-dotted buns.

Beetlebrow stared at the food being placed on the table. Her hands began gripping the silken seat of the divan. She looked across the multitude of dishes. The table-top was becoming swamped with silver plates, their rims shoulder-to-shoulder across its ebony surface. She felt the smell of melted fat and rich, meaty sauces filling her senses. She glanced at Pook. Pook was gazing at the food. Her brown eyes were wide.

Magell looked at Beetlebrow and then turned his focus towards Pook.

'Girls, please eat,' he said.

Beetlebrow's hands still felt dry from climbing the cliffs, side-stepping along the lip of rock above the waves.

'Do have you any bread?' she asked.

'Why, of course,' Magell said.

He clapped his hands again.

Beetlebrow saw a servant running in from the doorway and inclining his head down towards Magell's mouth. Magell's gaze was set on Beetlebrow's face as he whispered into the servant's ear.

The servant walked away again towards the door.

'It's just... if we were working for you,' Pook slowly said to Magell, 'we'd want to save some of our wages, and not spend them on food, especially all these rich things. We haven't got any money ...'

Magell glanced down at the plates and then looked at Pook again.

'Oh,' he said. 'Please, excuse me. It's my fault, I'm sure, for not explaining myself fully. My apologies: I should have made myself clear. All this food, it's all free. There is no cost; it's all for you.'

Beetlebrow's fingers grasped tighter against the divan as she stared at Magell.

'Please,' Magell said, looking at her. 'Eat all you like.'

Beetlebrow glanced at the table. She reached out her left hand. Her fingers hovered near the edge of a silver platter. She picked up a browned chicken leg from the pile. She felt the warmth of its meat against her cold hand. Its flesh was weighing down her fingers.

She glimpsed Magell nodding at her. Beetlebrow closed her eyes. She smelt oil and butter and aromatic herbs. Her teeth crunched through of the crisp, springy skin of the chicken and down into the soft, moist meat below. Unfamiliar flavours began singing across her tongue, surrounding her within its sensations.

She opened her eyes again, and saw Pook staring at the chicken leg.

'Eat something,' Beetlebrow mouthed.

'Please, my friends, don't stand on ceremony,' Magell purred. Beetlebrow glanced at him.

'And please, enjoy it...' Magell went on. 'In a palace under siege, a feast of this nature is a rare treat.'

Beetlebrow's teeth tore through the meat of the chicken. Her lips met the bone several inches below its yielding skin. She noticed Pook picking up a triangular slice of blue-frosted chocolate cake.

Beetlebrow gnawed around the bone of the chicken leg until it was stripped of meat. She grabbed a handful of bacon and hurried it towards her mouth. She felt the brittle, fat-lined rashers snapping under her teeth, and dropped the fleshless chicken bone onto a plate.

She glimpsed Pook finishing a slice of cake, leaning her right hand out towards the whitebait and begin crunching down into the deep-fried little fish.

A white-clad servant slipped back through the doorway. Beetlebrow watched him placing a small porcelain plate on the edge of the ebony table. At its centre was a square loaf of black-crusted bread embedded with sesame seeds. Pook took another handful of whitebait. She glanced at Beetlebrow. Beetlebrow saw the roundness of Pook's cheeks and the brightness of her eyes. She heard the fire crackling to her right.

Beetlebrow reached out towards the table again. She chewed chunks of ham and chicken and cake and chicken legs as she wiped sweat from her forehead. She felt like she was consuming the palace with every bite, taking in its ivory floors and silver walls by the mouthful. She felt the food passing into her skinny body. She could imagine its richness redeeming her years of starvation.

A servant placed more logs into the grasping flames of the fire. Beetlebrow took a fistful of chocolate cake. She knocked back several oysters.

She saw blurry figures in white taking the empty plates away from the ebony table. She looked down at the food again, grabbed a pie and bit down into its surface. She felt the crust crumbling on her tongue. Her teeth sunk through its soft jelly and reached the rich pork at its centre.

She grabbed another chicken-leg. As she sucked down the last piece of meat from its bone, she leant forwards and dropped it down onto the pile.

Beetlebrow sat back. She looked at the remaining plates on the table. Across their silver surfaces were crumbs of chocolate cake, the few remaining pieces of whitebait, five remaining pies, flakes of pastry, pieces of bacon and a stack of untouched chicken-legs. The loaf of black bread remained intact on its porcelain plate.

Beetlebrow's stomach felt hard and tight. She glanced at Pook. Pook's fingers were resting on her belly. Her feet were placed on the floor and her eyes were half-closed.

Beetlebrow looked at Magell. He was still smiling.

'What do you want with us?' she asked.

Magell looked at her and then glanced at Pook.

'What do I want with you? I have told you how talented you are. Now I need your help. But don't let me rush you. Have you both finished eating?'

'Yes,' Beetlebrow said.

Pook nodded.

Magell stood up. Beetlebrow heard the springs of his divan creaking.

'Please, come with me...' Magell said.

He walked away across the room. Beetlebrow stood up. She started stepping across the carpet after him. Her belly felt swollen and her legs felt slow. She had seen no blankets or sleeping mats on the floors of the rooms she had walked through, nor cooking pots above their fires. She felt fearful of these aimless rooms.

She glanced back at Pook. She saw her still sitting on the divan.

'We need to follow him,' Beetlebrow whispered. 'Anywhere he goes.'

'Yes,' Pook replied, her bleary eyes turning to share Beetlebrow's gaze.

Beetlebrow imagined hurrying after Magell with Pook at her side, and Pook's sluggish pace slowing her down. The sound of Magell's footsteps would become muffled between the carpets and tapestries, and the trail of his path lost among the endless corridors. Beetlebrow imagined drifting for days across gleaming floors as she and Pook tried to sight him again.

Perhaps there's been other people like us, she thought; countless numbers who had broken into the palace and could not find their way back out, their feet aching as they became desperate for a glimpse of the opening which had first brought them inside.

Magell stepped towards the door and turned the handle.

Beetlebrow looked at Pook again. 'We need to go.'

She glanced towards the door. She felt the palace slipping away from her hands. She imagined the floor falling away beneath her feet, and her body being dropped down into Floodcross's crowded streets, where noise and silence ruled. She knew her brothers would still be waiting for her back in the room where her mother had died.

Pook blinked. She slowly rose to her feet. 'It's just... I've never seen so much food in my life. I've never eaten so much.'

Beetlebrow glanced at the doorway. 'We've got to keep following him.'

Pook nodded.

Beetlebrow glimpsed Magell walking out the room. She started stepping across the carpeted floor. She felt her stomach weighing down like an anchor upon her slender frame.

She heard Pook following behind her. Beetlebrow sped up.

They followed Magell out of the room and into the light of torches beyond. Magell was walking along the marble floor of an empty corridor. He stopped by an open doorway and turned around.

Beetlebrow and Pook stood in front of him. Beetlebrow noticed the golden arms of a chandelier hanging above her head. She felt the warmth of the floor beneath her bare feet.

'I'm sure His Majesty will enjoy meeting you two,' Magell said, glancing towards Beetlebrow and Pook. 'The king has barely seen Stellingkorr, after all.'

Beetlebrow nodded. Her belly felt bloated and heavy. Her body was swaying left and right.

'You must excuse me now,' Magell went on. 'My... colleague, Ray Rez, will be in the next room. He'll tell you what we of the palace require of you; please, this way, girls...'

Magell pointed towards the white-walled room beyond the doorway. Beetlebrow saw dozens of gold-framed portraits of gnarled, white-bearded men displayed across its walls. She glanced across the canes, chains of office, sceptres and scrolls the painted figures were grasping in their hands. The men all appeared to be staring at one another.

'Until later, girls...' Magell said.

He turned around and walked away along the marble corridor. Beetlebrow and Pook stepped through the doorway of the white room and onto its black-slate tiles.

Beetlebrow glanced between its walls. The floor was empty. She looked at Pook. Pook raised her eyebrows. Beetlebrow shrugged.

She noticed a head and shoulders portrait on the left wall of the white room. It depicted a woman with short, side-parted black hair. Her smirking face was glancing out from the surface of the painting. On the right side of the woman's chest was a double-rose decorated in gold-leaf. Beetlebrow looked at the glinting hilt of a sword clasped in the woman's hand. Its silvery blade appeared to shine.

Beetlebrow faced Pook.

'Has anyone tried to search you?' Beetlebrow whispered. 'They haven't, have they?'

Pook was rubbing her tired eyes. 'Hmm?'

'It's like they think my knife wouldn't be able to hurt them.'

She heard a quiet pair of footsteps to her right. She faced towards the sound.

A wiry, white-haired man was standing in the middle of the white-walled room. He had thin black eyebrows and brown eyes. His lean face was contoured with wrinkles and his forehead creased with ridges. His grey tunic was tapered at the waist and his feet were bare.

'Newcomers!' he said, thrusting his right hand out towards Beetlebrow. 'I am Ray Rez; pleasure to meet you.'

Beetlebrow held out her right hand and looked up into his eyes. She felt Ray Rez's eager grasp gripping around her fingers and shaking her hand. His clasp made her arm feel like a child's rattle.

'After a year of being besieged, I've thought this situation would never end,' Ray Rez said with a smile. 'But with the help of you two girls, I believe we can bring this siege to a close.'

He glanced up at white marble ceiling and then looked at Beetlebrow and Pook again.

'Then,' he went on, 'I'm hoping to finally get to see the streets of Stellingkorr.'

He stepped towards Pook, took her hand and shook it. Beetlebrow saw her sleepy eyes snapping open wide.

'There's something you can do for us,' Ray Rez said. 'Something only you may be able to achieve. The delivery of a message to Dalcratty.'

Pook stared at him. 'You mean, you want to give us a job?'

'Yes,' Ray Rez replied. 'Oh yes.'

He was walking quickly towards a red velvet curtain on the right of the white room. Beetlebrow and Pook started chasing after him.

They passed a silver platter perching on top of a terracotta plinth. Beetlebrow noticed the piles of empty, golden-gilded oyster-shells on its surface as she and Pook stepped into the dank corridor beyond the red curtain.

The grey adobe walls to their left and right were daubed with the black smoke-trails of torches. Beetlebrow smelt clay and unwashed bodies; she felt moist, uneven earth under the soles of her feet.

She glimpsed Ray Rez walking through the gloom of the corridor.

'His Majesty King Ancissus left the city of Dalcratty as a teenager, thirty-two years ago, to become monarch here,' he said, 'when the previous incumbent, King Hartriss the Third, produced no heir.'

Beetlebrow and Pook followed after his steps. Beetlebrow noticed an open doorway to her left. She glanced inside. Three people were lying asleep on the dirt floor of the windowless room. Their bodies were lit by a single red stub of a candle. Beetlebrow noticed iron clasps bound around their wrists.

'It was decided that emergency fund – a great wealth of grain – should be set aside, for His Majesty to request if he ever needed it,' Ray Rez went on. 'It was hidden in a location, known only to him, somewhere near to Dalcratty, and the servants who ensured its secrecy were retired.'

He pulled aside the red velvet curtain at the end of the corridor.

Beetlebrow heard a flute and a harp harmonising together over a soft melody.

10
The message

Beetlebrow and Pook walked down the white corridor beyond the red curtain. Beetlebrow noticed the whale-oil lamps on the walls were half-dimmed. Ray Rez was stepping towards a white door on the right.

Beetlebrow saw two men sitting cross-legged up against the opposite wall. Greasy, greying hair framed their closed eyes; it draped down past the shoulders of their blue and silver robes. One man was playing a harp, the other a flute.

Beetlebrow heard the musicians reaching the end of the melody and return to the beginning of the tune.

Ray Rez sounded two light taps with his knuckles against the white door. Pook glanced at Beetlebrow and nodded towards the dark end of the corridor.

Beetlebrow saw a saffron-coloured dog trotting out from the shadows. Its body was about a foot long. Its face was lean and long-snouted.

'Tikk-tikk... tikk-tikk...' a high-pitched voice called out from the darkness.

A pale woman emerged from the gloom down the corridor. The light of the lamps began shining across her moon-shaped face.

Beetlebrow watched the woman crawling along the yellow floor-tiles, her purple silk dress stretching around the shuffling limbs of her skeletal body.

The woman drew close to the dog and lunged forwards. The three strands of pearl necklaces around her wrinkled throat clinked against the floor.

The women's dainty hands caught the tiny dog by its back legs. Beetlebrow glimpsed the little animal's front paws scrambling in the air as the woman lifted it up to her face, squashed its body against her round cheeks and pressed kisses against its squirming snout.

'Why would you want to run from me?' the woman cooed.

She looked down the white corridor. Beetlebrow met her gaze. The woman's grip tightened around the dog's belly. Beetlebrow saw her backing away into the dim depths of the passageway.

Ray Rez spun around. He faced Beetlebrow and Pook.

'You are not to talk to His Majesty King Ancissus,' he whispered. 'His Majesty shall talk to you... when he chooses to. And do not – I repeat do not – look at His Majesty's hands.'

'All right,' Pook said.

Ray Rez glanced at Beetlebrow.

Beetlebrow nodded.

Ray Rez opened the white door and stepped through into the bright, white room beyond. Beetlebrow smelt the sweet, heady aroma of frankincense. Ray Rez stopped a few paces beyond the doorway and crossed his ankles as he bowed towards the back wall of the room.

Beetlebrow glanced down at the cold white tiles under her feet. She wondered if they were made of ivory.

Ray Rez drew himself upright again and began walking down into the room. Beetlebrow and Pook started following after his careful steps.

A tall man was sitting upright on a wooden chair by the back wall of the white room. His head was bald, his complexion cream-coloured and his long black beard double-pointed. A purple silk loincloth separated his muscled torso from his bulging calves.

Ray Rez walked towards the centre of the ivory tiles and became still. Beetlebrow and Pook stopped to his right.

'My most humble greetings, Your Majesty,' Ray Rez said. 'We hail King Ancissus the Third, Lord And Regent of the Setting Sun.'

Ray Rez bowed low before the king; Beetlebrow thought his head was going to hit the floor.

'These are the two female subjects,' Ray Rez went on, 'the girls Beetlebrow and Pook, of whom we have spoken.'

He backed away from the room. Beetlebrow looked at King Ancissus. She felt his dark eyes burning through her. To Beetlebrow, his half-naked body appeared to be infused with riches.

She noticed two tattooed roses on the right side of his chest. The petals of the right rose were purple and those of the left remained unshaded against the king's pale skin. There was a rhino-horn bowl next to his bare feet. Several pomegranate halves lay within its black confines.

Ray Rez returned to Beetlebrow's side. The two musicians in blue and silver robes sat down cross-legged against the white wall to his left. Beetlebrow spotted the ancient scars around their eyes; she had heard of the children of servants being blinded, to be more discreet when they came to serve.

'You girls have succeeded in breaking through our defences, we gather?' King Ancissus asked, his voice soft and mild.

Beetlebrow glanced at Pook, and saw the frightened gaze of her brown eyes was set on King Ancissus.

'Yes, Your Majesty,' Pook replied. 'We want to work for you.'

'You must be very clever and resourceful girls,' the king said. 'We are most impressed.'

'Who d'you mean by "we"?' Beetlebrow asked.

'We are referring to our royal person, young lady,' the king replied.

Pook glanced at Beetlebrow. 'He means himself.'

Beetlebrow saw her meek smile.

'That is correct,' the king said. 'Now, girls, would you like to help us, and deliver a message that is vital to the kingdom?'

'Yes,' said Pook.

'Good,' the king said. 'Now... approach...'

Beetlebrow and Pook stepped towards him. Beetlebrow felt something soft under her toes. She looked downwards. She noticed a pure-white fur-rug beneath her feet. It was almost invisible against the tiles. She knew there would be many details hidden here among patterns she could not read.

She looked up at the king's gaze. She was two paces away from him when she noticed his eyes narrowing. She halted. Pook stopped beside her, and Beetlebrow saw the king's long, thin hands settling down onto the arm-rests of his chair.

'We need to inform you in advance that you will not understand the message,' King Ancissus said, 'and not only because you are children.'

Beetlebrow smirked.

'You girls have been able to enter our palace,' King Ancissus went on, 'bypassing the foreign besieging factions outside our walls. That indicates your great resourcefulness, stealth and courage. We require at this time such qualities in the person or persons who will cross the realm of the Dalcratty Empire to deliver a message to our first cousin in the east, His Majesty, King Hassan the Seventh, Lord And Regent of the Rising Sun, who dwells in the Empire's sacred mother city of Dalcratty.'

The king glanced at Pook. 'Our own messengers are apparently incapable of delivering our words to our cousin. Whole armies of soldiers have been destroyed trying to leave our Capitat. Perhaps there is wisdom in sending people who are less likely to be noticed, especially such resourceful girls as you appear to be.'

Beetlebrow saw the attention of his dark eyes turning towards her. She quickly nodded.

'We shall tell you the message now,' King Ancissus said.

'Listen closely now, girls,' Ray Rez whispered behind Beetlebrow.

The king's back straightened. 'The message must be repeated word-for-word to His Majesty, our cousin.'

'*By stumbling hearts,*' Beetlebrow heard King Ancissus intone, his voice becoming deep and rich, '*growth split sleep, and engraved the earnings two could not keep.*'

She saw dark lines gathering across his forehead.

'Repeat the message for us, please,' King Ancissus said.

'*By stumbling...*' Beetlebrow said.

She glanced right at Pook. Pook was still staring up at the king.

'*By... by stumbling hearts,*' Pook said. '*Growth slit* –'

'*Split,*' Ray Rez muttered behind her.

Beetlebrow noticed King Ancissus's long, bony hands grasping onto the arm-rests of his chair.

'*By stumbling hearts,*' she went on, '*growth split sleep.*'

'*And engraved the earnings...*' Pook said.

She glanced left, and Beetlebrow saw the strain in her eyes.

'*Two,*' Ray Rez whispered.

'*Two could not keep,*' Pook said.

Beetlebrow heard her exhale.

King Ancissus leant forwards. 'Again, if you please.'

'*By stumbling hearts, growth split sleep,*' Beetlebrow said.

'*And engraved the earnings two could not keep,*' Pook added.

'Good,' King Ancissus said. 'Very good. Working together, you remember it perfectly. Now, can either of you read and write?'

Beetlebrow shook her head.

'I can,' Pook said.

Beetlebrow glanced at her. 'Can you?'

Pook raised her left eyebrow. 'Yes.'

The king waved his right index finger at Pook. 'You must never write the message down. Do you promise that?'

'Yes,' Pook said.

'Very good,' replied King Ancissus. 'And now you've got the message right between you both, do not forget it.'

'I won't,' Beetlebrow said.

'I promise,' said Pook.

Beetlebrow watched King Ancissus working a thick silver bracelet from around the bony wrist of his right arm. When it was clear of his hand he held it out towards the room.

Beetlebrow walked away from Pook's side, stepping forwards a few paces towards the king. She looked at the silver bracelet he held between his slender fingers. It was horseshoe-shaped and had two pointed ends.

Beetlebrow glanced at the king's face. She noticed the sheen of pale make-up across his skin.

She reached out her left hand, plucked the bracelet from the king's grasp, and then stepped backwards. She enclosed the silver band within her fist.

'Bow to His Majesty,' Ray Rez whispered.

Beetlebrow and Pook dipped their heads towards King Ancissus for a moment.

The king rose to his feet, his elongated body unfurling from his chair. Beetlebrow watched his expressionless face soaring above her head. She saw his unfocused gaze turning towards the white door at the other end of the room. She noticed his pale hands stroking across one another.

Ray Rez touched her right shoulder. Beetlebrow turned around. The door at the rear of the room was open. The musicians had gone.

'Farewell, messengers,' the king said. 'We of the Dalcratty Empire are relying upon you.'

Beetlebrow glimpsed a white door opening in the white wall on her right. She saw a turquoise-tiled room beyond. Dozens of blue-robed, white-bearded men were circled around a six-foot-wide azure bowl.

Ray Rez placed his hands down on Beetlebrow and Pook's shoulders. He began stepping forwards. Beetlebrow and Pook started walking ahead of him back across the tiles.

Beetlebrow glanced right. King Ancissus's lean frame was stalking towards the bowl of the turquoise room. Beetlebrow watched the white door closing behind him, and its shape vanishing along the white width of the wall.

She felt Ray Rez's hand gripping tighter against her right shoulder. She faced forwards again, looking at the door at the rear of the room.

The three stepped out into the white corridor. Ray Rez pulled the door closed, and Beetlebrow heard wordless, guttural singing emerging from the room she had left behind.

11
The bracelet

Ray Rez started walking back along the white corridor. Beetlebrow and Pook followed.

Beetlebrow glimpsed the walls to her left and right. She saw oil-lamps dimming as the last of their fuel burnt away.

She gripped the bracelet in her left hand. Its hard silver surface felt cold and smooth. She looked at Pook, and saw her eyes were half-closed.

'We'll be able to rest soon,' Beetlebrow whispered. 'It can't be much further.'

She looked down the corridor. She felt the weight of the message lowering onto her shoulders, and she kept walking onwards.

She noticed Ray Rez standing next to the red velvet curtain and turning around.

Beetlebrow and Pook stopped in front of him.

Ray Rez wrinkled hands began clasping against each other, their liver-spotted skin tightening around his knuckles.

'There is...another matter,' he said, his head dipping downwards, his brown eyes looking out from underneath his black eyebrows. 'Usually a traveller of the Dalcratty Empire heading east would cross the Empire's trade-route from Byrehaven to Relleken, but... we will need you to go by a different route, and enter the north-eastern principality of Essum, and find a way into their prison.'

Ray Rez looked at the wall on his right. Beetlebrow followed his gaze, and saw the blankness of the milk-white wall.

'Why've we got to go to Essum?' she asked.

'There... there is an agent of the Dalcratty Empire incarcerated in the prison,' Ray Rez replied. 'I travelled with him, seven years ago, from Dalcratty. He and I came as representatives of His Majesty King Hassan to negotiate the re-opening of the old trade-route from the sea-port of Tirrendahl to the city of Essum. We were tasked with arranging this matter, so that the old commercial road from Dalcratty to Stellingkorr could be complete, as it was when the Empire ruled Essum, over a century ago. We – that is, the agent and I – carried with us a gift to Prince Tevyan, the regent of Essum. But... this gift was misunderstood.

It was comprised of a pair of antique vases, which our scholars had dated as being from the ancient days of Essum's previous regime. I shan't forget the look of disgust on Prince Tevyan's face when I presented these vases to him. He left the room immediately, along with his advisors and guards. I believe, looking back, that the existence of these vases was seen as an attack on Essum's history, where the only remaining artwork from the time before the Dalcratty Empire's occupation of the city was supposed to be represented by the Painting.'

'The painting?' Pook asked.

'Oh,' Ray Rez replied, 'you'll hear more than enough in Essum about their Painting when you reached that dreadful city.'

'So... this agent is in prison there?' Beetlebrow asked.

Ray Rez nodded. 'Yes. I... I could have stayed, and been jailed, like him, but I was given a chance to escape, and I took it. The agent's name is Bussert Maris. He was my friend. My close friend. And I left him behind.'

He faced Beetlebrow. She saw his wearied eyes glistening through the gloom.

'Bussert carried with him the passphrase for any messenger to be granted an audience with King Hassan,' Ray Rez went on. 'He kept the words of the passphrase secret, even from me. Bussert was the protégé of Jaderick Tench, so one would expect no less dedication, or secrecy. Tench was the chancellor of Hassan the Sixth, and under his tutelage many diplomats and spies were fostered to give strength to His Majesty's reign. Bussert was one of them, and you will need to hear the passphrase from him directly, otherwise you won't be able to see His Majesty, King of Dalcratty.'

Beetlebrow nodded.

'We understand,' Pook said.

'If you are able to reach Bussert Maris in Essum,' Ray Rez said, 'please do not mention my name. It will be much more painful for Bussert, in the prison, if he starts thinking about the times when he was free.'

Beetlebrow saw the lamps guttering on the white walls, sinking the corridor within the sepia glow of their dying light.

'It was sometime in the dark early hours of the morning when soldiers broke into our apartment,' Ray Rez went on. 'Bussert and I were in bed when we heard the door breaking down. We awoke as soldiers entered the room. Prince Teyvan's elite guard... they wear these golden masks on their faces. Even now, I can still see those glimmering, expressionless facades storming towards Bussert and I. The soldiers dragged us onto the floor and made us kneel down with our hands behind our heads. In their haste, in their haste... these soldiers had forgotten to secure the doorway to the balcony. I saw Bussert rushing to his feet and heading towards the soldiers. I still do not know whether he was causing a distraction, or was just trying to escape, but in the confusion I managed to slip away onto the balcony and scale down to the pavement below. Bussert and I had always said if we were ever separated in Essum, we would meet each other at the city's docks. That night I made my way there alone and I... I found a ship willing to take me to Byrehaven, and I took it. I was starving and penniless when I arrived in Stellingkorr, and I was received so kindly by His Majesty. I'm sure Bussert would understand, understand my struggle over these past seven years within this palace.'

He glanced down at the floor. 'Seven years. It feels so much longer ago. I was fifty-four when I left Essum, and Bussert fifty-five, but when I... when I look back at my time in the city, I picture us as young men.'

He exhaled. He looked at Beetlebrow and Pook again.

'Our spies embedded within Essum have told us Bussert is imprisoned in the city's secret jail. So please, if you able to see him... do not mention my name. The light of remembering our life together might make the darkness of the dungeon in which Bussert now dwells appear even deeper than it already is.'

Beetlebrow heard footsteps approaching from behind the red curtain.

Ray Rez pulled the sheet of velvet aside.

Beetlebrow glimpsed Magell walking along the bare earth of the dim, adobe-walled corridor beyond. He was holding his hands behind his back.

Ray Rez bowed at the waist towards Magell. Beetlebrow noticed Magell's mouth thinning out in a grim little smile as he nodded in reply. He stopped in the dirt of the adobe corridor.

Ray Rez glanced at Beetlebrow and Pook. 'Now, I'll need you to repeat the message for me. I need to be sure, girls, that you have it correctly.'

Beetlebrow glanced left, and saw Pook looking back at her.

'*By stumbling hearts, growth split sleep,*' Pook said.

'*And engraved the earnings two could not keep.*'

Ray Rez looked at Beetlebrow, and then at Pook.

'Thank you, girls,' he said. He smiled. 'May the spirits of the departed kings of Stellingkorr speed you on your journey.'

'Thank you,' said Pook.

Ray Rez turned around. Beetlebrow watched him walking away along the white corridor.

She heard Magell clearing his throat. Beetlebrow and Pook faced him.

Magell raised his right hand and beckoned them into the adobe-walled corridor. 'This way, messengers.'

Beetlebrow and Pook followed Magell back through the red curtain. Beetlebrow glanced over her right shoulder. She saw the white-walled corridor was empty. Its light had become faint and brown.

Magell walked back through the adobe corridor with Beetlebrow and Pook stepping behind his lead. He turned right through the room of paintings and entered into a bronze-painted hall. Beetlebrow and Pook followed him between pillars festooned with flowers.

Beetlebrow glanced through the wall of windows to the right of the room. She saw a square garden open to the air.

Three of its sides were bordered by plum-brick walls several yards high. Yellow and orange butterflies were swooping above the garden's paving-stones and segmented flowerbeds. Beetlebrow noticed a young man laying face-down on the patio beside a fig-tree sapling. He was wearing a white loin-cloth. A cracked jar was spilling just beyond the reach of his outstretched hand. Hundreds of black ants were swarming around the purple puddle surrounding the broken vessel.

Beetlebrow and Pook followed Magell through an arched doorway and into the shadowy confines of the adjoining room. Beetlebrow smelt ancient mould in the air. The dusty shelves from floor to ceiling were filled with vases and statues. She noticed depictions of warriors bearing spears, and of men embracing women.

'What're all these?' Pook asked.

'Gifts from friends and allies not important enough to decorate the halls at this time,' Magell replied. 'But revisions to history might require their presence one day.'

Beetlebrow glanced across the stone images of women and men. The women wore long draping clothes around their chubby-thighed bodies. The men's tall, lean bodies, chests and arms were segmented into muscles. Beetlebrow realised these statues were all depictions of people who had passed through the Dalcratty Empire, had achieved some great deed, and then had had their images hardened into stone.

She noticed Magell inching between the shelves. She watched him ducking and swerving across the room, his portly body inching past surfaces covered with matted layers of dust. He squeezed between two granite statues, climbed over a footstool, and stepped into a slender, egg-shell blue corridor beyond.

Beetlebrow and Pook slipped across the room after him, their slim shapes gliding between the dusty statues.

Magell wiped sweat from his forehead with a handkerchief. Beetlebrow and Pook approached. Magell scratched at his black and grey striped beard. Beetlebrow noticed a dark green patch of damp spreading out in an upper corner of the corridor.

'These shall be your last instructions before you meet the agent at the edge of the city,' Magell said. 'Are you ready?'

Pook nodded.

Magell unlocked a white door with a brass key and stepped through.

Beetlebrow noticed swirling arrangements of mounted spears, swords, axes and halberds covering the walls of the square room inside. Magell walked towards single caramel-coloured bench set against its back wall. He sat down on its varnished surface. Pook sat down beside him.

Beetlebrow leant against the opposite wall. She glimpsed weapons gleaming above her head.

'When you are travelling, do not accept instructions other than those which you receive from our agents,' Magell said to Pook. 'They shall know you are legitimate by the silver bracelet, and will not accept you as messengers otherwise, so keep it with you always.'

He glanced at Beetlebrow.

'Please,' Magell went on, 'if you could show it to me now...'

Beetlebrow held out the silver bracelet. She noticed the double-headed rose embossed at its centre.

She saw Magell holding open a small cedar-wood box between his hands. Three blood-stained silver bracelets were laying on the salmon-pink silk cushion inside.

'These have left been outside our gates in the past year,' Magell said. 'They were taken from the other messengers that set out for Dalcratty, soldiers and spies alike. There are ungrateful citizens in Stellingkorr, who do not appreciate all that the House of Rashem has done for them, all that it has sacrificed and fought and paid for, all to make their lives better. These people want this message to be stopped, so they can keep our good citizens hungry, and trick them into partaking in some sort of rebellion.'

His stubby fingers slipped across the lid of the cedar box and snapped it closed.

'Could I see those again?' Beetlebrow asked. 'For a moment, please?'

Magell looked at her for a moment.

'If you... like,' he said.

He opened the box and held it out towards her. 'No doubt these anarchists tried to use these bracelets for devious means, but without the passphrase to enter Dalcratty, these signs of His Majesty are merely symbols.'

Beetlebrow took the box from his hands.

Pook faced Magell. 'We'll not tell anyone we have the message. They won't know.'

Beetlebrow lifted the three silver bands away from their silk cushion.

'Good,' Magell said to Pook. 'Do not speak of it to anyone, not even each other. The rebels may overhear.'

He glanced across the four silver bracelets Beetlebrow held between her palms.

'I'd put your own bracelet away now, Beetlebrow, if I were you,' Magell said.

'Why was it Ray Rez who took us to the king, and not you?' Beetlebrow asked.

She saw Magell's gaze tighten its focus on her face. His lips pursed together. She slipped her left hand back into the inside pocket of her robe, put the two remaining bracelets back in the cedar box, closed its lid and held it out towards Magell.

His attention remained on Beetlebrow's eyes as he took the box back into his grasp. She noticed his fingers squeezing against its surface.

'Ray Rez is one of the Yotaran,' Magell said, his teeth gritting together. 'His people of this... religion... have worked alongside the House of Rashem for some decades now, and they are given certain privileges, such as proximity to His Majesty. These are advantages which others have had to work for, which deny others the chance to...'

He frowned.

'That isn't important,' he said.

He put the cedar box down on the ground, placed his right hand inside his cream-coloured robe and held out eight gold coins.

'Now, listen carefully, girls,' Magell said. 'There will much more money than this with the next agent, and there will be a great reward if you are successful in delivering the message to Dalcratty.'

Beetlebrow stared. She had observed the ivory floors, the silver plates and the breastplates of burnished bronze in the halls of the palace, but none had appeared as solid as the gold coins being offered to her now. She felt like the wealth of the building was draining down from the walls and trickling through her fingers.

Her feet started moving forwards. Magell placed four gold coins onto her open palms. She felt the thick metal circles sinking down against her hands. She knew each was worth several hundred loaves of bread.

She turned over a coin. On one face was a profile of King Ancissus. On the other was a double-headed rose in bloom. To Beetlebrow the images appeared as sharp as knives.

She glanced at Pook, and saw her gazing down at the four gold coins glimmering between her own hands.

'Now...' Magell said, 'it is very late, and we have beds ready for you in prepared rooms. You may stay until you feel ready to embark upon your journey.'

Beetlebrow thought of the room in Floodcross. She imagined waking up somewhere else. There would be no scent of pomegranates, and no touch of Lana's hand. There would be silence.

'We won't stop,' she said. 'We'll leave now.'

Magell looked into her eyes. 'We would not advise that. Sometimes... sometimes it's quicker to go slower.'

'Perhaps,' Pook said, 'we should stay and –'.

'We're going now,' Beetlebrow said. 'Before any rebels find out. It'll be safest.'

Magell glanced up at the weapons on the wall.

'You might be right,' he said. He flashed at grin at Beetlebrow. 'Yes,' he went on, 'small wonder you were able to infiltrate our palace where all others had failed.'

He nodded. 'You'll find the first agent in the northeast of the city, at the grey hexagonal tower in the Silkworks district. The agent is a man called Galba Yandarien. You'll be in good hands when you reach him. Yandarien is one of the most brilliant minds to have ever served the Empire. I was fortunate enough to study under him at Dalcratty's university, as the building was then. The education Yandarien gave me meant a great deal to a scholarship-boy, as I was. He will be able to tell you all you need to know about the passage east.'

Magell stood up. Beetlebrow saw Pook slipping her four gold coins inside her tattered sackcloth tunic and rising to her feet.

Magell started walking out the door into the egg-shell blue corridor. Beetlebrow and Pook followed.

'Whichever way you came here,' Magell said. 'Observing the same route back will probably be safest.'

He pointed to a red door on the right of the corridor.

'Goodbye, messengers,' Magell went on. 'May providence and good fortune guide you, and keep the message safe in your hearts.'

'Thank you,' Pook said.

Beetlebrow opened the red door. She and Pook walked into the square stairwell beyond the corridor. Beetlebrow heard echoes of their footsteps clinking down the metal steps.

She stopped and faced Pook.

'I know you're tired,' Beetlebrow said, 'but I think stopping anywhere's a bad idea. I want to feel safe before we slow down. I want to be out of here before we sleep.'

Pook nodded, her eyes closing for a moment.

'We'll cross the city,' Beetlebrow went on, 'and then we'll rest.'

She saw Pook stepping towards her. Pook opened her arms and brought Beetlebrow's slim frame close up against her skinny figure. Beetlebrow closed her eyes. She lay her head on Pook's right shoulder. She drank in the sweet scent of Pook's hair. She felt warmth kindling inside her body, and Pook's soft breaths brushing against her left cheek.

Beetlebrow thought about her own face, as she had glimpsed it in puddles and polished metal, and recalled the frowning expression and thick black eyebrows she had seen staring back at her.

Her body became stiff in Pook's arms. Beetlebrow's hands hung down by her waist, fearful of touching Pook and trying to bind her inside something she could never desire.

Pook released her clasp from her back. Beetlebrow looked at her face. Pook was smiling.

'Thank you,' Pook whispered. 'For this.'

Beetlebrow turned away towards the staircase.

She and Pook headed west across the grounds in the darkness, drawing closer to the sound of the sea. They passed the painted garden, stepped down the cliff-edge towards the shelf of rock, and began side-stepping back along its narrow length.

Beetlebrow shuffled left towards the city being revealed by the dawning day. She felt the salty wind drifting across her cheeks, and tiredness seeping into her thoughts.

She stared down into the gloom towards the sound of waves sidling alongside the base of the cliff. She felt the sheer edge of the lip of rock against her toes. She felt the urge to step down into the depths it offered.

She heard Pook side-stepping towards her. Beetlebrow kept moving left. She glanced down at the shadowed sand of the beach. She imagined how small the imprints of her feet would appear from this height.

Beetlebrow and Pook walked down along the rocks at the base of the cliff and stepped back down onto the beach.

Beetlebrow saw fishing-boats ambling out with nets and lobster-pots across the calm sea towards the emerging morning light. She felt coarse sand pressing underneath the soles of her feet. She lifted up her left foot. Dried smudges of green paint were still clinging to her heels. She started brushing away the grains of sand.

She noticed the bright rays of the dawn sun were spiralling out from the eastern horizon.

Pook stood in front of her. 'What do you think the message means?'

Beetlebrow lowered her foot. 'I don't know.'

'It sounds like a love letter to me,' Pook said.

'A "love letter"?'

'You know... when a boy fancies a girl, and he sends her a letter about it.'

Beetlebrow glanced away. She saw the black outlines of the city emerging through the dawn.

'You're right,' Pook said. 'We should go.'

Beetlebrow and Pook were silent as they walked back through the barricade and entered a cobbled street beyond.

Beetlebrow watched a gaggle of waddling geese being guided by their herder. She saw children running across the ground between the whitewashed walls and shuttered windows, and grey-haired men heaving barrels and hessian sacks along the surrounding streets.

'Here,' Beetlebrow said.

She led Pook towards the stall of a stout man selling fruit from wickerwork baskets. Beetlebrow slipped her left hand into the inside pocket of her robe. She felt the new gold coins against her fingers. The thick metal pieces felt cumbersome, with none of the ease which came with coppers. *Money ain't money if it ain't simple*, she thought.

A shadow fell across her body. The stallholder was backing away from his wares. Beetlebrow turned around.

She saw the cobbled street emptying of people.

Three men were standing in front of her and Pook. They were wearing red and brown uniforms. Beetlebrow noticed the shorter man of the three staring at her face. He had the crossed-swords insignia of a captain across the shoulders of his red tunic.

'We saw you leaving the palace,' he growled. 'We're here to escort you, messengers.'

12
Bottleneck Alley

Beetlebrow glared at the short man. She saw his sepia eyes scowling down at her from between his bald scalp, his snub nose and wispy black goatee beard.

'They didn't tell us about you,' Pook said.

'They never do,' the short man replied. 'Think of us as the back-up. We have informers telling us everything that's said in the palace. We're helping you, messengers, so do what we say and come with us.'

Beetlebrow saw the stalls were unmanned and the cobbles were empty. A wooden ball was lying on the ground where a child had left it.

The short man was stepping out ahead across the empty cobblestones. His gaze was peering into the nearby streets and alleyways.

Real police don't doubt themselves, Beetlebrow thought, *no matter what they do.*

A broad-shouldered man and a tall man pushed Beetlebrow and Pook out into the street.

'We can go by ourselves,' Pook said. 'We don't need –'

The short man looked back at her over his right shoulder.

'What you *need* is to be quiet,' he snapped.

'Where are you taking us?' Pook asked.

'Just shut up.'

The short man headed into a backstreet set between whitewashed walls. Beetlebrow felt gloved hands pushing against her back.

She and Pook entered the shadowed lane behind the cobbled street. The broad-shouldered man was walking to Beetlebrow's left, the tall man to Pook's right. Beetlebrow heard the three men's echoing bootsteps surrounding her body within their relentless press.

She glanced at Pook. Pook's eyes were facing down towards her bare feet. Her arms were loosely folded around her chest.

Beetlebrow looked forwards. She saw the short man marching between the backstreet's whitewashed walls. She noticed a familiar thread of ivy arcing across a bolted door. Her gaze darted around at the narrow lane. She recognised the entrance to Bottleneck Alley some yards ahead of the short man's path.

She remembered hurrying towards this passageway several weeks back with two stolen apples. The salesman had chased her through the streets. She had run into Bottleneck Alley. She had heard the salesman halting by its narrow entrance. She remembered feeling as thin as a knife as she had threaded along the gap between its walls, her slim shoulders rasping against its mud-bricks.

She listened to the bootsteps echoing in the narrow backstreet, and she knew all she wanted was to take Pook by the hand and lead her away from the circle of men.

Beetlebrow's right foot tripped in the dirt. She stumbled forwards. She watched the three men slowing down for a few moments.

She noticed the broad-shouldered man pausing a second longer than the other two. She glanced up at his face and smiled. She saw his shaggy black hair, his broken nose and the vertical scar across the centre of his upper lip. She began walking at her previous pace again. She watched the men stepping onwards down the backstreet.

She looked at Pook. Pook's brown eyes shared her gaze. Beetlebrow nodded towards Bottleneck Alley. Pook glanced ahead.

Beetlebrow saw brightness lighting up in her face. Pook looked at her again. Her arms unfolded, and her hands slipped down to her sides.

Beetlebrow looked up at the broad-shouldered man's face again. Her lips parted. Her smile was wide.

'It's a very pretty day today isn't it?' she said.

'I guess,' he mumbled.

'Can I hold your hand?' she asked, tugging at the right sleeve of his leather uniform.

'No.'

She glanced forwards again. Bottleneck Alley was a slit of blackness roughly five yards ahead along the lane of whitewashed walls.

She heard Pook's bare-footed steps walking by her side.

Beetlebrow smiled at the broad-shouldered man again.

'Can I hold your hand, please?' she asked.

She watched him glancing ahead towards the short man's back.

'All right, girl,' the broad-shouldered man whispered to Beetlebrow. 'But be quiet.'

He splayed out the fingers of his right hand. He held it down towards her.

'Not that one, silly,' Beetlebrow said.

She darted around his body, reappeared on his left and wormed the fingers of her right hand down into his grudging grip.

She glanced at Pook.

'Go,' Beetlebrow mouthed.

She saw the curve of a smile on Pook's lips.

The short man spun around. 'What you doing?' he barked.

The broad-shouldered man looked at him. 'Kid said she wanted to hold my hand.'

Beetlebrow saw the tall man glancing up and down the street.

'Where's the other one gone?' he said.

Beetlebrow glanced towards Bottleneck Alley. Pook's thin frame was squeezing between its narrow walls.

Beetlebrow slipped her knife out of her robe. She pricked its blade into the back of the broad-shouldered man's left hand.

'Ow!' he gasped.

Beetlebrow felt his grasp snapping away from her fingers. She darted left towards Bottleneck Alley. She saw Pook side-stepping along its length.

'Come back, you bitch!' a man yelled.

Beetlebrow stepped sideways between the walls of the alley. Darkness covered her face. She felt her ribs and shoulder-blades being pressed between the mud-bricks.

'Come back!' a man yelled.

'Come 'ere!' another shouted.

Beetlebrow glanced right, and saw the men's wide frames crowding around the neck of the passageway. She heard echoes of their voices clattering up the walls. She looked left. Pook was hurrying out into the light beyond the shadowed passageway.

Beetlebrow squeezed between the last mud-brick walls of Bottleneck Alley, its edges scraping against her body. She burst free. She hurried out into the sunlight of the dirt-row street beyond. She was panting as she stopped in front of Pook.

'Those men will have to circle around, won't they?' Pook said.

Beetlebrow nodded, breathing fast as she glanced around at the street.

The brown earth of its road was rutted between twisting rows of wooden shacks. Under an awning by a wall Beetlebrow saw a middle-aged woman sitting on the ground behind a red blanket covered with thin, green pears. Three seamstresses walked by from the left, holding their hands against their foreheads as they shielded their eyes from the sun. An old man in a long draping robe, his weathered face ingrained with dust, was turning a corner to the right.

Beetlebrow noticed Pook looking at her.

'What?' Beetlebrow asked.

'I didn't know what you were doing there.'

Beetlebrow shrugged. 'I was giving you a chance to get away.'
Pook stared at her for a moment.
'All right,' Pook said, and looked away.
Beetlebrow reached her left hand into the pocket of her robe. Her fingers glanced against the gold coins. She felt their heaviness. Her hand slowly returned to her side, and she looked at Pook.
'We'd best not use the money they gave us,' Beetlebrow said. 'It'll bring attention.'
Pook held out her right hand. Beetlebrow saw two copper coins in her palm.
Pook's lips parted as she smiled. 'Gozher didn't look like he needed these anymore.'

13
Selena

Beetlebrow and Pook bought two pears with Gozher's money; they bit down into the wet, ripened flesh of the fruits as they walked east through the city. Beetlebrow listened to the footsteps, rattling carts and overlapping conversations swirling between the people of the nearby streets.

In the afternoon they passed the open doors of a warehouse. Beetlebrow saw stout workmen trooping back and forth between its shelves carrying sacks and barrels and crates.

She noticed Pook glancing at a ragged man sitting outside on the broken planks of a wooden pallet.

Beetlebrow followed her gaze. The man's small, staring eyes appeared lost within his long, leathery face.

'What is it?' Beetlebrow asked Pook.

'I used to live round here,' Pook said.

Beetlebrow saw the man's looking down at the dirt by his bare feet, where the ground was too dry for even weeds to grow.

They entered the paved streets of the Silkworks district in the purple light of dusk. Stars were arriving as the sun disappeared above the lofty houses.

Beetlebrow glimpsed a willowy, bronze-coloured fox running out from a hole to her left and vanishing into the darkness to her right.

She looked upwards, and saw a grey tower rising above the sharp-cornered limestone buildings of the neighbourhood. She watched the six stone faces of the five-storey building slowly revolving to her progress through the wide, tree-lined avenues of the district.

'Keep in the shadows, away from any lamps,' she whispered to Pook. 'Red and browns grab people on the street here and blame them for robberies. It happened to my brother Joe. The police got reward money from a shopkeeper, and Joe got beaten up.'

'Do you have family then?' Pook whispered.

'Just stick to the shadows.'

Beetlebrow guessed Alder and Joe would be stalking through Floodcross by now, peering down alleyways and calling out her name.

As she walked through the evening darkness of the Silkworks district, she felt every step of her bare feet was taking her further away from the life of begging her brothers had planned out for her.

She imagined herself sitting cross-legged in the dirt of Floodcross's market, hoping every day for pity and a copper coin. She thought of her face becoming weathered, and her expressions wearing away, as the unceasing months and years kept her rooted down to a single spot by a wall.

She imagined staggering back up the stairs one night, the sound of the few coins she had managed to beg over the day shaking inside the ragged woollen confines of her robe. She imagined her feet stumbling underneath her wearied body as she finally trudged up the last steps and opened the door at the top of the building. She imagined collapsing down onto the floorboards, her face pressing against coarse wooden planks while exhaustion made her succumb to its pull. She knew, in her last moments of wakefulness, she would feel Alder and Joe's hands running through her pockets.

She heard Pook's steps walking by her side. Beetlebrow listened to her steady pace, and focused her gaze on the sight of the hexagonal tower surging above the limestone houses nestling around its base.

They approached the blue door at the foot of the tower. Beetlebrow noticed woodworm holes dotted under its peeling veneer of paint. She and Pook walked through the open doorway, stepping past the square block of purple-veined marble propping it open. Beetlebrow glimpsed a brass bell laying on its surface.

She smelt rotting leather as she stepped into the gloom of the entrance hall with Pook by her side. Beetlebrow felt cold tiles under the soles of her feet. She heard the wind whistling through the doorway.

A scrawny pigeon was pottering across the right of the black and white floor-tiles towards a pillar of brown books teetering by the black-slate staircase.

The blue door creaked.

Beetlebrow grabbed Pook's left hand.

Together they ran up the nine wooden steps of the staircase and hurried along the brown-walled corridor at its summit, their skinny bodies dodging between the piles of books and papers spread out across the carpet. Beetlebrow spotted a black door at the end of the hallway.

'In here,' she hissed to Pook.

Beetlebrow wrenched open the black door. She and Pook scurried inside. Beetlebrow glanced around at the room they had entered. It was roughly a yard square and twenty yards high. Its walls were lined with tightly-packed shelves of brown leather-bound books. Far above her head Beetlebrow saw silver clouds drifting above a square skylight.

She closed the door in front of herself, and saw darkness flooding across the room. She noticed a line of light budding underneath the blackness of the wooden rectangle. Its glow was spreading out across the wooden floorboards.

Beetlebrow glanced at Pook and nodded towards a dark corner on the left of the room. Pook hurried over into its blackness and squatted down.

Beetlebrow faced the door. She began stepping backwards. She pulled out her rusted knife. The line of orange light was becoming broader across the floorboards. She heard footsteps. Her shoulder-blades bumped against wooden shelves. She felt ensnared within the room's scents of leather and ink.

She kept her eyes on the door. She gripped the wooden handle of her blade in her left hand. She glimpsed the growing illumination slipping towards her toes.

The door opened. Beetlebrow saw a fresh-faced young woman standing in its frame. She was holding a stub of a yellow candle in her right hand. Beetlebrow saw the woman's sharp cheekbones, her short, black, side-parted hair and smirking expression.

'You certainly are a devious little creature, aren't you?' the woman said.

Beetlebrow heard the precise pronunciation of her words. The flame was reflecting vertical orange streaks within the woman's eyes.

'All the fancy buildings and houses in Silkworks and you've chosen this one to break into?' the woman went on. 'Unless you want mouldering ledgers or dead rats, I don't think you're going to find much worth stealing here.'

She glanced at the knife in Beetlebrow's hand.

'Well, what are you here for then?' the woman said.

'We were told to come to the tower to meet Galba Yandarien.'

'Well, I'm the one who does Galba's work round here,' the woman said. 'My name's Selena. If you really want to find Galba, you might try the Three Crows Inn. Or the Red Hart. Or Denzel's Long Bar.'

Beetlebrow's right hand slipped inside the pocket of the robe. She took out the bracelet. She saw its edge shining to the light of the candle.

'They told us to show this to Galba Yandarien,' she said. 'So he'd know who we are.'

Selena looked at the silver band.

'Oh!' she said. 'You're... yes. I understand.'

Pook stepped out of the dark corner. 'We need to know where to go next.'

Selena blinked.

She smiled.

'Let me get you some tea and some food,' she said. 'It's Drowston you're to go to next. The next agent is there.'

'Where's Drowston?' Pook asked.

'Just a few miles east of the city.'

A bell tinkled downstairs.

Selena stared out into the darkness of the doorway. Beetlebrow saw her fast breaths making white clouds in the air.

'Visitors don't come at this hour,' Selena whispered. 'Stay here, stay here.'

She ran out into the corridor. Beetlebrow and Pook stepped after her. Selena started hurrying down the stairs.

Beetlebrow and Pook stopped by the wooden railings above the staircase and looked down into the gloom of entrance hall.

Beetlebrow saw the light of the candle slowly moving across the black and white tiles below. She glimpsed Selena looking at the shadowed figures of two men standing in the darkness by the open door.

'Can I help?' she asked.

'Excuse me miss,' a growling voice replied, 'are you… are you Galba, miss?'

Beetlebrow's feet stepped back from the railings. She felt warmth draining away from her face.

'What is it?' Pook whispered.

Beetlebrow glanced right, saw Pook looking at her, and then stared down into the darkness of the entrance hall again.

'Galba?' Selena replied. 'No, no, he's not in today.'

'We're helping two messengers through the city,' a second man said. 'Two imperial messengers. They said they were coming here. We got separated. They'll want to find us.'

'Ah,' Selena said.

'Have they been here, the girls?' the second man asked.

'If you could just wait here a minute, please.'

Selena began walking back up the stairs. Beetlebrow saw her vague sphere of light trembling up the surrounding walls.

Selena walked out onto the threadbare carpet at the top of the steps. She looked downwards.

'I'm sorry…' she whispered.

'It's all right,' Pook replied. 'We know have to leave. We don't want you to get hurt too.'

Selena's mouth opened, and then closed again. She nodded. 'They did give you some money at the palace, didn't they?'

Pook nodded. 'Yes.'

'You'll need a gold coin each to pay the toll to leave the eastern gate of the city. Take a wagon along the road east. You'll be in Drowston within an hour. It'll take you most of a day on foot otherwise.'

'I don't like waiting, miss,' the first voice growled.

Beetlebrow heard the tread of heavy feet stepping onto the bottom of the staircase. She glanced up and down the corridor. She noticed a shuttered window to her left.

'In Drowston, look for a house next to a bakery,' Selena whispered to Pook. 'Under the sign of two roses, you'll find the next agent, a man called Darvan Kess, a scribe and an expert in Essum's affairs...'

Footsteps began stamping up the staircase.

Beetlebrow grabbed Pook's hand, ran towards the window on the left and shoved open its shutters. Pook straddled the sill and stepped out into the night.

Beetlebrow started lowering her down towards the dark ground inch by inch. She felt Pook's clasp slowly letting go of her hand finger by finger, and then heard her landing quietly in the murky grass below.

Beetlebrow stepped out of the window, turned around and hung onto the sill. She felt the wind buffeting against her body. She saw Selena standing in the corridor between the looming towers of books. Selena was looking towards the stairs. The gaze of her eyes appeared hollow.

Beetlebrow glimpsed a gangly man striding across the carpet towards the light of Selena's candle. Beside him was Alder.

Beetlebrow let go of the windowsill. She dropped down into the long grass in the yard of the tower.

She saw Pook, crouched in the gloom, looking up towards the glow of the square window above.

'Don't,' Beetlebrow whispered. 'We can't go back. We have to leave.'

'Leave?' Pook said, and faced towards her.

'Leave Stellingkorr.'

'I... I ain't been anywhere else,' Pook said.

'Me neither,' Beetlebrow replied.

The night was dark and clouds were hiding the stars. She looked towards the east.

14
The eastern gate

Beetlebrow's bony knees were pressing down the southern edge of a flat rooftop. Her slender hands were gripping around the last line of its terracotta tiles.

She glanced left, and glimpsed Pook sitting cross-legged in the darkness a few feet back from the precipice.

Beetlebrow looked down over the edge of the rooftop. Her hands grasped tighter against the tiles. She felt moss under her fingertips. She saw the street two storeys below. Her stomach lurched.

She glanced across the dozens of people standing in a line down the centre of the dirt-row lane. Their waiting bodies were lit by the torches mounted on the surrounding grey walls of square buildings. The queue remained motionless while their flickering shadows were cast left and right across the brown earth.

A lanky man was first in line. He stood roughly five yards away from the eastern gate. Beetlebrow spotted a grey-bearded policeman standing underneath the looming black arch, and beyond its darkness she glimpsed the road leading east to Drowston.

'There're red and browns down here too,' she whispered to Pook. 'I don't want to chance it.'

'We'll find a way out of the city,' Pook replied, her voice slow and drowsy. 'There has to be one.'

Beetlebrow heard the echoing sound of an isolated cough cracking across the silence below.

The grey-bearded policeman nodded towards the queue. The lanky man stepped forwards a few paces and placed four gold coins in his right hand. Beetlebrow watched the policeman peering down at the money in his palm. He glanced at the two small children standing behind the lanky man. They began wrapping their arms around the waist of a short, squat woman dressed in black robes.

Beetlebrow took out a gold coin from her inside pocket. In the blackness of the rooftop she ran her thumb across its thick edges.

The grey-bearded policeman jerked his thumb over his left shoulder. Beetlebrow watched the family of four grabbing their bags from the ground and hurrying under the gate.

The queue stepped forward a pace.

The grey-bearded policeman nodded towards the three slim young men standing at the head of the line. The three stepped forwards together. Each handed over a single gold piece.

The policemen bit into one of the coins. Beetlebrow saw him frown. The policeman looked back over his shoulder to the darkness under the gate.

Beetlebrow heard footsteps running out from the shadows below the arch. Seven policemen entered the light. They stormed across the dirt. Echoes of their pounding bootsteps were thumping across the surrounding walls. The seven surged around their grey-bearded colleague like a river flooding around the trunk of a tree.

The three young men started running away from the light of the torches. The rest of the queue remained in place.

Beetlebrow watched the seven police charging across the street. Two of the young men were shoved down face-first into the dirt. The third was felled with a baton-crack across the back of his head. The police dragged the bodies away into the shadows on the right of the street.

The queue moved forward a pace.

Beetlebrow's hands clenched together. She saw the line remaining as a trail of dark shapes down the centre of the light of the torches.

She heard a metallic sound from the left of the gate. She crawled over to the eastern edge of the rooftop and looked down into the blackness beneath its tiles. She heard a rumbling sound emerging from the ground two storeys below.

'Perhaps we should wait until it's light,' Pook said. 'Find some other way around the gate.'

Beetlebrow heard the rumbling sound stop. A grinding noise began. She leant down further over the rooftop. Her grip tightened around the terracotta tiles. She shuffled her knees up against the heels of her hands. She smelt an acrid stench coursing up towards her nose.

She saw a patch of dull orange light slowly rising from the lowest part of the wall.

'We can get down there,' Beetlebrow whispered.

'What did you say?' Pook asked.

'There,' Beetlebrow said, her gaze fixed on the growing square of light. 'Those are prisoners. I bet they've come from the sewage pits. They're pushing a cart under the wall. We can get through.'

She grabbed Pook by the left hand and ran across the rooftop towards its northern edge.

Beetlebrow grabbed onto the top of a terracotta drainpipe, swung around, and began descending along the dark face of the building, her hands grasping onto windowsills and bricks. She heard Pook climbing down towards her from above.

The rumbling sound stopped. Beetlebrow glanced left. She saw the square of light remaining still as it streamed out from the base of the shadowed wall.

She looked downwards. She saw the ground several yards below her feet. Beetlebrow let go of the drainpipe. She felt herself falling.

Her feet landed on the hard earth. Pain seized onto her shins.

She heard Pook dropping down beside her. Beetlebrow grabbed her right hand. Her legs were aching as she yanked Pook on towards the light.

She heard the prisoners' chains rattling away into the blackness to her left. Beetlebrow dropped down onto her hands and knees, pulled Pook into the square tunnel under the wall, and started crawling into the stench and darkness of its narrow enclosure. She felt a stone ceiling above her head and a coarse concrete floor beneath her knees. She kept hold of Pook's hand.

She heard the rumbling sound starting again; she guessed gears were grinding inside the wall.

Beetlebrow looked back west along the darkness of the tunnel. An iron door was drawing closed against the concrete floor. She saw the light of torches in Stellingkorr vanishing beneath its black descent. The door clanged shut. She felt its impact ringing across her teeth. She heard silence around herself.

'Pook?' she whispered.

'I'm all right,' Pook replied.

Beetlebrow let go of her hand, faced towards the blackness and began crawling further into its depths. She felt slime under her hands. She heard the humming rasps of flies buzzing past her ears.

She glimpsed a dim patch of light ahead, and she hurried towards its glow.

The stench of sewage increased. Beetlebrow's eyes began stinging. She started crawling faster along the tunnel. The walls pressing against her body felt like teeth trying to swallow her back inside the city.

She gasped as she tasted fresh air. She stumbled out of the tunnel on her hands and knees. The earth felt smooth under the touch of her fingers. She hurried to her feet. She was breathing fast.

Her first few steps outside the tunnel felt aimless. She realised she was walking beyond the streets of Stellingkorr. She felt like a baby bird discarding its downy feathers.

She sensed the heaviness of the silver bracelet and the gold coins in the pockets of her robe; by their weight, she knew she and Pook had escaped from the tight corners, dead-end roads and garbage-mired passageways of the city.

She looked at the iron sewage cart standing outside the tunnel, and then glanced north. She noticed an oxen-drawn wagon waiting outside the arch of the gate. The family of four were sitting in the back. To the east was the blurry sight of hundreds of tents spread out across the brown fields of dirt surrounding the city.

Beetlebrow heard a noise behind herself.

Pook crawled out of the tunnel, rose to her feet and then fell back down again onto her hands and knees and began coughing onto the earth.

Beetlebrow hurried towards her. She glimpsed Pook wiping her mouth with the tattered sleeve of her tunic.

'Not much further,' Beetlebrow softly said. 'We can stop soon, but we're not safe yet.'

'When will we ever be safe?' Pook asked.

Beetlebrow held out her right hand. Pook looked up into her eyes.

'We'd better go,' Beetlebrow said. 'They'll be someone collecting the cart from this side.'

Pook grasped onto her hand and slowly stood up. Beetlebrow glimpsed the red scrapes across her face and bloody rips along her knuckles. She looked at her hessian tunic. It was torn at the shoulders and smeared with brown streaks.

'Not much further,' Beetlebrow whispered.

They started walking towards the tented town, stepping through the dusty path winding between the triangular shapes and entering the illumination of its camp-fires.

Beetlebrow noticed a stocky, topless man to her left. White hairs coursed around his flabby chest. He was holding an empty frying-pan over a crackling fire.

He glanced at Pook, and winked.

Beetlebrow strode towards the man. She glared up at his face.

The man lowered his eyes. 'All right, all right, miss. Just being friendly.'

Beetlebrow walked back towards Pook and nodded towards the east. She looked at the blackness beyond the lights of the camp

'Not much longer,' she whispered. 'Then we can stop.'

She glanced back at the shadowed city-wall of Stellingkorr. She saw the night-time glow of the streets muting the light of the stars above.

She and Pook headed further between the tents. They passed two elderly women sitting on tall chairs, a thin man smoking a long clay pipe, and a beefy, bald man gutting mackerel as three thin ginger-and-cream cats weaved in and out of his hairy legs. Beetlebrow heard muffled talk and a guitar-player plucking at occasional notes.

She noticed a white-haired woman sitting on a three-legged stool to her left. She wore a widow's black headscarf.

Beetlebrow saw the two remaining fingers of the woman's left hand fiddling with a string of red beads. On a woollen rug by the woman's feet were pieces of dull cutlery, a heap of robes, bundles of firewood, blankets, several battered leather satchels and a pile of rusted, siege-engine cogs.

Beetlebrow pointed to a black leather satchel, two thick slate-grey robes and two grey blankets.

'Two silvers, four coppers,' the white-haired woman said.

Beetlebrow held out a gold coin. She felt its heaviness against her palm. The white-haired woman glanced at her trembling hand and then looked up at her face. 'Where did a young girl get this kind of money?'

'Does it matter?'

The white-haired woman took the coin. Beetlebrow saw her wrinkled hand clenching around its edges.

She remembered the copper Lana had given her yesterday morning. It had felt precious in her palm, to be able to get bread for her mother.

The white-haired woman bit the gold piece between her two front teeth, and then glanced up again. Beetlebrow saw her smiling a gummy grin by the light of her little fire.

She gave Beetlebrow twenty-seven silver and sixteen copper coins in change. Beetlebrow slid the pile of money, the robes and the blankets into the leather bag and swung it over her left shoulder. She glanced back at the white-haired woman. She saw her locking the gold coin in a wooden box.

Beetlebrow looked at Pook. She saw her eyes were nearly closed.

'We'll be beyond sight of the city soon,' Beetlebrow said. 'We can rest there.'

Pook nodded. Beetlebrow started walking eastwards. She saw no fires or lamps in her path.

She heard Pook trudging by her side. The sound urged Beetlebrow onwards into the blackness.

15

Gregory

Beetlebrow opened her eyes. She saw dull yellow and bright green strands of wheat reaching up towards the silver sky. She heard their stalks crisply rustling to the breeze.

She sat up in the shadows gathered below the canopy of the wheatfield. The cold morning air felt sharp on her cheeks. She smelt the richness of the earth underneath her body. She heard grasshoppers droning their separate songs.

She listened to the quietness around herself, and thought back to the room in Floodcross, where every day she had to start running as soon as she woke up, beginning her daily scramble between buildings and crowds of men as she tried to outpace starvation.

She noticed Pook lying asleep on the ground to her left, her skinny frame wrapped in her new blanket.

Beetlebrow stood up. She turned around. She took off her tattered rags and put on the remaining slate-grey robe from her bag. She held the copper coin her mother had given her. She looked at its dull sides for a moment, and then slipped it into her new robe.

She glanced at Pook. Pook's left hand was resting under her right cheek. Her lips parted. Her brown eyes opened.

'Hello,' Pook said, her mouth spreading out in a smile.

Beetlebrow watched her rising to her feet, her long, black curly hair trailing down across the front of her slate-grey robe. The garment was shapeless along Pook's body. It stopped just below her knees.

Beetlebrow stared. The stalks of wheat appeared golden behind Pook's slender frame.

Pook glanced downwards. Her gentle hands began brushing off dirt from her robe. Beetlebrow watched the brimming light making soft shadows across her face.

'It's so bright out here,' Pook said, knotting her hair up at the nape of her neck with her blue strip of cloth.

She faced Beetlebrow. 'What is it? You keep looking at me, and not saying anything.'

Beetlebrow glanced away. She felt a reply approaching her lips. She knew she would not be able to hold back a flood of words from following. She felt like she had her back pressed against a door, trying to block it from opening as the handle began to turn.

She noticed a single-file line of dried mud trailing east through the yellow strands of wheat; along its length she saw imprints of sandaled steps.

Her eyes remained lowered as she held out her left hand towards Pook's grey blanket.

'It's all right,' Pook said. 'I can carry it.'

Beetlebrow gestured towards the blanket again.

Pook handed it over. 'Thank you.'

Beetlebrow stuffed the two blankets in her leather bag and started walking along the shadowed path through the field.

The mud felt hard under the soles of her bare feet. Her shoulders glanced against the brittle stalks of wheat. Beetlebrow listened to them rustling and hissing to her touch.

She heard Pook following behind her.

'Did you know about all these fields?' Pook asked.

'No.'

'Me neither. I don't understand why bread's so expensive in the city, when there's all this. What do you think?'

'I don't know.'

They walked between the towering stalks of wheat as the morning passed by. Cold rays of sun drifted above their heads.

Beetlebrow watched the field ending on the grass verge of a dirt-road ten yards wide. Flat-roofed houses stood either side of its eastward course, the single lines of smoke from their chimneys drifting separately into the cloudless sky.

'This must be Drowston,' Pook said.

Beetlebrow saw an oxen-drawn wagon rolling along the dirt-road from the west of the road. She looked at the women and men and children sitting in silence at the back of the vehicle, their bodies squeezed between stacks of boxes and bags tied up with rope.

Pook stood by her side. 'You haven't said much today. Are you all right?'

'Yes.'

They stepped into a street of two-storey houses. Beetlebrow noticed packs of muddied men trudging back and forth through the town carrying scythes and sickles. She saw no women or children in their numbers. She felt the road tightening between the buildings.

'Let's hurry up,' she said to Pook.

She glanced at a street to her left. Its cobblestones sloped down between facing rows of elbow-to-elbow whitewashed houses. Beetlebrow looked at a clean-shaven man walking away from a counter halfway along its length. She noticed the square loaf of brown bread under the crook of his left arm.

She stared at the narrow house to the right of the bakery. Its red door was open. She saw a golden double-rose carved into a square of white porcelain above its frame.

'He must be here,' she whispered to Pook. 'The agent Selena mentioned.'

They stepped together down the slanted street. The houses to their left and right had shuttered windows and low wooden doors. Beetlebrow noticed the gangly man standing alone by a wall.

She grabbed Pook's arm and turned around. Together they walked fast back up the street and stopped by the red-brick wall around the corner.

'What is it?' Pook asked.

'There's a man there I've seen before. At the tower in Silkworks.'

'What's he doing?'

'He's waiting.'

'For us?' Pook asked.

'I think so.'

'This is where Selena said the scribe Darvan Kess would be. In the house with the double roses, right?'

'Yes,' Beetlebrow said.

'Then you stay here,' Pook replied. 'Keep watching the man. There might be another way into the building around back. I'll sneak around. I won't let him see me.'

Beetlebrow nodded. Pook turned away.

Beetlebrow stepped against the corner of the cobbled lane, her left shoulder pressed against its mud-brick wall. She glimpsed Pook's slim figure disappearing into the street to the right.

Beetlebrow peeked around the corner. She saw the gangly man leaning against the wall opposite the red door. His long legs were inclining away towards his sandaled feet.

He looked right. His gaze met Beetlebrow's eyes.

She stepped back from the corner. She glanced back along the road to the west, and then looked around at the unfamiliar turnings and alleys surrounding her. She began darting away from the corner, and then she stopped. She placed her trembling hands behind her back and looked towards the cobbled street.

She heard the crunch of sandaled feet growing nearer. She remained still.

The gangly man stepped around the corner. 'Hello!'

Beetlebrow saw his eyes poking out from between bushy black hair and a week's uneven growth of beard across his chin. He was clutching the strap of a leather satchel against the right shoulder of his cream-coloured robe. Beetlebrow noticed the satchel's brown surface shining with waxy polish.

'Are you from around here?' the man asked.

Beetlebrow grinned. She looked into his eyes. 'Yes.'

'You haven't seen two city girls come through here, have you?' the man asked. 'Wouldn't be locals. They'd be a few years older than you, I reckon; about sixteen or so, not a tiddler like you.'

Beetlebrow watched his right hand reaching down into his leather bag.

'I've been here for hours,' the man muttered, shuffling around in the bottom of the bag. 'So I know they haven't been here yet.'

His hand stopped.

'Ah!' he said.

He pulled out a silver coin. He brandished it in front of Beetlebrow's face.

'This... can be yours, if you have any information,' he said.

Beetlebrow stared at the coin. She widened her eyes. She glimpsed the man looking at her face, and then she quickly looked at him again.

'I haven't seen any city girls,' she said. 'I'd certainly tell you if I did.'

'Well, if you do, come back here, I'll be waiting.'

He slipped the shining coin back into his bag.

'Wait,' Beetlebrow said. 'You've been here all day?'

'Yes, that's right. Since midnight.'

'How about I watch the street for you for an hour or two? If you gave me a few coppers...'

'I'm not sure.'

'There isn't much money around here, and I'll wait here as long as you want, and if I don't see these girls by then, my dad's a watchman here. If these girls come through Drowston, I can find out.'

The man glanced over his right shoulder at the sloping street, and then looked back at her again. He nodded. 'All right... I suppose that would help. So you'd stay here, and watch this street for me?'

'If you gave me some money I would.'

'Well, wait here then. If you see these two girls, I'll be at the Crow's Tooth Inn. My name's Gregory of Dalcratty. You can ask for me there.

If these girls come through this street, and you tell me about it, you'll get the silver. If not, just stay here. Maybe you'll get some coppers if you wait.'

'All right,' Beetlebrow said.

'Good. Thank you, girl.'

Beetlebrow held out her right hand towards him, palm up.

'What?' Gregory smirked. 'Give you two coppers and never see you again? You'll get your reward if you're still here when I get back.'

He winked down at her. 'Nice try.'

He smiled, turned around, and started walking away into the west of the town. 'See you in a couple of hours.'

Beetlebrow watched his gangly frame ambling away across the dirt-road.

She faced towards the cobbled street. She saw Pook walking towards her. Beetlebrow smiled.

'Did you hear all that, with the man?' she asked.

Pook nodded. 'There's no way in the back.'

'Doesn't matter now.'

They hurried down the street and into the open doorway under the sign of the two roses, stepping from the light of the day into the gloom of the shadowed corridor.

16
Darvan Kess

Beetlebrow saw the banks of dust piled up along the feet of the windowless grey walls of a corridor less than two yards wide. On its right were four open doorways.

Beetlebrow and Pook passed by the first. Beetlebrow glanced inside. She spotted scuff marks on the white tiles of a square room; she guessed a desk had once stood there. In the second were stacked bundles of yellowed papers tied up together with hairy brown string.

They headed further down into the gloom of the corridor. Beetlebrow noticed fluffy mats of dust by her feet. She could tell people no longer walked across this hallway, where once many would have trodden, heading through with business of the Empire. She guessed there would many discarded rooms like this across the town and cities, hidden within structures proudly carrying the symbol of two roses above their thresholds.

Beetlebrow and Pook approached the third room along the grey corridor.

A thin scribe was sitting behind a narrow walnut-wood desk set between its widely-spaced walls. His narrow face was leaning down towards his desk, his nose only a few inches away from the small sheet of paper at its centre. His black beard was threaded through with seams of silver-grey. Beetlebrow saw his goose-feather quill, clutched in his right hand, twitching right to left across the ivory-coloured document.

Beetlebrow and Pook started walking into the room. Beetlebrow noticed an unlit stub of a candle on the edge of the desk. Beside it was a white plate – bearing a half-eaten chunk of bread and a wedge of pale yellow cheese – and a square, glass ink-pot.

She watched the scribe scratching out a few black, precise words across the sheet of paper as she and Pook approached. His gaze remained on his writing as his mouth opened. 'Are you lost?' he murmured.

Beetlebrow placed the silver bracelet down on the desk.

The scribe glanced up at her. His quill remained poised in the air as his eyebrows rose. 'A message from Stellingkorr...'

A single black spot of ink slipped away from the end of his quill and dropped down onto the walnut-wood desk.

The scribe looked downwards. With his blackened right thumb he blotted the splodge of ink.

'King Ancissus gave us a message to deliver to King Hassan,' Pook said. 'We need to know about Essum. There's an important painting there or something...'

The scribe blinked. 'Yes, Essum is the Painting City.'

'Well,' Pook said, 'that's where we've got to go next.'

'My word,' the scribe replied. He set his quill down on top of the square inkpot. 'I've been working here for five years, and I've not seen a message coming from the west for the last three. We only ever get missives from the east.'

Beetlebrow wondered how long it had taken him to become used to the settling dust in these quiet rooms.

The scribe glanced at Beetlebrow, and then at Pook.

'You're Darvan Kess?' Pook asked.

'Yes. And you're... from the palace?'

Pook nodded.

'You're both very young,' Darvan said.

Beetlebrow frowned.

'No matter, I suppose,' Darvan murmured.

'We need to know about Essum,' Pook said.

Darvan looked down at his quill. Beetlebrow followed his gaze. She saw the goose feather laying across the exact centre of the ink-pot.

'Why's it called the Painting City?' Pook asked.

Darvan looked up again.

'You need a complete history?' he asked.

Pook nodded.

'For more than six centuries Essum was part of our Empire,' Darvan said. 'Then – about a hundred and twenty years ago – the citizens of the city selfishly revolted against our rule. It was a bitter, bitter struggle, in which thousands died, but after a few years Essum managed to repel our troops and secede from Dalcratty's realm.'

He glanced at Beetlebrow, and then at Pook.

'When Essum's citizens had cleared away all traces of the Empire's rule from their streets,' he went on, 'they found a painting in the ruins of their city. Since this painting was obviously old, the newly independent people of Essum decided that it must be important. They therefore concluded, girls, that the Painting was part of the original, lost culture of Essum, from the halcyon days before Dalcratty took over.'

Beetlebrow glanced at Pook. 'Halcyon?' Beetlebrow whispered.

She looked back at Darvan.

'The word "halcyon", girls, means calm, idyllic and prosperous,' he said. 'It derives from the old name for a kingfisher. Our scholars in Dalcratty have determined that this singular bird only breeds when the waters around its nest are tranquil.'

'Right,' Beetlebrow said. 'So what's this painting, then?'

'Well,' Darvan replied, 'the Painting – it is always capitalised in the language of Essum – is about ten feet high and six feet wide. It is painted on a sheet of drab hessian cloth and shows a head and shoulders portrait of a man. Some details are completed in black lines – the right eye, the chin and the right ear – but most of the portrait is sketched with a diluted brown outline of paint; I believe this outline is called a wash.'

'Have you been to see it?' Pook asked.

'Many times, yes,' Darvan replied. 'Oh yes.'

He glanced down at his desk. 'When I first saw the Painting, I expected it to be mediocre. I assumed I'd see a dull image simply hanging from a wall. I was working in Relleken at the time, for the Dalcratty civil service, when I was told to travel to Essum and report back anything I could find to undermine the rule of Prince Tevyan. My wife – along with... along with Yacob, my baby boy – had died a few months before, of the sweating sickness, and I needed the distraction. I... was glad to be given the assignment.'

Beetlebrow saw his mouth flexing into a grim smile for a moment and then the expression bleeding away from his face.

'On my third day in Essum I joined the queue for the golden hall where the Painting is displayed,' Darvan went on. 'All day and all night this unceasing line of thousands – teeming with pilgrims waiting to see the famous portrait – snakes through the myriad streets of the city. It took me seven hours to reach the front of the queue. All around me I heard tourists, students, and citizens gabbling on about the magnificence of this portrait. I listened to them. I took notes. I kept my mouth shut.'

Darvan's gaze was focused on the blank white plaster of the ceiling. He raised his right hand to his mouth. His fingers tightened into a fist. Beetlebrow saw his distant eyes remaining still as he coughed into his hand.

'By the time I got inside the hall I was exhausted,' Darvan went on. 'I remember looking up at its walls, covered in gold leaf, and seeing a domed white ceiling rising thirty yards above my head. Dozens of soldiers were standing all around the golden hall. I knew I would have only a few seconds to look at the Painting; after a brief glance at the portrait a pilgrim is supposed to leave the building, or the soldiers will guide them to the door. You have to pay two silver coins to see the Painting, after all; it is basic economics to make the visit to the golden hall efficient, and unfulfilling.'

He lay his palms down flat on his desk.

'When I looked up and saw the hessian sheet hanging on the back wall I had to suppress a smile. The Painting was just an empty daub, I thought, just like I had been taught to believe by the civil service. At that moment I was convinced the devotion towards the Painting was created by Essum's government to bring tourists into the city.'

'So the Painting's actually boring, then?' Pook asked.

Darvan glanced down at the small sheet of paper in front of himself.

'Yes, I did think so, at first,' he murmured.

He glanced up at Pook again and leant forwards, his wiry fingers splaying out across the centre of his desk.

'But then I gazed up at the face of the man in the portrait and saw his right eye, outlined in black, bearing down on me,' Darvan said, 'and I found I just couldn't stop looking at the Painting. I felt myself somehow being... *taken over* by it, as if I were sinking into its pigments, into its brush-work and into its structure. The hessian sheet above me appeared like a vast beige ocean. I saw humanity in the man's black-painted eye. I saw wisdom in the man in the portrait's forehead. In the unfinished parts of the Painting I saw hope.'

He glanced up towards the ceiling again.

'It was then that I felt gauntleted hands on my shoulders,' he said. 'Soldiers were dragging me out of the golden hall. I felt furious, despairing, desperate; to leave the Painting behind felt like I was being pulled against my will down from a mountain top. The soldiers led me out into the street and threw me out onto the pavement. I didn't even notice them returning to the hall, but I suppose they must have done. I remember being out in the street after I had left the golden hall. I can't recall much of these moments, if they were indeed only moments. I do remember walking. I saw people around me – people with children and loved ones, shopping and deliveries – and they didn't appear real.'

'What did you do?' Pook asked.

Darvan glanced at Pook. His shoulders sunk as he exhaled.

He shrugged. 'What do you think? I joined the queue again.'

Beetlebrow saw his eyes had become dull and heavy.

'When I saw the Painting for a second time it drew me even closer towards itself and I surrendered willingly to its pull,' Darvan went on. 'I felt wholly free as I stood in front of such strength, such majesty. After a few seconds in the hall, soldiers dragged me out into the street again. They shouted at me, telling me to never come back. I ignored them, and joined the queue straight away, and waited for another seven hours to reach the front of the line. Over the next few days I managed to see the Painting five times in a row. I slept in the street and queued and did nothing else. I must have eaten during this time, although I don't know what. Possibly I didn't eat at all. All I remember doing was waiting up to see the Painting, basking in front of its brilliance, before being escorted out of the hall and taken back out into the street again.'

Beetlebrow glanced at Pook. She saw her nodding at Darvan. Pook's eyes were wide. Her mouth was frozen in a smile.

She shared Beetlebrow's gaze. Pook raised her eyebrows. Beetlebrow smirked, and faced Darvan again. She saw his glazed eyes staring towards the back of the room.

'It was another Dalcratty agent, in the end, who came and took me away from the city,' Darvan went on, his ink-stained hands slowly rubbing against one another. 'I wanted to fight against this agent, but I was too tired to resist, too worn out to even speak. This agent... he brought me back to Relleken. That was six years ago now. I haven't been back to Essum since. I couldn't risk it. I know I'd just return to the queue. I know I'd want nothing more than to wait to see the Painting again, and to feel alive for those few seconds every day.'

He looked down at his desk again. He straightened a stack of papers. He glanced at his ink-pot. His right hand reached out towards it. His fingers creeped several inches towards his quill, and then his hands withdrew from the surface of his walnut-wood desk.

Beetlebrow heard the hush in the building. *Darvan must hear this every day*, she thought. She felt the silence growing. She was reminded of seeing her mother lying on the floor.

'So why do we need to know this?' she asked Darvan.

'What you must understand, here, is the power the Painting can have over people,' he said. 'The citizens of Essum base their entire lives around this single portrait. Every inch of its hessian surface is important to them. Each brushstroke and mark has been exhaustively pored over by the scholars in the city, who believe each detail is imbued with great significance.'

'Studied in what way?' Pook asked.

'Well, for example, there was a school of thought concerning the forehead of the man in the portrait,' Darvan replied. 'The followers of this school exclusively studied the three lines across the man's brow. They believed that the original artist – whose name is unfortunately unknown

– was trying to convey that the people of Essum should think deeply about their surroundings, as the man in the Painting was evidently doing. The forehead-cult was a very popular faction in the city, until Prince Rashine made the Sixth Addition to the Painting, nearly thirty years ago, painting a thin black line on top of the brown wash line which denoted the man in the portrait's jaw. Ever since this amendment was made, the government of Essum has tried to concentrate the study of the Painting on Prince Rashine's Addition above all other details in the portrait. And when Prince Rashine died, soon after making his Addition, his infant son Tevyan inherited the title of regent of the city, and continued to enforce his people's focus on the line of the jaw.'

'And do they paint things in Essum then?' Pook asked.

'Only copies of the Painting. Every year thousands of young men come from up and down the coast and beyond the sea to pay for an education which can only be obtained within Essum. We have even heard of some people from the Dalcratty Empire studying there, although anyone attempting this would need a great deal of money to obscure their origins, as any citizen of our Empire discovered in the Painting City is likely to be executed by Essum's police, due to ancient resentments towards the Dalcratty occupation. But the people of most city-states and empires are free to enter Essum. They can study there too; if they can afford the fees.'

'So what do they study there?'

'Well, all over the city, brush-makers, paint-mixers, painters and art critics run academies and schools and universities to teach these students what they believe the Painting demonstrates, and what they have decided its original artist intended to express. Many of these students return to their homes after their education is finished – or when their money runs out – but some hope to go on, after many decades of training, to design brushes and research new colours or – if they are highly skilled – to produce copies of the Painting. These reproductions are painted on stretched sheets of white canvas which, by tradition, are kept at twenty inches high by twelve inches wide.'

'So these copies aren't as big as the Painting itself?' Pook asked.

'Oh, no, no, no, no... of course not, my girl,' Darvan replied. 'To make copies of the same proportions as the Painting would be sacrilegious. The great size of the Painting is unique, and cannot be replicated, but in all other ways the copies are identical to the original portrait. In Essum it is seen as the supreme achievement for a citizen to duplicate the Painting in every detail, with the most expensive reproductions being the ones where no sign of the copyist's artistry can be discerned. The true professionals sell their work at the tourist market in the west of the city.'

'And what're these Additions?' Pook asked.

'Ah, yes,' Darvan replied with a smile. 'Every couple of decades, after long debate, the current prince might make a small amendment to the portrait. Six of these Additions have been made over the past century, although no changes were made in the fifty-four-year rule of Prince Okab, grandfather of Prince Tevyan. The people of the Painting City believe when their sacred portrait is finished they will have total knowledge of all of human experience, and since they all think themselves part of the continuing work of the original artist, each citizen feels they are they are becoming greater and more divine with every Addition.'

Darvan glanced at Beetlebrow, and then he looked at Pook again.

'And you've come at the right time, messengers,' he said, 'or the wrong one: we've heard Prince Teyvan will paint the Seventh Addition in two weeks' time.'

'So how do we get to see Bussert Maris?' Beetlebrow asked.

'Ah,' said Darvan, faintly smiling. 'The Maris problem.'

He picked up his quill and rolled it between his palms.

'We know, for certain, that Bussert Maris remains imprisoned in Essum. The government of the city say they have no prisons. They're very proud of this claim, as they believe it shows their peaceful and artistic nature. But it's a lie. We, of the civil service, know there is a hidden jail somewhere in the Painting City. Essum likes to keep political prisoners close to hand, in case they might need them, to backdate some new precedent or history. Wherever this prison is, Bussert Maris will be confined within its walls. Essum will think him too valuable to execute in secret, which is what their government does with most people who break the laws of the city.'

Darvan opened a drawer on the left of his desk. Beetlebrow heard his hands rustling around amongst the papers inside. Darvan closed the drawer again. He placed five gold coins on the desk beside the silver bracelet.

Beetlebrow stared at the money. The fingers of left hand twitched down by her waist.

The desk appeared dull beneath the gleaming surfaces of the coins. Beetlebrow tucked the thumb of her left hand against its palm and squeezed her fingers around it until she became still again.

'I know what message this is,' Darvan said, 'and its success is vital.'

Beetlebrow forced her gaze away from the coins and looked into his eyes.

'The Byrehaven to Relleken route has always been too close to the southern empires – the Batjud and the Con'eth,' Darvan went on, 'but their strength is growing and the payments needed to keep their privateers away are becoming prohibitive. Our trade route is being threatened. I think the future of the empire may depend on this message. A lot of money's gone into Tirrendahl already, and the investment needs to pay off.'

He gestured towards the money.

Beetlebrow snatched up the gold coins and bracelet from the desk. She slipped the silver band back inside the pocket of her robe and placed the coins under the blankets inside her leather bag.

'As citizens of the Dalcratty Empire,' Darvan said, 'the best thing way for you to conduct yourself in the city of Essum is to avoid drawing attention to yourself, and to not tell anyone that you come from the Empire's territories. Maris and Ray Rez didn't do that – they came into the city with open hands – but ... well, those two were very clever with Prince Tevyan, with their gifts and their flattery, although the final bribe they offered... well, the prince obviously thought its worth too low. Be very careful, messengers. And don't show those Dalcratty coins in Essum. People have been killed on its streets for far less. There are plenty of places to have your money exchanged before you reach the Painting City. Head east along the road from here and in a day you'll reach Kosair. From there you can get a cart to Byrehaven, and then sail up the coast to Essum. Going by sea is the only way to avoid the plain to the north-east of here. The plain was the part of the old trade route between Kosair and Essum, but it dried up once Essum succeeded from the Empire, and it appears nothing can grow on it anymore.'

'Thank you,' Pook said.

Darvan dipped his head. 'My pleasure. Talking about Essum is one of the few... satisfactions I have.'

'Is there anything else you can tell us?' Beetlebrow asked.

'My information about the royal family in the Painting City is scarce, as you might expect,' Darvan said. 'But Prince Tevyan's recent divorce from his wife, Princess Atalia, might be something you could use to your advantage. The princess married the prince twelve years ago, when she was eleven, and he seventeen. Princess Atalia is very naive, by all accounts, as she hasn't known any other life. Getting close to her might give you access to information about the prison.'

'Thank you,' Pook said.

Beetlebrow and Pook walked back out through the dusty corridor and into the sun-lit street beyond. Beetlebrow glanced left and right. The sloping cobbled row was empty.

'He talked lot, didn't he?' she said to Pook. 'About the Painting city and that. When someone talks that much, I don't want to trust them.'

Pook glanced forwards. She halted.

Beetlebrow saw her looking at the wall opposite the red door.

'What is it?' she asked.

'A snowpetal,' Pook whispered.

She hurried across the street and crouched down below a pair of green shutters.

Beetlebrow stepped after her across the cobblestones. She looked down at the ground by Pook's feet. By the base of the cracked whitewashed wall was a line of weeds. At their centre was the thin green stalk of a plant bending down beneath a heavy head of blue and white flowers.

'Snowpetals,' Pook said. 'They come out around my birthday.'

Beetlebrow looked at her face. Pook smiled up at her.

'How old are you going to be?' Beetlebrow asked.

'In a few weeks... sixteen.'

Beetlebrow grinned. 'You're younger than me...?'

Pook stood up. She flashed a smile at Beetlebrow, and started stepping down the street towards the bakery. Beetlebrow hurried after her.

'How old are you, then?' Pook asked.

'I turned sixteen two months ago.'

Beetlebrow remembered waking up just after dawn and seeing her mother quietly opening the door. Lana had glanced over at Alder and Joe, lying asleep against the wall on the right of the room, and then faced her daughter again with a finger held to her lips. Beetlebrow had looked into her dark-brown eyes. Her mother had stepped into the room and walked in silence across the floorboards.

Beetlebrow had sat up in her blanket to her mother's approach. She had noticed a brown bun topped with white icing in Lana's left hand. Beetlebrow had stared at the sugary coating of the square little cake. She recalled how pure and smooth it had appeared. She had grinned as Lana handed it to her. Beetlebrow had begun to split it in half between her fingers when Lana shook her head. 'No,' she whispered, 'it's all for you.'

Alder had woken up with a cough. Beetlebrow had turned away from the room, faced into a corner and wolfed down the iced bun before her brother saw what she had been given. She had swallowed hard and then quickly wiped away any crumbs from her hands and lips.

Beetlebrow remembered how white the icing had looked. She could not remember its taste.

Pook faced the two-foot long counter-top beside the open window of the bakery. She placed her elbows on its white surface.

Beetlebrow peered through into the lemon-yellow walled room beyond the counter. She saw the slim teenage baker sweeping across the white floor-tiles of the bakery with a stiff-bristled broom, his black pony-tail swishing left and right behind his back.

'One loaf, please,' Pook called over the counter.

'I thought you were older than me,' Beetlebrow said.

Pook's eyes thinned out as her white, even teeth parted wide into a grin. 'Why's that?'

'Well, you...' Beetlebrow said. She glanced away. 'You're taller than me.'

She looked at Pook again and saw her smile. Beetlebrow laughed. 'You just look older.'

The baker wiped his hands on his apron as he approached the other side of the counter. 'You don't want to come back later, do you? I've not done today's batch yet.'

'Is there anything left?' Pook asked. 'We're not fancy.'

'Tell you what, you might be in luck. I think I've got a loaf left over from yesterday.'

'Hey!' shouted a voice to the right.

Beetlebrow faced towards the sound. A tall man in white was stalking down the cobblestones.

He strode past her and slapped his hands down on the counter. He turned the gaze of his glaring eyes down towards Pook. Beetlebrow looked across his long white robes and the shiny curls of his black hair.

'I'll take that last loaf, if you don't mind,' he snapped to the baker.

Beetlebrow noticed the two stout men behind him. They were carrying muddied scythes and shovels over their wide shoulders.

'Did you ask him to hold it?' Pook asked the man in white.

He glanced at her. 'Yes, I did, you cheeky slut.'

The teenage baker hurried towards the other side of the counter with a square loaf in his hands. The man in white snatched it from his grasp and flung a copper coin in his direction.

'Thank you, sir,' the baker said.

The man in white began striding back up the street with the two stout men walking by his side.

Beetlebrow saw Pook standing by the counter. She was staring at the copper coin in the palm of her left hand.

Beetlebrow's fingers tightened into fists. *Pook had enough cash for the bread*, she thought. *She was first in line.*

She spun around. She felt heat scorching like a brush-fire across her senses. Her teeth gritted together. She started running up the street.

'What did you say?' she barked at the man in white.

'It's all right...' Pook said. 'Leave him...'

The man's sandaled feet stopped. He turned around. Beetlebrow saw the two stout men becoming still behind him. The man in white looked down at her. She watched his sneer become a smile.

'What did you call her?' she snapped.

'A slut,' he said. 'And what are you going to do about it?'

Beetlebrow pulled out her thin knife.

'What do you think you're going to do with that, street-rat?' he said.

Beetlebrow plunged the blade into the top of his thigh.

She saw his mouth opening wide in a soundless scream. She felt the knife sinking deep through his flesh. The man in white's knees buckled. He fell backwards onto the cobblestones, the shining blade jammed in the scarlet-spurting wound in his leg.

Beetlebrow glared up at the two stout men. They started backing up along the street, before turning around and hurrying away along its path.

Beetlebrow heard the man in white whimpering. She looked downwards. His fingers were wrapped around the slim knife sticking vertically out of his thigh. Blood was dripping down through his white robes and pooling around the round islands of cobblestones.

Beetlebrow pulled her blade out of the man's leg. His scream wrenched his mouth fully open.

She stared down at his wide eyes. She felt sweat adhering her grey robe against her body. She heard swift breaths coursing through her nose. Her mouth was dry and her limbs felt numb. She saw the handle of the knife in her left hand.

Pook grabbed her right arm. Beetlebrow felt her grasp against her sleeve of her robe.

'Let's get you out of here,' Pook whispered.

Beetlebrow saw the stillness of her brown eyes.

Pook turned around and pulled her away from the street, tugging at Beetlebrow's hand towards a weed-flooded alley between two white wooden houses.

'I don't know... what happened,' Beetlebrow said.

Pook glanced back at her.

Beetlebrow tightened her clasp around her fingers. She felt her feet walking across the dirt, their heels pressing down into the soil. 'The way... the way he spoke to you...'

Pook slowed her pace down to a walk and looked back at her again. Beetlebrow saw her eyes glancing across her face, and then losing their sharpness.

'You scared me,' Pook whispered. 'I think you scared yourself too.'

Beetlebrow did not know where Pook was leading. She felt like shutting her eyes and being taken wherever Pook chose.

Pook glanced back into the streets they had left behind. 'We need to get away. Now.'

Beetlebrow felt Pook pulling her onwards through the town.

17
The little house

Beetlebrow looked up at the last few houses of the east side of Drowston. Their square shapes loomed above rectangular lawns of short grass. Their shuttered windows appeared like staring eyes.

She glanced down at the knife in her left hand. Dark red blood was gleaming along its slender length.

'Let's hide in here,' Pook whispered.

Beetlebrow saw Pook taking her towards a single-storey building in a field of slick, waist-high grass. Its shutter-less rectangular window showed the beige plaster walls of the room inside. Beetlebrow's view of the little house was trembling. She felt the firmness of Pook's touch squeezing against her hand, and then letting go.

She heard Pook stepping behind her. Pook's fingers pressed gently against her shoulders and urged her inside the building.

Beetlebrow staggered forwards. She felt dry earth underneath her feet as she stepped across the dirt floor of the single room, between the tangles of unkempt weeds, pottery shards, rags and discarded hessian sacks. She saw black marks from ancient fires scored against the wall at the back.

'We should be safe here,' Pook softly said. 'I can't hear anyone following us.'

She stepped in front of her, and touched her left hand. Beetlebrow's fingers loosened. The knife fell away from her grasp. It landed down flat in the dirt.

Beetlebrow looked right. She stared beyond the shadows of the room towards the afternoon light outside the window. She saw the houses of Drowston.

She thought of all the streets she had known in Stellingkorr; the alleys and the thoroughfares, the avenues and tunnels and waste grounds she had walked though with her mother by her side. Lana had told her all their names.

'We could've walked away from that man,' Pook said.

Beetlebrow felt her heart thumping against her ribs. She looked down at her knife. She saw the rusted blade laying beside pieces of grey pottery and spiky shards of green glass.

'We would have been safer if we'd just walked away,' Pook said.

Beetlebrow squeezed her eyes shut, and shook her head. 'You're all I have. I can't lose you.'

Pook smiled. 'Well, I don't want to lose you either.'

'No... I can't lose you. I just can't. My mum... she died the morning I met you. I didn't have anyone else. She was... she was... '

Beetlebrow glanced at the wall at the back of the room. She noticed the mark of burn across the beige plaster; a scorched black bulb rising to a pointed peak.

'She had a perfume,' Beetlebrow went on. 'It smelt of pomegranates. I used to smell its scent and know she was near.'

She realised how far she had travelled away from Lana and her brothers and the streets of Floodcross. She remembered leaving the doorway at the bottom of the building as soon as her mother had died, and then stepping across the market towards Pook and then taking her hand and leading her north towards the royal palace.

She looked into Pook's eyes. Beetlebrow sensed the ground beneath her bare feet.

'We have each other,' Pook said.

'Yes, I know,' said Beetlebrow. 'But...'

She looked at Pook's cheekbones, her brown eyes and the mole on her upper lip. She smelt the scent of Pook's body. She heard her steady breaths, and felt her own breathing beginning to slow down.

'But what?' Pook said.

'But it's more than that.'

'Tell me,' Pook whispered.

Beetlebrow heard the stillness in the room.

'I won't know if you don't tell me,' Pook said.

'I... I've seen girls with their friends sometimes,' Beetlebrow slowly said. 'I'd hear them talking together.'

She glanced towards a beige wall, and then looked at Pook again. 'I thought if I had the chance to have friends, then I'd say what I'd heard them say. And then I met you, and all those things they said sounded so small. What I've felt... I didn't know the words. I haven't heard anyone say those sort of words before.'

Pook stepped closer towards her. Beetlebrow felt the warmth of her body. She noticed the sepia threads circling around the brown irises of Pook's eyes.

'What would you like to say?' Pook said.

She glanced at Beetlebrow's mouth.

'There are too many things...' Beetlebrow said.

She faced downwards.

'So tell me,' Pook said. 'Tell me everything you want to say. I'm here.'

Beetlebrow looked up again. She saw Pook gazing into her eyes.

'I want to tell you about...' Beetlebrow said, 'what you give me when you look at me, and you smile. I feel... I realise it's me who made you smile.'

She felt Pook's soft breaths against her mouth.

'And what else?' Pook whispered.

'And I want to kiss you.'

Beetlebrow's head moved forwards an inch. Her lips touched Pook's lips. Beetlebrow felt their softness.

She closed her eyes. She felt Pook's arms wrapping around her back, and their bodies binding closer together. Beetlebrow's hands slipped around Pook's waist. She felt the curve of her soft hips under the touch of her fingers.

Pook gave her a last peck of a kiss before their lips parted, and then looked into her eyes.

Beetlebrow felt exhaustion weighing on her shoulders. She glanced down at her hands. She saw they were trembling. She felt her eyes closing, as if being drawn downwards by an unseen touch.

'You should sleep,' Pook whispered.

Beetlebrow nodded, her head dipping.

She lay down on the dirt-floor. Pook placed a blanket across her body.

Beetlebrow felt her eyes shutting. She saw Pook sitting beside her. Beetlebrow's eyes slowly closed.

18
Outside Drowston

Beetlebrow woke up with sweat all over her. She rose to her feet. Her eyes were drawn to the window of the little room. She saw the dark blue moonlight outside. Dense grey clouds were gathering above Drowston.

She turned around. Pook was curled up asleep inside her blanket against a beige wall at the back of the room. Beetlebrow saw the crinkled grey blanket lying beside her. She looked down at her own left hand. Dried blood was splashed in patches along her fingers. It appeared inky black in the light of the moon.

She remembered her knife plunging into the man in white's leg. She thought of the scrapes along Pook's knuckles, scored as she had dragged her beneath the city-wall of Stellingkorr.

She looked at Pook's face. Beetlebrow imagined her blunt hands trying to touch her, and her sharp fingers tearing through Pook's skin. Beetlebrow's hands curled into themselves like sheaves of paper burning at the edges of a fire.

She turned away from the room and walked out the doorway. She felt the wind pressing against her body. She felt wet grass brushing against her ankles. She glanced over her right shoulder and saw the square, black shapes of the houses of Drowston being pierced by the orange light of lamps.

She heard Pook walking across the grass behind her. Each of her footsteps sounded calm.

Beetlebrow stepped further away from the little building. She looked at the glow above Drowston. 'We were both scared earlier. I don't want you to feel like you... we can go back to the way it was, if you –'

She felt hard fingers grabbing onto her left hand.

Pook turned her around.

Beetlebrow saw her standing close to her body. Pook's lips pressed hard against her mouth.

Beetlebrow shut her eyes. She felt herself sinking into Pook, dissolving into her body. She sensed Pook's tongue against her own. It felt like the glowing branches of a new fire, keeping her protected against the cold outside, and inciting the embers beneath the old ashes into flames.

Their teeth clicked together, and Pook's lips unsealed from her lips. Beetlebrow kept her eyes closed. Pook exhaled through her nose, a sound almost like a laugh, and then pushed her mouth against Beetlebrow's mouth again for a moment.

Their lips separated. Beetlebrow opened her eyes. She looked at Pook. She saw her long, black, untied hair and broad smile. Beetlebrow felt her wet lips, parted from Pook's mouth, stinging to the touch of the wind.

She remembered stepping nimbly along the cliff-top above Stellingkorr's beach. She did not trust her voice to be as precise as her feet had been.

Beetlebrow glanced away. 'I'm... not good with... talking...'

She felt Pook touching her hands. Beetlebrow squeezed her fingers in her own, and gazed into Pook's eyes.

'You and me,' Beetlebrow said.

She saw the brightness in Pook's expression.

Beetlebrow glanced down at her own grey robe. She felt her heart beating fast.

She grasped the coarse woollen material of her robe by her knees and pulled it upwards. She felt the garment moving away from her legs. Her thighs were tingling. She lifted her robe up over her stomach. She felt the chilly night air against her skin.

She pulled the robe over her head. She held it crumpled up in her left hand. She noticed Pook gazing at her unclothed body. Beetlebrow knew the night was cold. She looked at Pook, and did not feel cold.

Pook pulled her own grey robe over her head. She let it fall down onto the grass. Beetlebrow saw her standing naked in the dark blue light. She glimpsed the excitement and fear in Pook's eyes.

Beetlebrow looked down at her left hand. Her fingers opened. Her robe dropped onto the ground. It felt like the breaking of a chain.

She stepped towards Pook and placed her arms around her waist. She felt Pook's hands clasping around her back.

Beetlebrow noticed the black wisps of hair in Pook's armpits. Their foreheads touched. Their hips pressed together. Beetlebrow looked into Pook's eyes as her right hand slid around the back of her neck and swept up through her thick black curly hair.

She smelt the sweet scent of Pook's sweat. She felt the touch of Pook's fingers moving down towards her thighs. She looked at her face and saw a desire mirroring her own. Pook's mouth slowly opened, her lips quivering with the hope of a kiss.

19
Kosair

They left the outskirts of Drowston in the morning light, walking east as the afternoon rose, crossing fallow fields and quiet rivers.

Beetlebrow watched Pook bending down by the sandy bank of a stream. Pook scooped her cupped hands into the water. She sipped from their contents.

Beetlebrow saw the water shimmering with white illuminations. Its glow reflected dappled patterns across Pook's face. Beetlebrow stepped towards her. She looked at the light she contained between her fingers.

Pook glanced up, and gestured the water towards her. Beetlebrow knelt down beside her, and drank from her hands.

They entered the town of Kosair in the late afternoon, stepping into a twisting street of yellow dirt bordered by three-storey, whitewashed buildings.

Beetlebrow felt crumbled earth underneath her toes. She smelt the oily odour of frying food drifting down the road with the western breeze. She looked northwards. Beyond the white buildings the emptiness of the yellow plain appeared to stretch all the way to the horizon.

Beetlebrow glanced at Pook. Pook wet her lips with her tongue. Beetlebrow smirked.

She heard carts rattling through the yellow streets of the town, their metal wheels rumbling under the passengers they carried on their backs. The white oxen pulling the vehicles, with trudging shoulders and humbled eyes, were grunting and lowing to the swish of cracking whips.

'We'll need to take one of these wagons to Byrehaven,' Pook said.

Beetlebrow spotted four thin teenage boys waiting beside a brown, mud-brick wall on the other side of the street. Their leather sandals were brightly polished and their clean tunics were tightly tailored to their slender frames. She noticed jars of vivid powder-pigment, brushes and bottles of oils clutched in the teenagers' hands, and the white canvases gripped under their arms.

She watched two beige-skinned oxen shouldering eastwards along the street. The cart behind the beasts drew up alongside the line of teenage boys. The driver yanked at the reins. The cart's wheels creaked as they settled down into the yellow dirt.

Beetlebrow saw the boys handing silver coins to the driver and clambering up onto the rear of the vehicle.

She felt something sharp crawling over her toes. She glanced downwards. A black scorpion was scuttling over her right foot. It was carrying a squirming multitude of pale babies on its back.

Beetlebrow looked at the cart again. She noticed a square of wood nailed to its side. Black letters were painted across its surface.

'What's the sign say?' she asked Pook.

'*Byrehaven Three Days, Two Silvers*,' Pook said.

'And Essum is north from there, up the coast,' a man's voice called.

Beetlebrow saw the gangly figure of Gregory stepping towards her across the dusty street, the shine on his leather bag reflecting the late-morning sun.

'It's all right,' she whispered to Pook. 'We can fool this one.'

She noticed a stocky, black-bearded man walking beside Gregory. Beetlebrow stepped backwards.

Her heels struck a wall. She felt coarse mud-bricks pressing up against her shoulder-blades.

She faced the two men striding towards her; Gregory glancing left and right along the street, and Alder's heavy-lidded, mahogany-brown eyes glaring down at her.

Beetlebrow felt as if the four walls of the room in Floodcross were closing around her body again, tightening around her chest until she could no longer breathe.

Gregory and Alder stood in front of Beetlebrow and Pook.

'I heard it was a couple of girls trying to take this message to Dalcratty,' Alder said, staring down at his sister. 'The rebels were asking around the neighbourhood, paying for information, and they said one of the girls had big black eyebrows, and I guessed it might be you. Who else but you could hurt our people by doing the dirty work of the royals?'

He smirked. 'Me and Gregory have been following you since Stellingkorr.'

Beetlebrow felt his shadow looming over her face. She glanced to her left, and saw Pook standing by her side, her back against the wall.

'This is your sister then?' Gregory asked, looking at Alder.

'That's right,' Alder said, twisting the red beads at the ends of his black beard. 'Or half-sister, if you like... me and my brother raised her, not that I see any thanks from her.'

'Liar!' Beetlebrow snarled.

'Alder...' Gregory softly said. 'Give these girls some space.'

Alder frowned. 'Why should I?'

'The elders only allowed you to come with me if you followed my orders,' Gregory replied. 'So, I'm saying now, just... step away for a bit.'

Alder scowled. He turned around and walked out into the street. Beetlebrow saw him stopping in its dusty centre.

Gregory glanced back at Alder for a moment, and then looked at Beetlebrow again.

'See here,' he said, 'I don't care about your family problems, or whatever it is between you and Alder. That's not important. And I don't care that you tricked me back in Drowston. I'm willing to ignore that if you do just the right thing now, which is to give up the bracelet. We know you can't carry the message any further without one of those bracelets as proof along the way, so I'm giving you the chance, girls, to hand it over willingly. This message is bad, girls, and it'll hurt our people.'

Beetlebrow saw Alder striding back across the street towards her. She reached inside her robe. Her fingertips glanced against the edge of her knife. Its cold, sharp metal felt reassuring to her touch.

Alder stopped to Gregory's right. He scowled at Beetlebrow and then looked at Pook.

He jerked up the side of his black robe to show the pink scar shining above his right knee.

'Beetlebrow's dad did this to me, did you know that?' Alder said, his forehead wrinkling. 'That dirty pimp, with the eyebrows just like hers, did this to me! I was twelve, and I wouldn't share my bread with Beetlebrow, and he stuck me with a knife. That's the kind of company you're keeping, the daughter of a piece of filth like him!'

Beetlebrow saw a white speckle of spit fly out from between his gritted teeth.

'And she stole from us,' Alder went on, 'she stole the last bit of money from Mum's dying hand! Took it for herself, Beetlebrow did. Beetlebrow the thief, we used to call her.'

Beetlebrow looked down at the dusty yellow dirt by her feet. 'Pook, he's not telling the truth...'

She glanced left. Pook's brown eyes were glaring up at Alder. Beetlebrow saw her bare feet standing in the earth as solidly as the roots of an ancient oak.

'That's your problem, Alder,' Gregory said.

Alder's staring eyes turned away from Beetlebrow. He frowned up at Gregory's face.

'You can't let these petty things go,' Gregory went on, 'It's not about you, this mission, and you'd better get that into your head. You told the elders in Stellingkorr you wanted to help our rebellion, but I've not seen you showing it. All I've seen you do in these last few days is talk and talk and visit brothels. You don't want to help us be free from the House of Rashem – you'd prefer to be out drinking and smoking with whores. It's no rebellion to take drugs and have sex with trollops. You talk about revolution because the word sounds good, but even revolutions take hard work. You don't do anything really helpful for our people. Why? Because you're bone-idle. Bone-idle and you don't want risk breaking a sweat.'

Alder flashed a last scowl at Beetlebrow and then turned round.

'Who do you think you are,' Alder muttered, 'to tell me what to do...?'

Beetlebrow watched him walking away again. He glared up at the passengers of an ox-cart as their vehicle rattled by.

Gregory faced Beetlebrow and Pook again. He held up his hands.

'Look. Ignore him, all right?' he said. 'Listen to me, because what I've got to say is important. I understand – I really do – how it might've seemed at the royal palace. They fed you, they treated you nice, made you feel special, and you think the House of Rashem is doing good. But they're not.'

'They told us this message would help people,' Pook said.

Beetlebrow saw her staring at Gregory. She felt a warm glow rising in her chest.

'If it's going to bring wheat into Stellingkorr,' Pook went on, 'how can it be bad?'

'Yes, yes,' Gregory nodded. 'I know how it sounds. The royals have a good story. We've heard it told by their spies and soldiers, but we'd expect this sort of talk from them. The royals had to convince you though, and you've obviously bought into their lies, girls. So let me tell you the truth about this message.'

Beetlebrow frowned.

'They said this wheat would help people, right?' Gregory asked.

Pook nodded. 'That's right.'

'But what people?' Gregory went on. 'It can't help everyone in the Empire, can it? Someone's going to end up deciding how it's split up, and whoever that is, they're going to put their thumb on the scales. We reckon the Empire's going to sell this wheat once they find it. Either that or barter it away for political favours.'

He glanced over his shoulder towards Alder. Beetlebrow saw her brother standing in the yellow dirt of the street. His back was turned. He was shifting the weight of his stocky body from one bare foot to the next.

'And another thing,' Gregory said to Pook. 'Have you two girls even thought how this cache of wheat's going to be moved from Dalcratty to Stellingkorr? To try to shift something that huge across the Empire'd take weeks, at a massive cost, and they'd risk losing it to bandits, or to pirates or privateers as they ship it across the Central Sea from Relleken to Byrehaven. Prince Tevyan controls all trade across the northern stretch of the sea. He's got it locked up in their route from Essum to their protectorate, Drayzhed, in the north coast of the eastern continent. His ships are patrolling the Central Sea at all times, waiting to plunder any Dalcratty vessels. And the southern empires are gaining more power every day. I've seen their ships patrolling south of Relleken, seen it with my own eyes. To try to get this wheat across the Central Sea, between those two powers, would be too risky. The Dalcratty Empire'd have too much to lose. So it makes sense that they won't take this wheat to Stellingkorr. We, though, want to give it to the people who need it, the starving and the homeless of our cities. We want to give it to them direct.'

Beetlebrow heard an ox-cart rolling across a street to the south. She felt its weight shaking the crumbled yellow ground beneath her toes.

'King Ancissus told us you just want power for yourselves,' Pook said.

Gregory nodded. 'I guess that's true, in a way. But not like them. Not like them. Listen... I'm from Dalcratty. The House of Rashem are the same there; they started in Dalcratty, after all. I travelled out west to talk with our allies in the other cities of the Empire. The rebellion elders in Stellingkorr told me about this wheat, and asked me to help them seize it, because what the people in Stellingkorr want is the same as what we want in Dalcratty. We don't desire the Empire's palaces or its wealth: we just want to own our own land, to be able to plant our crops on it, to raise our families on it, and bury our dead on it, without these royals taking their taxes. We're not philosophers or poets in the rebellion: we're farmers and grave-diggers, born with a shovel in our hands. Whatever you two believe about the message, we are your people and the House of Rashem are not.'

Beetlebrow heard a rumbling sound to her left.

She saw a cart led by a team of four white oxen rolling into the street. A line of young men paid their silver coins and climbed up into the back of the vehicle with their boxes of vials, jars of bright powders and paintbrushes. Beetlebrow noticed one young man clasping a small vial of turquoise pebbles against his narrow chest.

She felt the Painting City drawing closer, its colours becoming bolder in the air, like the orange tint of the afternoon sky turning red as the evening grew inescapable. She looked at the earnest faces of the young men sitting on the back of the cart and imagined vivid colours in the streets of Essum among many-hued buildings.

'Did you know that the House of Rashem don't even want to share the sun in Stellingkorr?' Gregory went on. 'They call it the false sun, as if it's not the same as the one in Dalcratty. These royals even keep themselves indoors so they don't get darkened by its rays.'

Alder stepped past him. 'That's enough talking. You can't persuade my sister with no fancy speeches. She hasn't the brains to understand what you're talking about.'

He grabbed Pook by the back of her long black hair.

'Let her go!' Beetlebrow barked, lurching forwards.

Alder bound his skinny right bicep across Pook's neck. Her blue rag spilled down into the dirt as he stepped backwards into the street, his staring gaze focused on his sister's face.

'Let her go!' Beetlebrow shouted, advancing towards Alder, her left hand inside her robe.

Alder stopped in the middle of the street. Beetlebrow sped forwards. She saw Pook's curly hair trailing down over her eyes and parted lips.

Alder squeezed his arm against Pook's throat.

'No further,' he growled to Beetlebrow, 'or I break her neck.'

Beetlebrow stopped.

She glared at Alder's face. She glimpsed the short, square-sided, black club in her brother's right hand, and Pook's blue rag, drifting along with the yellow dust of the street and tumbling away west between the whitewashed houses.

'One of you has the bracelet,' Alder said, 'and I bet it's you, Beetlebrow, because it's just like you to take something like that for yourself. Now give me the bracelet, give me it now, and I'll let your creepy little friend go.'

'Let her go and we'll talk,' Beetlebrow snapped. 'I ain't doing nothing if you're hurting her.'

'You're going too far, Alder,' Gregory said. 'These are children, they're not soldiers –'

'Let me be, you ponce!' Alder shouted. 'You've had your chance. You just talked and talked and you got nowhere.'

He released his arm from around Pook's neck. Pook tumbled down onto the ground, and Beetlebrow ran forwards.

Pook landed on her hands and knees. Her brown eyes rose to meet Beetlebrow's gaze.

Alder swung his club downwards. Beetlebrow heard the club crack against the back of Pook's left shin. Pook screamed. She fell face-first down into the dirt.

Beetlebrow knelt down in front of her. She lifted Pook's head up from the ground. Pook's eyes were closed. Her face was covered with a thin layer of yellow dust. Dark blood was trickling down her left leg.

Beetlebrow saw Alder's stout frame approaching. He was holding open the palm of his left hand.

'The bracelet, Beetlebrow!' he shouted. 'Give it to me. I know the agents along the route to Dalcratty won't believe you're a messenger if you haven't got one of them silver bracelets, so hand it over. You're not going any further with this message, girl. All this talk of kings and rebellions, it's all above your head. You're a child; you don't know what you're doing. So let a man decide for you.'

Beetlebrow noticed Gregory striding towards him.

'Stop!' Gregory said. 'Stop this now! This is too much, they're just kids.'

Beetlebrow saw the gaze of Alder's heavy-lidded eyes turning towards Gregory.

She clasped her left hand around Pook's waist, slipped her right arm around the back of her own neck and stood up. Beetlebrow felt her body shaking under her grasp. She heard her struggling to breathe through trembling tears.

Alder began stepping towards Gregory. He swung his club. Beetlebrow heard it smack against Gregory's forehead. She saw his gangly frame crumpling down onto the dusty earth.

Beetlebrow looked down at Pook. She saw two glistening lines of tears cutting through the dry yellow dirt along her cheeks. Beetlebrow reached her right hand inside her robe. Pook's bleary eyes were looking at her face. Pook nodded.

Beetlebrow took her hand out of the pocket.

'No,' Pook whispered. 'Not that. Don't…'

Beetlebrow gestured the shining silver bracelet towards Alder.

'Here,' she said.

Alder stared into Beetlebrow's eyes.

'Good girl,' he said, stepping forwards and snatching the bracelet from her grasp.

Beetlebrow saw Gregory sitting alone in the dirt road between the whitewashed houses. The palms of his hands were pressed against his eyes. Drips of scarlet blood were spilling down through his fingers.

Beetlebrow glanced at Pook.

'I had to,' Beetlebrow said. 'There's nothing else. Alder's right.'

She saw her brother raising the square-sided club above his head.

'Now,' Alder snarled, 'you'll get the punishment you should've gotten back in Floodcross.'

Beetlebrow reached her right hand into her leather bag and felt the mass of coins inside. Her fingers closed around a bunch of cold metal pieces. She pulled her hand out of her bag and flung a fistful of silver coins at Alder's face. She saw the discs battering against her brother's cheeks.

Alder flinched. His feet slowed. He stood still. He glanced down at the coins in the dirt.

Beetlebrow reached back inside her leather bag again. She glimpsed Alder's knuckles whitening around his grip on the club.

'Think you can buy me off, do you?' he said.

Beetlebrow's fingertips touched the thick edges of a gold coin. She felt the embossed portrait of King Ancissus on one of its sides. She clasped the gold coin in her left hand and pulled it out her bag.

She looked at Alder and threw the gleaming metal disk at his face. She saw it strike his right eye.

Alder yelled. He staggered backwards.

Beetlebrow took out a second gold coin from her bag. She whipped it at her brother. It struck the bridge of his nose.

Alder screamed, wrapping his arms across his face.

Beetlebrow gently lowered Pook down onto the ground, grasped the leather bag with both hands and ran towards Alder. She rolled up the bag lengthwise, screwing it up tight within her grasp, and stepped towards Alder.

She swung the bag towards her right, and then brought it left against Alder's face. It struck his chin. Beetlebrow heard the coins inside the bag clinking to the impact. She felt the blow shaking up her arm.

She saw her brother falling sideways and landing face-first in the dirt.

She noticed the bracelet gleaming in his right palm. She bent down, her left hand reaching out towards the silver band.

She saw Alder's dazed eyes opening.

Beetlebrow stepped backwards across the dirt.

Alder pressed his hands down flat on the yellow ground. His feet wobbled as he began to stand up, a snarl on his bloodied lips.

Beetlebrow quickly turned around. She hurried back towards Pook and helped her up to her feet. Pook's head was hanging downwards.

'Can you walk?' Beetlebrow whispered.

Pook nodded.

Beetlebrow kissed her right cheek.

She felt sweat coursing down her face as she started walking fast through the streets with Pook limping by her side. They staggered past the carts and pedestrians and white houses of the town. Beetlebrow looked north. Her feet were aching. She saw the miles of yellow earth ahead.

Beetlebrow kept stepping northwards at the edge of town. She glanced at Pook, and saw her eyes were closed. Beetlebrow heard the noise of the town fading behind her feet. She saw no people ahead.

She felt dusty ground underneath her toes. Her mouth felt dry. She swallowed her saliva.

Beetlebrow kept moving forwards. Pook's body felt heavy in her arms. They stepped together onto the plain. Beetlebrow heard the sounds of Kosair slipping away, and the wind whistling across the flat landscape.

They staggered onwards across the barren yellow dirt as the evening grew. Beetlebrow saw the sun dipping down across the blue sky. She watched the light descending into the west. She felt sticky sweat tightening against her armpits.

'Stop,' Pook whispered. 'Please. It really hurts.'

Beetlebrow slowly lowered Pook down onto the ground. She watched her stretch out her legs across the dirt. She saw the purple bruises covering her left shin.

She glanced around at the empty expanse of yellow earth. She thought of the rivers they had crossed outside Drowston. She remembered Pook kneeling down beside a stream.

There isn't even any water to wash the wound, she thought.

She looked back towards the south. She saw miles of yellow dirt in her wake. The distant whitewashed houses of Kosair appeared like pebbles.

She sat down cross-legged beside Pook.

Beetlebrow reached into her leather bag and brought out the bloodstained bracelet. The symbol of two roses caught the last light from the dimming sun.

Pook looked at her face.

'Just need to shine this one up,' Beetlebrow said, 'and then it'll look like the other one did.'

She saw Pook's smile surfacing for a moment.

'There're two of us,' Beetlebrow went on. 'So I thought we'd need two bracelets. I took the second one from Magell in the palace. I didn't think he'd miss it.'

She slipped the bracelet back into her bag.

She saw Pook glancing down at her bloodied leg.

'I see why you wanted to leave Stellingkorr,' Pook softly said. 'With a brother like him, I'd leave too.'

Her eyes squeezed shut. Beetlebrow held onto her hands. She looked at Pook's knuckles, scabbed and reddened from the city-wall of Stellingkorr.

'That was then,' Beetlebrow said. 'Now there's us, and there's the message.'

She put her arms around Pook's shoulders. Pook leant back against her body, and stared out into the emptiness of the yellow plain.

'I had a family too,' Pook slowly said. 'We had a flat in Silkworks. Me and Mum and Dad. It was Mum who taught me to read. She thought it would make me a good wife one day.'

She slid her head under Beetlebrow's chin.

'When Dad got sick,' Pook went on, 'we only had Mum's wages. They were much less than Dad had earned. Then Mum and Dad started drinking. They forgot about me. I had to leave.'

She circled her arms around Beetlebrow's waist.

'I was begging in Floodcross when Gozher started talking to me,' Pook said. 'He gave me a few scraps of bread. He wasn't all bad, you know.'

She glanced back at Beetlebrow.

'There's worse people than Gozher, I suppose,' Beetlebrow said.

She felt Pook squeezing her hands tighter around her waist.

'Sometimes he'd give me a few coppers to cook for his girls, or clean out their rooms,' Pook said. 'They were nice to me. Most of them anyway. The older ones at least. Gozher would always ask me if I wanted to stay in the house, but I knew what that meant. At least with the begging I could be in control. Even if I starved.'

Beetlebrow watched the sky darken. The stars came into view and the sun vanished. She felt the plain becoming cold, and the warmth of Pook's body remaining by her side.

'We'll keep going north-east,' Beetlebrow said. 'Alder'll be after us in towns. There's gotta be something in this plain. I don't know if we can walk to Essum, but... there has to be something before the Painting City. We'll find it.'

'I think it's too far to walk to. And we've no water. No food either.'

'We'll find something.'

They lay down on the hard yellow earth. Beetlebrow cradled Pook's head inside her left arm. She heard her breaths slowing down.

Beetlebrow looked up at the stars. Her mouth felt parched. 'We'll find something.'

She glanced across the darkness of the plain. Beetlebrow felt grateful for the night. Her words could lie where her eyes could not.

20
The plain

Beetlebrow saw a degraded bud of light appearing in the eastern horizon. The surrounding yellow earth emerged from the darkness.

She stood up. She looked to the east and west and north and south. The horizon was blank in all directions.

She thought back to the packed streets in Floodcross, pressed up against one another like the fractured halves of broken bones. She saw the distance spreading out everywhere around her, and longed for the security of buildings.

She heard Pook coughing as she woke up.

'Let's start walking,' Pook said.

'We can rest a whi-'

'We need to keep moving.'

Beetlebrow nodded.

Pook draped her right arm across her shoulders. Beetlebrow gripped her left arm around her waist. Together they stood up. Beetlebrow saw the sun shining out bright and cold.

Pook's eyes were half-closed. Her face looked thin and drawn. Beetlebrow glanced downwards. Red and purple bruises had bloomed along the length of Pook's left shin.

'Here,' Beetlebrow said.

She reached into the pocket of her robe and felt the fig inside. She took it out and handed it to Pook. Pook slowly took the little fruit between her fingers. She started nibbling at its purple skin. She glanced at Beetlebrow.

'No, it's all for you,' Beetlebrow said.

The sun passed into the west as Beetlebrow and Pook walked north-east across the plain. Beetlebrow closed her eyes. Her head felt light. She could smell salt in the soil. She opened her eyes again. She saw blurry yellow earth surrounding her.

She wondered if people had stayed here when the trade-route had been closed between Stellingkorr and Essum.

Perhaps they'll be people in the miles ahead, she thought, *who'd been born here and wanted to carry on living with what they knew.*

She imagined glimpsing a house emerging from the eastern horizon, and then hurrying towards it, her mouth dry and her body tired. She thought of watching its square shape unfolding against the yellow earth. She and Pook would be staring, as they approached, while the house revealed itself to be four walls without a roof. They would walk inside its doorway, step across its arid floorboards and look out into the yellow plain through its empty window-frames and doorways.

She saw Pook's eyes squeezing shut.

Beetlebrow became still.

'Why are we stopping?' Pook whispered.

'You need to rest.'

'Oh.'

They sat down on the ground.

'You could've told me about the other bracelet,' Pook said.

Beetlebrow glanced towards the west. She thought of the touch of her mother's hands.

'I've not been very good at telling the truth, in the past,' she said. 'I got so good at holding back. With my brothers... growing up, I couldn't say anything. And with Mum, I just tried to hide anything bad from her. I felt I had to do that. She was already... hurting enough.'

Pook's eyes remained closed as she nodded.

'I don't want to be like that with you,' Beetlebrow went on.

She felt Pook's head leaning against her right shoulder. Beetlebrow began to stand up. She felt her muscles straining. Her shoulders softened. She sat down again, and squeezed her arms around Pook's waist.

21
The fire

Beetlebrow and Pook staggered onwards across the plain, stopping at nights, walking whenever Pook had the strength.

Beetlebrow lowered her down onto the ground in the evening of the third day. The dark blue sky was cloudless. Beetlebrow's tongue felt dry. She opened her mouth. Every breath she took felt harsh against her throat. Pook's arm slipped away from around her shoulders.

The earth felt cold against Beetlebrow's body. She looked downwards. She saw her coppery hands outlined on the yellow earth. She saw her dirt encrusted fingers splayed out across the ground.

She looked at her knuckles, red and torn.

She tried to lift her hands from the dirt. She watched them remaining still. She thought about all the other people who would have died out here, sinking into the ground without being heard of again.

All was dark. She could not see Pook. Beetlebrow opened her mouth wide. She called out Pook's name. She could not hear her own voice.

She glanced upwards. Blackness was pressing down on her. *The stars should be there*, she thought.

A mahogany-coloured shape blossomed in front of her eyes. It split into two pieces left and right. A dark smear appeared at its centre.

She watched the mahogany shape rising up again. She noticed a mass of black fish-hooks on its surface. She realised they were hairs on the back of a man's hand.

Her numb limbs left the ground. Her body felt weightless. Beetlebrow looked downwards. The yellow earth appeared to be several miles below her feet. Large fingers were gripping her shoulders. She felt water against her lips.

'Drink,' a deep voice said.

Her hands reached out into the darkness ahead. Her fingers clenched around the rough, stitched sides of a leather pouch. She heard water sloshing around inside. She held the vessel against her lips and felt liquid on her tongue.

She took a long gulp. She leant backwards and gasped, feeling exhaustion surrounding her body. Tiredness closed her eyes. Sleep approached. She knew she had no strength to fight against its pull.

Beetlebrow opened her eyes. She saw a pile of branches burning several yards ahead of her body. Glowing threads of hawthorn twigs were entwined at its centre. She heard the branches buckling under the heat. She watched the red flames rising, peaking and then darting away into the blackness surrounding the fire.

She looked down at her body, sitting cross-legged on the yellow earth. She felt the grey blanket wrapped around her shoulders.

Her gaze levelled. She held out her hands towards the fire. Her palms faced its flames. She felt the cleansing heat lapping against her fingertips.

She heard footsteps approaching. Her hands pressed against the ground. She started to shuffle backwards across the dirt.

A tall man emerged from around the right side of the fire. The left side of his rail-thin frame was dipped in shadows. She glimpsed the man's fawn-coloured headscarf.

She watched his lanky frame leaning down towards her. He was holding a blue, two-handled cup in his mahogany-shaded hands. She watched the cup growing nearer to her face. She saw thick black hairs across the back of the man's hands.

The cup was placed against her mouth. It began tipping down towards her lips.

She took a sip of the bitter liquid inside. She felt the cup being taken away again.

She dribbled out a clove. It fell over her lower lip and down her chin.

'Good…' the tall man murmured, the bass-baritone word booming out across the stillness.

Beetlebrow saw the blurry, dark shape of his lofty body standing up in front of the flames.

'Pook,' she croaked.

The tall man remained still.

'Pook,' Beetlebrow repeated. 'The other girl.'

The tall man stepped away into the surrounding blackness.

Beetlebrow saw Pook lying asleep on the ground several yards to the left of the fire. She was wrapped in her grey blanket.

Beetlebrow felt relief flooding through her body. Her shoulders slumped downwards.

She watched the orange fire-light tumbling against Pook's slim frame like waves splashing across a shore-bound rock. She noticed Pook's left leg, wrapped in white rags, was sticking out straight along the earth.

Beetlebrow opened her eyes. The sun was up and the fire was dead. She realised she had been asleep.

The tall man was walking towards her.

She looked at the creased, cotton fabric of his long, fawn-coloured headscarf. Between its folds she saw the tall man's pin-prick eyes, his beaky nose, his wrinkled-slashed cheeks and a black beard pointing down several inches beyond his narrow chin. Through his parted lips she spotted a crowded array of tombstone teeth.

She felt her blanket falling away from her body. The tall man's hands were holding onto her shoulders. Beetlebrow wanted to tear his grasp from her body, and take Pook's hand again, and hurry away, as she had back in Floodcross, on the day when they first met.

She glanced left and right. She saw the emptiness in the surrounding plain. She felt her sight spinning. She felt nausea in her throat. She was breathing fast.

'Be calm,' the tall man said. 'You're dizzy. You need to be still.'

Beetlebrow shut her eyes. She glimpsed the yellow earth of the plain swaying in the blackness beneath her closed lids. She felt her balance teetering. The tall man's hands remained on her shoulders.

'Be still,' he said.

She felt her body becoming still. She thought of Pook. Beetlebrow's eyes opened again. She looked down at the yellow earth. Her bare feet were standing flat on the ground.

The tall man removed his hands from her shoulders.

Beetlebrow looked at his tawny-coloured robes, trailing down to his sandals, and then glanced upwards. She saw the tall man's face silhouetted in front of the burnished golden circle of the sun.

'We don't stop long,' he said. 'We're heading to Essum, the Painting City.'

He walked away from Beetlebrow. She watched him stopping beside a grey mule.

She saw the black leather saddle on its back. A tiny child, swaddled head-to-toe in black clothes, was sitting on its front half. Pook was sitting behind her.

Beetlebrow started stepping forwards. She looked at Pook's long curly black hair, trailing down the back of her slate-grey robe. She saw Pook's head resting against the child's left shoulder.

Beetlebrow felt coarse-grained dirt scratching against the soles of her feet. She heard the wind catching at the tall man's long robes.

Pook's head slowly turned. She looked at Beetlebrow. Beetlebrow saw her brown eyes. They were mere slits between their cinnamon-shaded lids.

Pook mouthed, 'Hello.'

'Hello,' Beetlebrow quietly said.

The tall man looked at Pook. 'If you think you're going to fall,' he said, 'hold onto Ava.'

Beetlebrow glanced at the child's black-clothed frame. She guessed Ava to be three or four years old.

The tall man faced Beetlebrow.

'Walk?' he asked.

Beetlebrow glanced at Pook. Her left leg, wrapped in white bandages, was stretched out stiffly alongside the grey mule's belly.

Beetlebrow looked at the tall man again. 'Yes.'

'Good.'

He pointed north-east. 'Essum.'

His lanky frame bent downwards. He hooked the bridle out from under the mule's neck.

He stood upright again and wrapped the strip of raw-hide leather three times around his right hand.

Beetlebrow watched the tall man yanking on the bridle and walking away towards the north-east. She saw Pook sitting on the back of the saddle.

The mule was trotting behind the tall man's steps. Beetlebrow kept her eyes on Pook as she began to follow behind the animal's trudging path.

22
Porridge

Beetlebrow's feet were stumbling. It was past noon. The plain appeared endless.

She saw the tall man letting go of the bridle. She noticed two plump water-pouches bound with leather straps to the mule's saddle. One was grey and the other black.

The tall man untied the grey pouch from the saddle and lifted it up to Ava's mouth. Beetlebrow saw Ava's small hands grasping onto the leather vessel. She drank a mouthful and then let go of the pouch.

The tall man handed it over to Pook. Pook took a gulp.

The tall man stepped towards Beetlebrow.

She took the water-pouch from between his large hands. The tall man stood beside her while she took a long drink from the water within.

She lowered the pouch. She wiped her mouth with the back of her right hand, and looked up at the tall man's face. She saw his unsmiling teeth peeking out from between the folds of his fawn-coloured headscarf.

'I'm Beetlebrow,' she said.

She noticed his gaze turning to the water-pouch in her grasp. She slowly handed it back to him.

'What's your name?' she asked.

The tall man glanced at her. He did not reply. He started walking away towards the north-east. The bridle was wrapped around his right hand.

The mule's bony frame began plodding behind him.

Beetlebrow watched the yellow plain growing wider as Pook's dark shape grew thinner in her sight. She started walking forwards, heading after the dull tapping sound of the hooves stepping through the dirt.

She watched the sun pivot across the sky as the hours drifted by.

The day began fading. Beetlebrow felt her eyes closing. Pook remained asleep against Ava's left shoulder.

The tall man handed the grey water-pouch to Beetlebrow. She took a long drink from its contents, and then returned the vessel into his waiting hands.

'Why don't you ever use the black water-pouch?' Beetlebrow asked.

The tall man glanced at her. 'That's for emergencies.'

He tied the grey pouch back to the saddle. He started walking into the north-east with the mule stepping behind him, and Beetlebrow followed.

The sun went down. She felt cold. She looked into the near darkness ahead. She heard the tall man's sandaled footsteps pattering beyond the mule's gentle tread.

'We should stop,' Beetlebrow said.

She stood still. She heard a breeze hissing across the plain.

Through the murky blue dusk she glimpsed the black shape of the tall man letting go of the bridle. She watched him lifting Pook down onto the ground.

She saw Pook's right foot tensing in the dirt beside her bandaged left leg. Beetlebrow hurried forwards.

She glimpsed the tall man walking away into the gloom to her left. She noticed Ava's small, black-clad frame was still sitting on the back of the mule, and there were leather straps fastened across her body, securing her down to the saddle.

Beetlebrow stepped towards Pook in the near darkness and pulled her close against her body. She smelt the scent of Pook's sweat. Beetlebrow glanced down at the white rags wrapped around her left leg.

'It was him,' Pook whispered. 'He bandaged me up.'

Beetlebrow looked right. The tall man was kneeling down several yards away from the mule. He was grinding the sharp end of one stick into the side of another.

Beetlebrow held Pook around the waist. Pook wrapped her left arm across her shoulders, and together they walked across the dusty earth towards the tall man. Beetlebrow felt the softness of Pook's skin through the thin woollen material of her grey robe. She heard Pook's left foot shuffling beside the slow steps of her right.

They sat down in the gloom beside the tall man. He began laying a bed of dry brown moss around the pile of smoking sticks. Little flames started scorching across the wispy fronds. The tall man placed wooden chips around the flaming patches of moss.

Pook looked at Beetlebrow, puckered her lips, and leant towards her. Beetlebrow pulled her head back, and glanced at the tall man. He was placing branches around the growing fire.

'We need to be careful,' Beetlebrow whispered to Pook. 'I just think we need to...'

'Be careful,' Pook whispered. She nodded. 'Yes.'

The tall man stayed knelt beside the rising flames. He placed a black pot upon a tripod of wooden sticks. He poured oats, raisins and water inside. Beetlebrow watched him stirring at its contents for several minutes until they steamed.

He walked over to Beetlebrow and Pook. He handed them each a wooden spoon and a blue bowl filled with cream-coloured porridge.

'Thanks,' Beetlebrow said.

Pook smiled. 'Thank you.'

Beetlebrow felt the warmth of the bowl against the palms of her hands. She looked down at the spongy mush inside, and sunk the spoon deep down into its gloopy depths. She watched the tall man walking back towards the shallow fire.

She glanced at Pook, and saw her head hunched over the bowl, stuffing spoonful after spoonful of porridge into her mouth.

The tall man placed a square, tassel-cornered cushion beside the fire and sat down at its centre.

Beetlebrow noticed him staring into the flames, his face in profile, his nose jutting out above his wide mouth, and his teeth dimly visible behind his parted lips.

The tall man flung out a handful of dry leaves into the fire's glowing orange base; they vanished in a moment's flash of light.

Beetlebrow ate a spoonful of porridge. It tasted of raisins and honey. She felt its warmth sinking through her body. She licked the sticky white paste from the spoon. Its wooden surface felt coarse against her tongue.

She looked at the tall man.

'Tastes good,' Beetlebrow said.

She heard the fire snapping. Embers were darting into the inky blackness above its light.

'I'm Beetlebrow,' she said. 'She's Pook.'

The tall man stared into the flames.

'Won't you tell me what you're called?' she asked.

She saw his black eyes, glinting with light, piercing towards the fire.

'What does it matter what my name is?' he quietly said.

Pook placed her spoon back into her bowl.

'You're travelling to Essum?' she asked.

The tall man nodded. 'Yes.'

'And you're taking us with you?'

'Yes.'

Pook stared at him.

'Why?' she asked.

'You had no water.'

'How long will it take us to reach the Painting City?'

'Your leg is badly bruised. You can't travel for now. Not without my mule.'

'What do you want with us?' Beetlebrow said.

The tall man glanced at her.

'I couldn't let you die,' he said.

He handed around the grey water-pouch. Beetlebrow and Pook each took a drink from its contents, and then handed back the vessel.

Beetlebrow looked at Pook's face. She saw the purple rings under her eyes, and a dab of porridge to the right of her mouth. She reached out her left hand towards Pook's face and wiped the porridge away with her thumb. Pook's smile rose. Beetlebrow glanced at the tall man. His pin-prick eyes were staring at the flames.

Within an hour the fire was becoming low. Beetlebrow felt her eyes drawing closed.

She noticed the tall man lying asleep on the ground beside the embers. She glanced at Pook. The right side of Pook's face was shadowed while its left was lit by the faint orange glow from the remains of the fire.

Beetlebrow felt Pook's hands touching her waist, and her soft fingers drifting across her skin. She heard the branches crackling.

Beetlebrow's throat was dry and her lips were chapped. She leant towards Pook. She saw Pook's brown eyes become lit with flames as their mouths drew together.

23
Yellow earth

Beetlebrow woke up in the brightness after dawn. She saw the yellow plain surrounding her.

She noticed a blue bowl to her right. It was covered with a square of thin white cotton cloth.

She saw Pook sitting to her left. She was looking into Beetlebrow's dark-brown eyes.

'Was I asleep?' Beetlebrow asked.

'Yes,' Pook replied. She smiled. 'Most of the night.'

Beetlebrow looked at the tall man, sleeping on the ground several yards away from the grey ashes of the fire. Beside him was the bundle of dark blue, cream-white and vivid orange-coloured blankets. Ava was sleeping in their middle. Her body and head were clothed in black. Beetlebrow noticed her eyes were closed between the folds of the dark material.

She looked at the tall man, silently slumbering on the ground, and imagined chains around her wrists, connecting his hands to hers. She glanced up at the flat north-eastern horizon beyond his lanky frame.

She looked at Pook.

'This man – how long's he been with us?' Beetlebrow whispered.

'Three days, I think,' Pook replied. 'Maybe four.'

'What's he told you about himself? Has he said what he's doing out here?'

Pook shook her head.

'Do you know what's wrong with Ava?' Beetlebrow whispered.

'No,' Pook replied. 'But there're going to Essum.'

'What do you think he wants with you and me?'

Pook opened her mouth. She closed it again. She stared into Beetlebrow's eyes.

'He saved us,' Pook said.

Beetlebrow heard trails of wind lapping across the plain.

She nodded. 'All right.'

She lifted the white cloth from the bowl. She saw clear water underneath. Ribbons of white sunlight were flexing across its surface. She took the bowl in her hands. She felt its hard ceramic lip pressing against her teeth. She gulped down half the water and then handed the bowl to Pook.

She heard footsteps crunching across the dry earth. She saw the tall man walking towards the mule. His back was straight and his body was lean. He was carrying Ava in her arms. Her black-clad body was cradled against his chest. Her head was slumped against his right shoulder.

Beetlebrow glanced at Pook. The bowl was empty.

She placed Pook's right arm over her shoulders, clutched her left arm around Pook's waist and stood up.

She looked at the tall man. He was strapping Ava to the saddle. Beetlebrow saw the edges of his tawny robe furling to the wind. She started stepping towards him.

'Wait!' Pook hissed.

'What?' Beetlebrow whispered.

'You need to slow down.'

'Why?'

'You're walking too fast,' Pook whispered. 'It's hurting.'

Beetlebrow looked at the tall man, standing by the mule, and her grip tightened around Pook's waist. She took another step forwards.

'Let go,' Pook whispered. 'Please.'

Beetlebrow took her arm away from Pook's waist. She watched Pook limping towards the mule. Beetlebrow stood still.

The tall man looked at Pook. He reached out his hands. Beetlebrow saw Pook shaking her head, and then grabbing onto the saddle and hauling herself up onto the back of the mule behind Ava.

The tall man wrapped the bridle around his right hand. He started walking towards the north-east. Beetlebrow saw the strip of rawhide leather tightening behind his path. The mule stepped forwards, and Beetlebrow began to follow.

The sun soared upwards across the plain. The tall man passed the grey water-pouch around. Beetlebrow took a long gulp from its contents. She felt its weight. The pouch was half-empty.

She glanced at the saddle. The black water-pouch remained full. Beetlebrow gave the grey vessel back to the tall man.

She noticed him squinting up at the looming sun.

The tall man stepped back towards the mule. He tied the grey pouch to the saddle and then stood beside Pook and wound a long black scarf around her head, enclosing her hair and her neck and ears within its single length of fabric.

'Thank you,' Pook said.

The mule was sniffing down in the dirt, its nostrils flaring as they searched across the ground.

The tall man yanked at the bridle.

The mule was jerked forwards. Beetlebrow started walking behind its path, tramping north-east across the yellow earth.

24

Water

Beetlebrow watched the sun seeping down towards the western horizon. The tall man stopped. He placed the coloured blankets on the ground. He gently lowered Ava down into their middle.

Pook climbed down from the saddle. Beetlebrow glimpsed her feet slowing as they neared the earth.

Pook glanced at her and smiled. 'Over here.'

Beetlebrow stepped towards her.

The tall man started to make a fire.

Beetlebrow stood beside the mule. Pook draped her left arm around her shoulders. Together they walked over to the tall man.

They sat down beside the budding flames. Pook unwound the black scarf from around her head and tied up her long black curly hair at the nape of her neck.

The tall man stood up and walked away into the south.

'Where are you going?' Pook called.

Beetlebrow heard her words fading out across the silence of the plain. She noticed the flat grey water-pouch trailing from the tall man's hand. She saw his body leaving the light and entering the blackness beyond.

She stared into the darkness to the south. She listened to the quietness. She wondered what else the tall man was hiding inside his silences, as he led the mule onwards, day after day.

'We can't do anything,' Pook said.

Beetlebrow saw the tiredness in her eyes.

'We just have to wait for him to come back,' Pook went on.

Beetlebrow lay down in her blanket. She turned onto her side. She faced north-east.

She felt Pook lying down behind her. Pook's left arm reached over Beetlebrow's waist. Her questing hand curled across her skinny belly. Beetlebrow entwined Pook's fingers within her own.

Ava coughed.

Beetlebrow leapt up from her blanket. She started stepping away from the warmth of the fire. She felt the chill of the ground against the soles of her feet.

She glimpsed the mule standing behind the pile of blankets. Beetlebrow noticed its eyes glinting to the orange light of the fire. She heard Ava's slow breaths.

Beetlebrow knelt down beside her. She saw Ava's eyes through the slit in the headscarf. Around their black centres were yellowed whites.

Beetlebrow glanced south. She saw only darkness. She faced Ava again.

'Your dad will be back soon,' Beetlebrow quietly said.

She looked at Ava's eyes. They appeared glassy, their gaze empty. Beetlebrow forced a smile.

She turned around and walked back towards the light of the fire. She felt heat splashing across her face as she approached its glow.

She awoke before dawn.

She saw the tall man sitting down by the ashes of the fire. His knees were huddled up in front of his chest. Beetlebrow noticed the flat skin of the grey water-pouch hanging from his right hand.

'Hey,' she said.

The tall man glanced at her, his small eyes looking out through his fawn headscarf.

Beetlebrow nodded towards the water-pouch. 'It's empty, isn't it?'

The tall man faced the ashes. Beetlebrow watched him staring at the remains of the fire.

Her gaze burned at him. Beetlebrow placed her left fist into the palm of her right hand and squeezed her fingers around it. She heard the tall man's silence boiling through the air.

'We need to start the other pouch,' she said.

The tall man shook his head. 'It's for emergencies.'

'We need to keep moving, then.'

'We can't travel today. She's too weak.'

Beetlebrow saw him glancing over at Ava. She followed his gaze. Ava's black-clad frame appeared like a shadowed patch of earth.

'We can't find water if we stay still,' Beetlebrow said.

'I know.'

The tall man turned away from her, knelt down and began enticing a smoking bundle of twigs alight on the ground.

Pook limped over towards Beetlebrow and kissed her left cheek. Beetlebrow clasped her left hand in her own. Pook sat down to her right.

The tall man dropped a bundle of branches on top of the smoking twigs. He began drawing a spindly stick out from within the burning stack of branches.

'What's your name?' Beetlebrow asked.

The tall man jabbed the stick into the centre of the blaze.

'Did you hear what she said?' Pook asked.

The tall man glanced at her. 'Is Beetlebrow a name?

'It's what I got called,' she replied.

The tall man faced back towards the fire. 'My name is Peddar.'

He slid the stick deep into the flames. Beetlebrow saw his gaze returning to the sleeping figure of Ava, as if sight of her was the only nourishment he needed to survive.

25
Levep

Beetlebrow watched the sun rising and the ground appearing underneath its rays. She saw the colour of the plain turning from brown to red to yellow. The blue sky looked as empty as the yellow earth.

Peddar sat down cross-legged beside Ava.

'We can't stay still,' Beetlebrow said. 'If we stop, nothing will change.'

'We gotta keep moving,' Pook added.

Peddar's focus remained on his daughter. 'Ava can't travel today.'

'We need to keep moving,' Beetlebrow said. 'We can't last otherwise.'

Peddar shook his head. 'Ava is too ill.'

'Can we at least open the other pouch?' Beetlebrow asked.

'No. I decide when we use it.'

'It's for emergencies. This is an emergency.'

Peddar shook his head.

'Then we have to keep moving,' Pook said, 'and find some more water.'

Beetlebrow saw her eyes focusing on Peddar's face.

'If don't get somewhere soon, we'll die,' Pook went on.

Peddar took the flat grey water-pouch from the saddle and sat down beside Ava. He squeezed the vessel between his hands. Beetlebrow watched him placing a white rag underneath the pouch. She saw a dribble of water emerge from within its leather container.

Peddar glanced at Beetlebrow and Pook, and then looked down at Ava again. He began slowly unfolding the black headscarf from around his daughter's face. Beetlebrow saw the sheen of sweat covering Ava's yellowed cheeks and the dark-brown dots of freckles around her button nose. She guessed Ava to be seven or eight years old.

Ava's eyes remained closed while Peddar wiped the rag across her face.

Beetlebrow watched several drips dropping down from the white material. The round blobs of water glittered in the air before they landed on the dusty surface of the yellow ground and withered away into the parched soil.

Beetlebrow raised her hands to her cheeks. Her skin felt as hard and cold as stone.

The evening dragged its darkness across the light of the day. Beetlebrow sat down in the dirt. She felt its dust under her feet. She saw the night arriving. The distant stars appeared still and bright.

Her hands began twitching on the yellow soil, fiddling with dry fragments of earth between her fingers.

She stood up, and started stepping through the gloom. She noticed a pale branch on the ground by her feet.

Her walk slowed. She picked up the branch. She saw another and grabbed it. She began scrambling across the soil until her arms were full of twigs and roots.

She built up the fire. She watched it tearing through the wood and releasing warmth and smoke.

She heard Pook's limping steps walking towards her. Pook stood behind Beetlebrow and wrapped her arms around her shoulders.

Peddar rose to his feet. He took a flattened hessian sack from the mule's slim saddle-bag. He stroked the thin hairs under the animal's neck, and then turned over the sack. A few oats floated out down to the ground. The mule lowered its head. Its fat tongue licked the specks of white dust from the yellow earth.

Peddar folded up the hessian sack and placed it back in the saddle-bag. He walked over to Beetlebrow and Pook, snapped a hard biscuit in two, handed them each a half, and then sat down beside Ava again.

Beetlebrow chewed on her half of the biscuit. She felt its mild taste of oats and corn-flour coursing across her famished senses. She thought of the food in Stellingkorr's palace. The chicken legs, and the pies.

She saw Peddar staring up at the stars. A flash from the fire illuminated his wrinkled face for a moment.

'It's going to rain soon,' Pook said. 'I can smell it in the air.'

'It'll take us six more good days of travel to reach the Painting City,' Peddar said. 'By my measure.'

He looked towards the fire. 'We came up from a village near the town of Levep. I didn't want to go into Empire territory, and I'd heard there were medicines in Essum. I hope... I'm hoping there's something there that might cure her. Perhaps their scholars have gained some forgotten knowledge from the Painting.'

He glanced at Ava, and then bent down and kissed her forehead. He pulled a small grey blanket from the mass bundled around his daughter and lay down on the ground by her side.

Beetlebrow swallowed her saliva. She felt it scraping down her dry throat.

She glanced at the saddle on the back of the mule. The plump black water-pouch weighed against its straps. The flat grey water-pouch hung beside it.

Beetlebrow looked upwards. She saw the stars as single spots of light striking out from the blackness above.

'He'll never leave Ava,' she whispered to Pook. 'She'll not survive, and he'll stay with her.'

Pook's left hand reached out towards Beetlebrow's right. Beetlebrow clasped her fingers inside her grip.

'Maybe tomorrow,' Pook whispered, 'Ava'll be well enough to travel.'

Beetlebrow squeezed Pook's hand, and then lay back in her blanket and closed her eyes.

Her throat was dry and her stomach was empty. She felt the heat of the fire lowering. She guessed Peddar had placed his daughter in front of its warmth.

She remembered walking out the room while her mother lay on the floor. She remembered heading down the steps while Lana was growing cold upstairs.

She opened her eyes. She saw the fire settling down in front of herself, and Peddar and Ava sleeping several yards away to its right.

Beetlebrow reached out into the blackness until she felt one of Pook's hands in her own, and then she wrapped her fingers around it.

26
The blackness in the east

Beetlebrow woke up seeing the three-quarters moon looming above the darkness of the plain.

She noticed the grey mule standing several yards away from the embers of the fire. Its muzzle was low to the ground, chewing at the leaves of a terse little green shrub.

Beetlebrow saw Pook sleeping by her side. She saw the red marks along her knuckles. Beetlebrow felt a twinge of pain across her own bruised hands. She remembered grasping onto the sight of the palace in Stellingkorr, and the view taking her beyond the streets of Floodcross.

She stared into the darkness in the north-east, as if her eyes could adjust to its blackness and see Essum within reach.

She touched Pook's left cheek. Pook's groggy eyes slowly opened. Beetlebrow put a finger against her lips.

They slowly folded up their blankets, placed them in the leather bag and started walking towards the mule. Beetlebrow saw its ears turning towards the sound of their footsteps while its eyes remained downcast.

'What if Ava gets better?' Pook whispered.

Beetlebrow tied her bag to the saddle. She heard the leather straps straining. 'What if she doesn't?'

'We can't leave them to die.'

She felt the silver bracelet in her pocket pressing against her chest. The route east felt as slender as an alleyway, and she knew Peddar and Ava could not squeeze between its narrow walls.

It's me and Pook who need to survive, she thought.

She remembered sitting beside Lana when Alder and Joe had stepped out the door, and holding onto her mother's hand as Lana's eyes began to close. Beetlebrow imagined talking to her, and keeping her awake, as the day rose, and the copper coin remained in her pocket.

She grasped Pook's hands. She felt their softness. She looked into Pook's brown eyes.

'We're carrying this message,' Beetlebrow whispered. 'It's more important than us, or anyone else.'

She saw Pook glancing at Peddar and Ava, lying asleep on the earth to the right of the embers of the fire.

Beetlebrow squeezed her hands. 'We're going to have to leave some people behind.'

Pook looked towards the blackness of the north-eastern horizon. Her limping feet wandered forwards a few steps, and then she walked towards the mule, clambered onto its back and sat down on the rear of the saddle.

Beetlebrow untied the black water-pouch. She walked over to the sleeping figures of Peddar and Ava, placed the pouch on the ground beside their blankets, and then stepped back towards the mule.

Pook grasped Beetlebrow's hands and helped her up onto the front of the saddle. Beetlebrow's legs slid down against the mule's sides. She felt its coarse hair brushing against her shins and its bony ribs by her bare feet.

She glanced at Peddar and Ava, lying on the ground to her left, and imagined them waking up at dawn. The morning light would expose the surrounding emptiness. The absence would be stark against the yellow dirt of the plain.

Beetlebrow thought of stepping down from the saddle, and lying on the ground beside the tall man and the little girl, and waiting through the days ahead for Ava's eyes to open again.

She felt Pook's hands squeezing around her waist. Beetlebrow looked north-east, and pressed her thighs against the mule's hard flanks. She felt the animal stepping forwards, its hooves shuffling against the dusty ground.

She flicked the bridle. The mule started trotting out across the yellow earth. Beetlebrow looked at the blackness in the plain. She saw the dark ground and the north-eastern stars above. They appeared to promise Essum.

27

The mule

Beetlebrow woke up sitting on the saddle, Pook's arms wrapped around her waist.

Her legs felt numb against the mule's flanks. She knew she had been holding the bridle for close to three days. The strip of raw-hide leather, bound around her hands, felt soft against her palms until it moved away from the calluses it had worn down into her skin, and then it felt as sharp as a blade.

She thought back to the puddle of beige water they had found the day before. Her right hand drifted down to the empty grey water-pouch strapped to the saddle, and then she looked towards the flat north-eastern horizon.

She felt Pook's hands tightening against her belly.

'Bee?' Pook whispered, her voice sounding dry and spare.

Beetlebrow smiled at the name. 'What is it?'

'Can you smell that scent?'

Beetlebrow sniffed. She sensed salt from the earth, the sweat from their bodies, and the musky stench of the mule. 'What?'

She heard the mule's hooves trotting onwards and the wind rushing against her robe.

She watched the sun rising up in the east as the morning wore out. She felt her face being bathed in the slow, heavy light of the afternoon.

She smelt a briny odour in the wind. 'The sea.'

'Yes,' Pook whispered.

Beetlebrow slapped the mule's right side. Its flesh felt bony against her palm. The mule issued a hollow, wheezy bray, its hooves biting down into the dirt as it galloped into the blankness in the north-east.

Beetlebrow watched rectangular shapes growing out of the horizon for several hours. An expanse of grey flagstones rose up from the yellow emptiness.

Thousands of people in white clothes were walking back and forth across a teeming plaza filled with hundreds of white stalls.

Beetlebrow saw wooden counters, below white canvas awnings, flashing with a gleaming traffic of gold and silver coins. She heard voices talking of vivid reds, ivory, linseed oil, horse-hair and ebony. The plaza looked to her like the flame of a candle, illuminating all within its reach and ignoring anything beyond its grasp.

She looked north. She saw roads filled with hundreds of oxen-driven carts and carriages. The vehicles were emptying people into the plaza like rivers spilling water into the sea. She heard the rumbling of wheels and the chatter of voices. Her sore hands gripped tighter against the bridle.

The mule's front hooves stepped onto the flagstones at the western edge of the plaza.

Its head yanked left.

Beetlebrow wrenched the bridle right. She heard the mule's quiet, moaning bray. She noticed the crowd turning towards her, their eyes beginning to focus on her face.

'Let's get down from the mule,' Pook whispered.

Beetlebrow nodded.

She felt Pook sliding away from the back of the saddle, and then she dropped down onto the shining granite flagstones.

She watched the height of the crowd soaring above her head. Their hands, elbows and white robes bunched around her body.

She helped Pook to step slowly down onto the flagstones. She noticed her left leg was bare, its shin swollen and red.

'I didn't think I needed the bandages anymore,' Pook whispered.

Beetlebrow glanced back at the miles of yellow plain in the west. She imagined the thin material of the bandage becoming brittle as it lay in the dryness of the soil along with everything else left behind.

She watched the sun carrying away its light towards the empty horizon. The soles of her feet were tingling. She smelt sweat, frying food and coming rain. She looked at Pook.

She saw the thin layer of yellow dust across her cheeks and dried, flaky white patches around the corners of her lips.

'Water,' Pook whispered, looking downwards. 'We need water.'

Beetlebrow gulped, and felt the tenderness of her throat.

Pook took her right hand in her grasp. Beetlebrow's left hand held onto the bridle. She looked down at her feet, blistered and covered with yellow dust. Her toenails appeared orange against the spotless grey surface of the granite flagstones.

She felt a dull ache in her hips and a strain along her legs. She looked across the surrounding streams of tall, chubby people; they appeared like hulks of ships drifting though an ocean. She remembered the fishing boats around Stellingkorr, hugging close to the shallow waters of the coast-line, able to dart between rocks and rip-tides. She recalled leaving

Floodcross with only a copper coin and a knife; from this nothingness, everything felt equal to the reach of her hands.

She and Pook threaded south through the plaza. Beetlebrow saw the thick sandals of women and men stamping across their path. She heard conversations of prices and gluts, warehouse fires and import taxes. The air felt humid in the shadowed spaces in-between the drifting crowds.

She noticed a salesman was standing next to a barrel. He was selling water by the tankard. Beetlebrow led Pook by the hand towards him.

She moved the shoulder-strap of her bag closer towards her neck. She felt the heaviness of the gold coins inside. She remembered Darvan Kess, in his dusty office, telling her people had been killed on the streets of Essum for bringing Dalcratty money into the city.

She stood in front of the salesman. 'We've been travelling a long time. My friend needs water. We haven't got any money –'

The salesman shook his head. 'No cash, no water.'

Beetlebrow gripped Pook's hand tighter. Together they walked onwards through the plaza.

A silver-haired man was standing on a wooden crate between two stalls. His long, draping, white robes were edged with gold.

He spread his arms out wide as he intoned, 'His Most Gracious Majesty Prince Tevyan will make the Seventh Addition to the sacred Painting in two days' time.'

Beetlebrow spotted a line of scarlet, semi-circle marks in the dirt by her feet. She stopped, and glanced back along the flagstones. She saw the trail leading up to the mule's hooves.

She let go of Pook's hand, and stepped back towards the animal.

She saw its chestnut-coloured eyes trembling. A froth of white foam was spewing from its mouth. Beetlebrow looked downwards. The mule's hooves were shredded, bloodied stumps.

Beetlebrow reached up her hand and stroked the mule's furry neck. A clump of its thin grey hair fell away to the touch of her fingers. She glanced around at the crush of people walking between the stalls. Amongst the white-clad bodies she glimpsed glass jars and boxes.

Her shallow breaths felt clogged with dirt. She looked at Pook.

'The mule,' Beetlebrow said. 'I noticed the blood on its hooves the day before last.'

Pook's eyes closed. 'I did too.'

Beetlebrow looked around at the stalls in the market, and then faced Pook again. 'We need local money.'

Pook nodded.

'We're going to have to...' Beetlebrow said, glancing at the mule.

'Yes,' Pook whispered.

They started walking south through the plaza. Beetlebrow heard the noise of the crowd falling away as their numbers thinned out by its southern edge. She smelt the sweet, coppery scent of blood.

They stepped into a narrow alleyway pressed between flat grey edifices of concrete-brick walls. Beetlebrow felt the bridle tightening against her palm of her right hand. She wound the bridle three times around her knuckles as she and Pook stepped deeper into the dark yellow dirt between the walls of a smoke-blackened alleyway. Beetlebrow heard the mule's staggered progress trailing behind her bare heels, and she tugged the bridle.

She noticed Pook turning right along the backstreets.

'This way,' Pook whispered.

Beetlebrow followed her around the corner.

She saw a bald-headed man hacking at the flayed, pink carcass of a lamb hanging from a hook on a wall. The man's brown leather apron was sprayed with blackened stains. His face and hands were covered with speckles and splatters of dried blood. Beetlebrow noticed the white clay pipe in the top-pocket of his robe.

'How much is this worth?' she asked, nodding towards the mule.

The man squinted at the animal. He rubbed his nose with his bloody, cleaver-bearing hand. He glanced down at the mule's legs, peered under its foaming lips at its teeth, and then looked at Beetlebrow again.

'Seven coppers,' he said.

'Fifteen.'

'Nine.'

'Twelve.'

'Ten.'

'All right,' Pook whispered. 'Ten.'

Beetlebrow nodded.

The butcher counted out ten copper coins between his blood-stained fingers onto her dirt-encrusted palms. She noticed each of the dull metal pieces had a rectangular hole at its centre.

She handed the bridle to the butcher. She saw him leading the animal through a low doorway into the gloom of a grey-walled corridor between lines of bony-shouldered cows. She watched him tugging on the bridle, and the mule tottering behind his steps, its trembling legs slipping across the red and brown puddles on the floor.

Pook grasped Beetlebrow's arm and stared into her eyes.

'Let's get back to the market,' Pook whispered.

28
Sellessen

They passed locals in ragged grey robes buying empty oyster-shells. Beetlebrow heard conversations about where they were going to display them in their homes.

She felt smooth flagstones under the soles of her aching feet. She heard salesmen arguing over the strength of horse-hair or pig-bristles, the yellow tint achieved by urine or gold, and gossiping about the waning and rising fashions for turquoise, cochineal and purple.

She noticed a group of young men climbing down from the back of an ox-cart. They held leather bags, glass jars of pigments and stacks of thickly-bound books in their hands. She saw the young men's beaming faces glancing around at the merchandise of the plaza.

Her gaze drifted across the market, taking in the teeming stalls, bright colours and well-fed people wandering across its flagstones. The clusters of stalls appeared to her like pools of wealth gathering themselves away from the barrenness of the plain. She squeezed Pook's hand, and they turned away from the buying and selling.

Beetlebrow noticed a section of the market separated out the rest of the stalls. She guessed it to be about thirty yards square. Across its flagstones several dozen white-bearded, white-robed men were sitting on wooden stools. In front of each man was a white canvas propped up on a pinewood easel. She saw the copies of the Painting were about twenty inches high and twelve inches high. Each man was holding a wooden palette in their left hand and a thin black brush in their right. Beetlebrow noticed the cleanliness of their fingers.

With flowing black swoops of their brushes the men were slowly painting a left eye, a left ear, three frown-lines and a curving jaw-line across the centres of their separate canvases. Beetlebrow saw the rest of the portraits being detailed in faint lines of brown wash. On the centre-right of each canvas was a double rose decorated in gold-leaf.

She spotted a tall man frowning as he snatched his canvas down from his easel. She noticed a tiny black splodge on the right cheek of his painting.

The man snapped the wooden frame over his right knee and threw it down onto the gleaming flagstones. A plump young man in white picked up the pieces, walked over to an iron barrel and threw the mangled hash of torn canvas and wood inside.

Beetlebrow saw dozens of identical head and shoulders portraits being displayed above a stall to her right. The single eyes in the paintings were staring down at the people crowding beneath their gazes.

She watched a tourist placing four gold coins down onto the counter below. The salesman pointed to the middle of the three rows of canvases. The tourist gestured towards the top row.

'Seven,' the salesman said.

The tourist placed three more gold coins on the counter. The salesman took the money, reached up above the stall, lifted down a copy of the Painting from the top row, wrapped it up in a sheet of white silk and handed it over to the tourist.

Beetlebrow looked at Pook. Pook was staring at the ground. Her brown eyes appeared weighted down with fatigue.

'We'll get something to eat,' Beetlebrow quietly said.

As they stepped beyond the throngs of tourists and towards the smell of frying food, she heard Pook's steps limping by her side.

She spotted pies and battered fish, pastries and steaming meats being sold from tables at the northern edge of the plaza. Beetlebrow bought a pair of coal-seared kebabs and two wooden tankards of water. The salesman asked for six copper coins. Her hands felt tired as she gave him the money.

She lifted up the tankard and started sipping at the water. She tasted mud on her tongue. She turned away, and spat down onto the flagstones. She looked inside the tankard. The water inside was clear down to the bottom of the vessel. She glanced at the ground. She saw the mark of her yellow spit against the grey stones.

She looked at Pook, swigging at her water and biting through the pitta of her kebab down to the grey slices of meat inside.

'What's it like?' Beetlebrow asked.

Pook nodded as she chewed, her cheeks full of bread and meat.

Beetlebrow smirked. She bit down into her kebab as she stared east along the plaza.

'The prison'll be down there somewhere,' she said.

She bought two more tankards of water. Her left hand slowed down as she handed over the copper coin, and the salesman snatched it from her grasp.

Beetlebrow spotted Pook leaning against a grey wall. Pook was gulping down the final bread of her kebab. Beetlebrow approached. Pook's lips parted. Beetlebrow gazed into her eyes.

'What?' Pook asked.

'I just haven't seen you smile for a bit,'

They finished their water and handed the tankards back to the salesman.

'Let's start searching for the prison,' Beetlebrow said.

Pook chuckled. 'We've just got here. Let's look around first.'

They walked back into the centre of the plaza. Beetlebrow watched the crowds of men and women closing around her body; she felt safe as she became swallowed amongst the streams of people consumed with the air of buying and selling.

She and Pook headed under the white awning of a stall. Beetlebrow looked across the hundreds of glass jars lined up along the long white tables beneath the canvas canopy. She saw their hues passing from black on the left through to purple, red, orange, yellow and white on the right.

She glanced up at the salesman behind the counter. He wore a white apron over a clean white robe. A white cloth cap was set on top of his thin, creased face.

He peered down at Beetlebrow. He folded his wiry arms. She lowered her eyes.

She lifted up a square jar from the front shelf of the stall. She looked at the inch-thick layer of pomegranate-pink pigment inside and turned the jar upside down. The slab of paint remained in place. Beetlebrow stared at it for a moment, and then quickly put the jar back down in its place in the spectrum.

She noticed a jar of yellow paint. She wondered if the colour inside the glass was as dry as the soil of the plain. *Peddar and Ava will still be out there*, she thought.

She smelt boiling cabbage. Beetlebrow looked to her left. Under the shadow of a balcony, a man in a white robe was ladling out watery soup for a line of silent, ragged dozens.

Beetlebrow felt raindrops landing on her shoulders. She looked at Pook, and nodded towards a stand on her left.

They stepped across the darkening flagstones and under the cover of the next canopy. Beetlebrow smelt wet earth. She heard the droplets splatting against the waxed canvas awning above the tables. She saw the queue for soup remaining huddled by the wall while women and men in the plaza began escaping from the coming shower under the shelter of the stalls.

She noticed a short, plump man standing on the right of the stall. His thin grey hair was fluffed-up over the bald patch at his crown. He was revolving a bunch of silver coins in the centre of his right palm.

A tall young woman was leaning down towards the stall, her black dress tightening along the curves of her thin hourglass frame.

Beetlebrow watched the woman's lithe fingers hovering over the blonde heads of the brushes. She heard the golden bracelets along her arms jangling back and forth to the motions of her indecisive hands.

The woman glanced right at the grey-haired man. He nodded at her.

The woman faced the stall again and picked up two brushes. Her bracelets massed together at her left wrist. Beetlebrow watched her handing the pair of brushes to the chubby salesman behind the counter.

'Just these two, please,' the woman said.

The salesman bowed his head. The grey-haired man gave him three silver coins. The salesman smiled. He folded thick brown paper around the two brushes, tied up the package with white string and handed it over to the woman. The grey-haired man began ambling away across the flagstones into the slackening rain. The woman followed. Beetlebrow saw her keeping her pace three steps behind his heels.

'Are any of these brushes different?' Pook whispered to Beetlebrow.

Beetlebrow looked across the stall again. Each of the hundreds of brushes across the tables had a square, yellow half-inch thick head of hairs affixed on top of a black, wooden handle.

'I think if we could tell the difference, we'd've been here too long,' she said.

She heard bootsteps to her left. Four soldiers in blue and white uniforms were hurrying between the stalls. She saw their tall figures swarming around the half-starved frame of a ragged young boy. She guessed him to be around five years old.

A soldier stuck out his right boot in front of the boy's ankles. The boy tumbled forwards. His face struck the ground. A spurt of scarlet blood shot out of his nose. It splashed across the grey flagstones.

One soldier sat down on the boy's tiny waist. A second soldier pressed the heel of his right boot against the back of the boy's left hand. Beetlebrow saw the boy's fingers sparking open. A black-handled brush fell out of his grasp.

'These townies should mind their place,' the second soldier muttered, scooping up the brush.

'Just like the jaw-line of the Painting tells us,' the first soldier replied.

Beetlebrow watched a lanky man, wearing a white apron and white cloth cap, jogging across the flagstones. He stopped beside the boy. The second soldier handed the lanky man the black-handled brush. He took it with his left hand. 'Thank you, thank you so much, officer.'

Beetlebrow spotted a silver coin flashing in his right palm. She saw him shaking the soldier's hand and then walking away holding only the brush.

The four soldiers wrenched the boy up to his bare feet. Beetlebrow noticed his bony ribs protruding from tears in his thin, grey tunic. A blackened gash stretched down the centre of his face.

She glanced down at the flagstones. The red line of blood was being diluted with each new drop of rain.

She heard the deep, droning toll of a bell ringing three times.

She looked around at the plaza. She noticed the orange light of torches peering out through the drizzling twilight between the stalls. Students were turning away from the market, salesmen were counting their stock and tourists were walking back towards the lines of waiting ox-drawn carts.

She watched the crowds of people heading away from the coming darkness. The separate glows of the stationary torches were concentrating light away from the departing figures. She felt her body sinking down into the gloom collecting above the flagstones.

Pook grabbed her left hand. Beetlebrow felt herself being pulled her into a shadowed space between two stalls.

'What is it?' Beetlebrow asked.

Pook's mouth quickly pressed against her lips. Beetlebrow felt the rain on her cold skin. She felt the heat of Pook's tongue. The warmth of her breath brushed against her mouth.

Beetlebrow glanced right at the dull orange light of the market. She saw the crowds seeping away from the plaza.

She felt Pook putting her left hand over her eyes.

'They can't see us,' Pook whispered. 'Forget them.'

Beetlebrow closed her eyes and kissed Pook. Pook let go of her hand, and planted a last little peck on her lips.

'Now... we need to find somewhere to sleep before it's dark,' Pook said.

The rain was thinning out as they walked between the stalls packing away for the evening. Beetlebrow and Pook headed through the light and the noise of the departing crowds – between the artists ordering their assistants to pick up their canvases and brushes and the paint-sellers offering their last deals of the day – and stepped into the bright eastern edge of the plaza.

They walked into the gloom offered by the quiet darkness of a narrow street. Beetlebrow felt herself becoming surrounded by rows of three-storey, grey mud-brick apartment buildings. She saw ladders with broken rungs leaning against their walls.

'We might have to search for this prison street by street,' Pook said.

They stepped east along the dirt-row, between mounds of rotting garbage, floating piles of decomposing vegetables and heaps of soiled clothes.

Beetlebrow glanced upwards. She noticed children sitting on the rooftops of nearby buildings. Their legs were dangling down over the wooden edges.

She stared across the shapes of the surrounding buildings, and imagined seeing the landmarks of Floodcross set against this dark blue sky. She felt as if the turns and exits of the streets of Stellingkorr were inscribed on her body like the scars on her knuckles. *All its passageways and alleys*, she thought, *and I remember the name of each one.*

'Kid, can you help?' said deep voice rumbled.

Beetlebrow glimpsed the bull-like shoulders of a muscular man kneeling down in the dirt to the left. A gaunt young woman was sitting up against the wooden wall beside him. Beetlebrow noticed a pair of high-heeled, black shoes held between the delicate, long-nailed fingers of her right hand.

'She's fainted,' the muscular man said. 'Can you get some water? I can't leave her by herself.'

Beetlebrow looked at him. His scalp was shaved down to stubble and his black beard was squarely cut half-way along his throat.

She glanced away from his broad shoulders and stocky build, and tried to focus on his wide, terracotta-shaded face. She saw, in his gaze, the frightened eyes of a lost boy.

She looked at the woman. Her legs were twig-thin and her knees were muddy. The woman's skin was copper-toned and her blue-black, shoulder-length hair was slick with sweat.

She looked back at Beetlebrow, and then lowered her eyes and crossed her arms over the bare shoulders of her short grey robe.

'It's going to be all right, Sellessen,' the muscular man whispered to the woman, his wide hands holding her skinny arms.

Beetlebrow noticed the red burn-marks across his palms.

'We'll get some water,' she said.

She looked at Pook. Pook's brown eyes were wide. She shook her head.

Beetlebrow glanced up at the square black shapes of the surrounding buildings. She looked at the children perching high above the street.

'We need some help in this city,' she whispered. 'If we help these people...'

Pook shook her head again. 'I don't feel safe with these two.'

Beetlebrow stepped towards her and took her hands in her own.

'Please,' Beetlebrow said, gazing into her eyes.

She felt Pook's grasp trembling under her touch. Beetlebrow tightened her hold. She realised Pook's hands were still, and her own fingers were shaking.

She glanced at Sellessen and the muscular man, and then looked back at Pook again.

'Please,' Beetlebrow repeated.

Pook stared at her face for a moment, and then nodded.

Beetlebrow stepped out into the street. She spotted a dented metal cup in a patch of spiky weeds beneath a wooden window sill. She hurried across the road and picked up the vessel. She dipped it in a rain-water trough, and then headed back towards the wooden wall.

She approached the gloom of the dirt and knelt down beside Sellessen. Sellessen's sepia-coloured eyes looked up at her face. Beetlebrow held out the metal cup. Sellessen took it with both hands. She glanced at Beetlebrow for a moment, and then looked down at the vessel and lifted it up to her mouth.

'Thank you,' the muscular man said to Beetlebrow. 'Most people would just've walked by.'

'We just moved up here from Levep,' she replied.

She saw Sellessen frown, and lower the cup from her lips.

'The people in Levep were only interested in money,' Beetlebrow went on, 'but we heard people are working for something more important here.'

Sellessen smiled.

Beetlebrow grinned back. She glanced over her shoulder. She saw Pook, standing alone in the street, thinly smiling in return.

29
Paint

Beetlebrow watched the muscular man rising to his feet, his wide shoulders towering above her head.

'I'm Beetlebrow,' she said. 'This is Pook.'

'I'm Tulliver,' the man replied.

He looked at Sellessen. 'How you feeling?'

'Still a bit weak,' Sellessen replied.

She lifted up the cup, drank down the last of the water and then placed it in the dirt. 'I just want to get home now.'

Tulliver held her hands as Sellessen stood up. He glanced at Beetlebrow and nodded towards the east of the darkened street.

'I need to get my girl home,' he said, wrapping a beefy arm around Sellessen's shoulders.

'Do you know somewhere we can stay for the night?' Beetlebrow asked. 'We'll be looking for jobs in the morning. We're hoping to work for the princess.'

Sellessen faced her. 'Princess Atalia?'

'Yes.'

Sellessen nodded. 'We always help people who help the Painting. You and your sister can stay with us tonight. But just for the night though.'

Pook smiled. 'Thank you.'

'How do know we're sisters?' Beetlebrow asked.

Sellessen shrugged. 'Just a good guess. Why else would two girls be travelling together?'

Tulliver held Sellessen by his side as he turned around.

'This way,' he said.

Beetlebrow nodded.

Tulliver's broad-shouldered frame began walking away down the street beside the short, narrow-hipped Sellessen.

Beetlebrow looked at Pook, and saw the fear in her eyes.

'We need their help,' Beetlebrow whispered. 'This place, it's all so new.'

Pook glanced at the diminishing figures of Tulliver and Sellessen and then faced Beetlebrow again.

'I don't always agree with your plans, but... you've given me so much,' Pook whispered. 'I promised myself I'd follow you, wherever you go.'

Beetlebrow heard a creaking noise to her right.

A door opened in the shadowed swathe of a wall.

Beetlebrow looked into the high-ceilinged room beyond the doorway. She saw dozens of thin figures standing in silence by the faint light of guttering candles. The workers' scalps were piebald and their cheeks sunken and pale. Their bony arms were stiffly turning long wooden spatulas inside steaming metal casks of bubbling liquid. The oily stench of paint hit Beetlebrow's nostrils.

She spotted a skinny woman stumbling out the doorway. Her hands were blackened and her ragged grey robe was stained blue and orange. She was rubbing her reddened eyes and coughing into a stained rag.

Beetlebrow watched her wandering away west down the street.

The door shut again. The wall to the right rejoined the darkness of the neighbourhood.

Pook squeezed Beetlebrow's left arm and nodded east down the street. Beetlebrow spotted Tulliver and Sellessen stepping into an alley between two lines of broken wooden fences.

She held Pook's hand. They began to follow. They headed into the alley.

Beetlebrow listened to the planks rattling to her left and right. She heard a man's echoing shout sounding out in the distant streets she had left behind.

She saw Sellessen and Tulliver threading around the puddles of a patch of clay-brown waste-ground beyond the fences. She noticed four wooden shacks squeezed together between a set of grey concrete-brick walls. In the waxy, fleshy odour in the air Beetlebrow recognised the scent of a factory where hogs were processed into lard.

She saw Sellessen and Tulliver heading towards the boxy shack on the left of the waste-ground. She looked across the single-storey structure. Built from horizontal layers of wooden shards, the shack appeared to her like stacked rows of rotten teeth.

She heard a child's distant cry to her right.

Sellessen lifted up the hessian sheet hanging over her doorway and glanced back at Beetlebrow and Pook.

'Come on in,' Sellessen called.

Beetlebrow and Pook hurried forwards. They ducked under the hessian sheet and stepped inside the dirt-floor shack.

Beetlebrow smelt burnt sunflower oil and fried offal. She saw two yellow candles, set on an upturned crate to her right, illuminating the whole of the room by their light alone.

She heard a mumbling noise to her left. A skeletal man was lying down along a row of hessian cushions lined up against the wooden wall. His hairless head was without eyebrows or lashes. She noticed the vacant expression of his sepia-coloured eyes.

Sellessen sat down on a cushion behind him.

She looked up at Beetlebrow and Pook. 'This is my brother, Gan.'

She looked down at her brother's face and smiled.

'I'm going to turn in,' Tulliver said. 'I'm up early.'

Beetlebrow saw him walking into the rear of the shack, his burly shoulders hunching over beneath the wooden ceiling. He sat down against the wooden wall at the back of the room, folded his arms and closed his eyes.

'Tulliver does the dawn shift at a brush-makers,' Sellessen said to Beetlebrow.

'Are you feeling better?' Beetlebrow asked.

'I just get tired, is all,' Sellessen replied. 'My heart ain't good; always been that way. I get tired, and I feel faint. It comes when I work too hard.'

'What work do you do?'

Sellessen smirked. 'Oh... me and Tulliver, we have a thing. I lure men into alleyways, or somewhere else quiet, down by the Love Lane district, and when they follow me in there, Tulliver's beside me, with a club!'

Beetlebrow forced a chuckle. She glanced at Pook. She watched Pook hurriedly nod and smile at Sellessen.

'It always works,' Sellessen went on. 'When someone's half-naked they don't want to argue, so I get their cash, and nobody gets hurt. Unless they're stupid.'

'So you just pretend to be selling your body?' Pook asked.

'That's right.'

'But... but you don't wear make-up?'

Sellessen frowned. 'You're going to have to leave them ideas behind now you're in Essum. Make-up takes away from a woman's natural beauty.'

Pook glanced at Beetlebrow.

'Does the Painting tell you that?' Beetlebrow asked Sellessen.

'In a way,' Sellessen replied. 'There aren't any women in the Painting, so we know women shouldn't be illustrated, with eye-shadow and rouge and all them other foreign things.'

Pook looked at Sellessen again. 'I'm sorry,' Pook said. 'I... I've got a lot to learn.'

'Yes, you have.'

Beetlebrow heard a dog barking some streets away. She listened to the silence separated inside the shack.

'Does it work then, tricking the men?' she asked Sellessen.

'Oh yes,' Sellessen replied, her smile resurfacing. 'It's good money. I know lots of girls on the street who have it off with men for cash. Some have boyfriends, but they don't have the sort of relationship I have with Tulliver. He ain't pimping me out. We work together, and no-one touches me but him.'

Beetlebrow looked at Tulliver. She saw his eyes were closed. She noticed an earthenware jar on thin wooden shelf several feet above his head. The stems of a pennyroyal plant, with flowers like mauve bubbles, were springing up above the bulbous vessel.

'Sometimes I go out by myself,' Sellessen went on, 'if Tulliver's on shift, or if Gan has one of his turns, because then he needs someone with him, and then Tulliver stays home.'

She glanced down at Gan's face. 'When that happens, it's me with the club. But I still wouldn't let the punters touch me. I'm lucky with the man I've got.'

She grinned up at Beetlebrow and Pook. 'You two have boyfriends?'

Beetlebrow and Pook shook their heads.

'The students are a good bet,' Sellessen said. 'They're loaded. They pay a fortune to be taught here, because in Essum they'll learn all there is to know about everything in the world from studying the Painting. They can't get that sort of knowledge anywhere else.'

'There aren't any prisons here, are there?' Pook asked.

'That's right, we don't have prisons in Essum,' Sellessen said with a smile. 'People obey the law here.'

Beetlebrow noticed her fingers stroking across Gan's forehead. His eyes began closing. Beetlebrow heard laboured breaths seething through his nose.

'We heard the announcement for the Seventh Addition...' she said to Sellessen.

Sellessen beamed. 'Isn't it exciting? I've been waiting so long for this. I have so many hopes for the new Addition. I remember when I heard the Sixth being announced, and I remember going to see it, months later, when Mum had saved up enough money for me to visit the golden hall. Seeing the strong single line of black paint across the jaw changed my life. I was only a little girl then, but His Highness Prince Rashine's

Addition has guided me every since. With that confident black line, His Highness shows us the independence and strength we have, as proud citizens of Essum. I think of that black line every day, normally just as I wake up.'

She glanced down at Gan. 'One day I want to buy a copy of the Painting. We've been saving, me and Tulliver. But the good ones ain't cheap.'

She looked up at Beetlebrow and Pook again.

Beetlebrow nodded.

'You're free to learn about all this,' Sellessen said, 'now you're finally in Essum.'

Beetlebrow saw the zeal in her eyes.

Sellessen looked down at Gan. 'No matter what you do, we're all serving the Painting,' she said, 'even if...'

Beetlebrow noticed a line of saliva dripping down from between Gan's parted lips.

'... you have to sacrifice,' Sellessen went on, 'it's worth it for what the Painting gives us, lifting us up beyond wanting wealth, and material goods, and all the other things foreigners are interested in.'

Beetlebrow heard the stillness in the air. 'What wrong with him?' she whispered.

'He worked for a paint factory,' Sellessen slowly replied. 'He worked there eighteen years. Started when he was thirteen. The factory began putting these new metals in the white paint, and they didn't tell no-one. Gan lost a tooth one day, and then another three the next, and then most of the rest went too. He would make a joke about it, saying he'd save money on food, because it took him twice as long to chew his bread.'

Sellessen exhaled. Her shoulders slumped. 'Gan was so lively when we were kids. I'd be up every night waiting for Mum to come home from working the streets, I'd be crying with worry, and Gan's three years younger than me, but he'd make me smile until I weren't afraid no more. I can still see it now. Even when Gan got older, and got a wife and kids, I still saw him as the little boy cracking jokes and clowning around in those long nights, all to make me feel better, and help me sleep.'

Gan slowly looked up at her, and returned his sister's stare with a gummy smile of four higgledy-piggledy yellow teeth.

'After a while Gan lost all his hair, and then he started getting these headaches,' Sellessen went on. 'He couldn't concentrate on the work no more, so the factory manager fired him. Gan's missus – that dirty bitch – said Gan was lazy, and kicked him out of their flat, so I brought him back here to live with me and Tulliver. So he was here, sleeping a lot, and every day he was talking less, moving less. And one time I just saw him, lying here on these cushions, and it hit me: Gan wasn't who he was anymore...'

She looked up at Beetlebrow and Pook again.

'But it's all worth it for what the Painting gives to Essum,' Sellessen said, 'and what it brings to us all. You said you wanted to work for Princess Atalia?'

Beetlebrow nodded and smiled as her thoughts began stitching together her next lie. She recalled what Darvan Kess had told her back in Drowston, as he had sat alone in his office. She widened her smile. 'We heard about Her Highness's divorce, and we just really felt for her.'

Sellessen glanced down at the dirt. 'The poor Princess Atalia... Her Highness came from one of the old families of Essum, from before the occupation, when things mattered, and people were honest. Now Her Highness is in the old palace to the north, and Prince Tevyan is all alone in the old Dalcratty palace in the eastern edge of the city. I often worry how cold he must get at night.'

She looked up at Beetlebrow again. Beetlebrow narrowed her eyes, slowly nodding as she tried to deepen her focus on Sellessen's face.

'So do you think it'd be hard for us to get work with the princess?' Beetlebrow asked.

'When I tried to find a job at Her Highness's palace, they told me they had enough women working there already,' Sellessen replied. 'They've got lots of maids and seamstresses, apparently, but not enough stable-lads and carpenters. It's easier for boys to get jobs in royal service, because most boys just want to mix paint or make brushes. Isn't that right, Gansey?'

She looked down at her brother's face. Her fingers began stroking across his forehead again.

She glanced up at Beetlebrow and Pook again. 'I'm worn out. You two, sleep wherever you can find space.'

30
The princess's palace

Beetlebrow awoke in blackness. She felt Pook's head leaning against her left shoulder. She heard the wooden walls rattling to the wind, and Gan's snores issuing from across the room. He snorted, and then his guttural breathing began again.

She heard heavy bootsteps walking across the bare earth down the middle of shack.

She circled her left arm around Pook's shoulders and reached her right hand inside her robe for her knife.

'Tulliver?' Beetlebrow whispered.

She heard the bootsteps stop.

'That you, kid?' Tulliver whispered through the darkness. 'Sorry if I woke you. I'm heading out for me shift.'

'We're coming too,' Beetlebrow said.

She nudged Pook with her elbow. 'We're getting up.'

'All right,' Pook hoarsely replied.

They gathered up their blankets into the leather bag and followed the sound of Tulliver's footsteps beyond the hessian sheet and into the puddle-covered waste-ground outside.

Beetlebrow felt a breeze pushing against body. She smelt the stench of the hog-rendering plant to the west, and saw the stars were dimming against the light emerging through the dark blue sky.

She glimpsed the shapes of the surrounding streets growing more distinct. She heard an owl hooting somewhere to her left, its piping calls drifting across the slumbering neighbourhood.

Tulliver stopped at a four-way intersection of dirt-row lanes. The dark silhouette of his muscular frame turned around. Beetlebrow glimpsed the three-storey buildings behind him. They appeared as squares of blackness below the brightening day.

'These streets are called Four Eyelashes,' Tulliver said. 'Turn north from here, keep walking beyond the Cutters district and Pewmark Road. After a mile or so you'll see the Princess Atalia's palace. You can't miss it; it's taller than anything else in the neighbourhood. There'll be some light be the time you reach it.'

'Thanks,' said Pook.

'Thank you,' said Beetlebrow.

"Ere, take these,' Tulliver said.

Through the darkness he handed a bundle over to Beetlebrow. Between her fingers she felt two soft pairs of thin leather shoes wrapped in a clean length of cloth.

'Some old things of Gan's,' Tulliver said. 'Sellessen wanted you girls to have them. Gan don't get out much anymore. You'll need these at Her Highness's palace. You won't be hired there barefoot. And if you do get a job at the palace, please come back to the house and tell Sellessen how Her Highness looked. My girl, she's mad on the royals. She'll want the details about her dresses and her manners and all that; how Her Highness smelt, how she walked.'

Beetlebrow held out her right hand. She felt Tulliver's large grip grasping around her fingers for a moment and then letting go. The handshake was brief, and Tulliver's hands cold and hard.

'And see the Painting, soon as you can,' he went on. 'So you can understand all the work we're doing here.'

'Thank you, Tulliver,' Pook said. 'We will.'

'Stay safe,' he replied. 'You and your... sister. Best of luck to the two of you.'

Beetlebrow heard his footsteps walking away across the gloom of the street.

'What did he give you?' Pook asked.

Beetlebrow handed over the bundle. She saw Pook's high cheekbones and slim figure vaguely defined against the darkness. She heard her unfolding the fabric around the shoes.

'It's a tunic,' Pook said. 'A man's tunic.'

'And that's good?'

'You remember what Sellessen said, about it being easier for boys to find work at the palace?' Pook asked.

'Yes?'

'Put this on.'

Beetlebrow shrugged. She slid the tunic over her grey robe and pushed her arms through its long sleeves. She felt the body of the garment draping down against her shins.

'Now, your knife,' Pook said.

Beetlebrow handed her the knife. Pook raised it up towards Beetlebrow's head. Beetlebrow stood still while she felt Pook sawing through her hair. She remained in places for several minutes while Pook tugged at the long black strands, cut them away and threw them aside.

Pook lowered the knife. 'There.'

Beetlebrow reach up her hands and touched the sides of her hair. She felt where its long black strands had been. She found Pook had cut her hair down to roughly an inch in height all over. To the touch of Beetlebrow's fingers, it felt soft in places and bristly in others.

Pook gave the knife back to her, handle first. Beetlebrow saw the blade glinting in the dark blue light.

'Now me,' Pook said.

Beetlebrow chuckled.

'What?' Pook asked.

'You look too much like a girl. I don't think you could pass as a boy, like I could.'

'No?'

'No.'

Pook glanced down at the knife. 'Perhaps I don't need to. Then, I'll be able to go in the kitchens, and the laundry-rooms, and you'll be able to go to the stables and... other places boys work in a palace. However we find out about the prison, as a boy and a girl we should be able to go everywhere.'

'The shoes will be too big though,' Beetlebrow said.

She tore away the sleeves of her tunic, hearing the thin material ripping under the grasp of her fingers.

They stuffed the ragged pieces of cloth inside the two sets of soft leather shoes until they fit their feet.

'Ready?' Beetlebrow said.

'Yes.'

They started walking north through the city, heading through the paved streets in the pale yellow light of dawn.

Beetlebrow saw herds of thin people in plain grey robes hurrying towards the back doors of limestone buildings. She noticed women kneeling down on marble doorsteps raising white froths with furious scrubbing-brushes.

She watched the square, four-storey structure of the white palace rising above the red-brick buildings of the neighbourhood. She thought the houses in the surrounding streets looked like ripples circling a pebble dropped down into the centre of a lake.

Beetlebrow looked across the smooth surface of the palace and felt her steps becoming firmer upon the pavement. *A place like this is built too large for people to live in*, she thought, *and they don't know what to do with all the space inside.* She remembered sitting down in the room in Floodcross with Alder and Joe and the one lock on the door keeping her confined within its walls. She knew she and Pook could escape from any condemning hands along a palace's lengthy corridors and forgotten rooms.

They slipped into a shadowed alley beside the four-storey building.

Beetlebrow peered around the corner. She saw white clouds of mist drifting across the clean, grey flagstones outside the flat-topped privet hedge surrounding the palace grounds. She heard birds chirruping and handcarts trundling along the nearby cobbled lanes.

She noticed a group of five women and three boys walking up the street from about thirty yards away. She looked at their plain grey robes, their thin black shoes, yawning faces and reddened eyes.

She felt a breeze drifting across her scalp. She ran her fingers along her shaven head, and looked back into the alley.

She saw Pook leaning against the wall. Beetlebrow noticed her hair was tied up behind her head with the black headscarf.

'How do I look?' Beetlebrow asked.

Pook glanced up at her hair, and then looked across her grey tunic and down at her thin black leather shoes.

'Not bad,' Pook smiled. 'For a boy.'

Beetlebrow's expression sharpened. She tugged at the collar of Pook's robe with her right hand and kissed her hard.

Beetlebrow smirked. 'Not bad, eh?'

Pook's lips curled. 'I don't usually like kissing boys.'

Beetlebrow's smile drained from her face. 'Have you kissed someone before, then?

'I had a girlfriend, in Silkworks, a year or so back,' Pook said. 'She lived a few doors down from us.'

Beetlebrow heard the single tolling of a bell sweeping away all noise in the neighbourhood within its clear, deep tone.

She glanced around the corner and out into the street. She saw the group of women and boys were roughly twenty yards away from the neck of the alley. She felt her breaths becoming shallow, as if there were no air outside the alley and the only way she could inhale was to face Pook again.

The sound of the bell was still resonating through the air as she looked at Pook again. She saw her still leaning against the wall. Pook's stare was set on the palace.

'So what happened?' Beetlebrow asked. 'With the other girl?'

Pook frowned. 'You and me've got to get into the palace. We haven't time to talk about this now.'

'We do have time. What was she like? What did she look like?'

'Well... we couldn't see each other often; we had to hide from our families that we were seeing each other at all.'

'What was her name?'

'Nina,' Pook said.

'Did you love her?'

Pook glanced away for a moment, and then she looked into Beetlebrow's eyes again.

'I thought so at the time,' Pook said, 'but....'

'But what?'

'Then I met you.'

Beetlebrow blinked. 'So... what happened with you and her?'

'Her parents made her marry a merchant's son. I wasn't allowed to see her anymore. I think Mum and Dad kind of guessed about me and her, but... they thought I'd grow out of it.'

'Do... you miss her?'

'Not now.'

Beetlebrow heard footsteps nearing the entrance of the alley. Her attention tightened on Pook's face.

'So we walk with these servants into the palace,' Beetlebrow quickly whispered, 'do whatever jobs we get ordered to do and snoop around where we can. Hopefully we'll hear something about the prison, or talk to this princess. And I'll meet you by the west side of the palace when two bells strike for the afternoon shift.'

She heard the group of women and boys nearing the neck of the alley. Beetlebrow and Pook walked out into the street and stepped between their numbers, keeping pace with the servants' sluggish steps as they trudged down the flagstones. Beetlebrow glanced around at the silent women and boys. They were all looking ahead.

She followed their gaze, and saw the black gate in the middle of the privet hedge. A soldier in a silver and white uniform was opening its metal wings from within the palace grounds, and seven soldiers were standing abreast across the white gravel pathway inside.

Beetlebrow and Pook stepped with the group of servants across the threshold of the gateway. Beetlebrow's feet left the smooth flagstones of the street behind. She entered onto the white gravel path. She felt its stone pieces crunching under her thin shoes.

'Morning ladies; morning boys,' one of the soldiers said.

'Good morning,' several servants replied.

'Morning,' Beetlebrow said.

She saw the gravel path tapering away towards the palace. The square building's white surface, roughly a hundred yards ahead of the gate, was slashed with dark vertical windows.

She glanced across the empty acres of short grass bound within the span of the flat-topped privet hedge.

'You, boy!' a man's coarse voice called out from the right. 'I need a hand over here!'

Beetlebrow noticed a thickset man looking at her from the grass a few yards away from the edge of the white path.

'Yes, you! Short hair!' he called.

The thickset man was holding out his right hand and beckoning in her direction. Beetlebrow felt the gesture passing through her body. She recalled Pook placing the tunic on her body and cutting her hair. *This isn't my lie*, Beetlebrow thought, *and it doesn't feel truthful.*

She glanced left, and met Pook's gaze.

Pook smirked. 'I'll see you later, boy.'

Beetlebrow grimaced and stuck out her tongue. She turned right, stepping off the gravel path and left the group of servants behind.

She looked at the thickset man. His black hair was swept back over his forehead with grease and trailed down against his shoulders. Stubbled cheeks flanked his messy goatee beard. His skin was dark brown, his eyes were beady and his nose broken to the right. Beetlebrow noticed the looseness of the shabby grey robe around his prominent belly.

'Right, boy,' the man said. 'Follow me.'

Beetlebrow glanced back over her right shoulder. She saw the women and boys walking towards the palace. They were all wearing grey robes and black shoes. *Pook must be one of them*, she thought.

She faced forwards again. The thickset man was striding across the grass towards a flowerbed below the privet hedge. Beetlebrow started stepping after him.

The thickset man halted. He turned around and faced her. She stopped a few paces away from him.

'You're kind of small, aren't you?' the thickset man said.

Beetlebrow scowled.

'Not your fault, I guess. Now, boy, this week I need some help.'

He stared at her face for a moment. 'Have I met you before?'

'No.'

'Oh, thought I had. Right, I'm Zello, head gardener.'

Beetlebrow held out her right hand. Zello glanced at it, looked into her eyes and then shook her hand.

'Right,' he said, 'you know what a weed is, do you, boy?'

'My name's Bee –'

'You know what a weed is?'

'An ugly plant nobody wants?'

Beetlebrow saw his gaze reading across her face.

'Ah, good, you're sharp,' Zello said. 'You should see the fools they try to send me here... delicate lads daydreaming about vermillion or impasto...' He snorted a laugh, '... when they should have their eyes on greenfly and slugs. The last one who worked here, a skinny young lad by the name of Trestor, or something stupid like that, said to me, "I don't want to work with my hands, in case I hurt them, 'cos then I won't be able to paint". Can you believe that? What a little sod, eh?'

'Well, I ain't worried about that. I can work with my hands, no problem.'

Zello gave a brusque nod. 'Good. Very good. Which part of the palace were you working in before, boy? I hope they appreciated you.'

'I was just doing odd jobs in the main building.'

'Well, enough chit-chat, boy, let's get to work,' Zello said, walking away.

Beetlebrow glanced back across the grounds of the palace. The white gravel path was empty.

She saw Zello kneeling down in front of a flowerbed. Beyond his chubby frame, she noticed pink and yellow petals dwarfed by plumes of green bushes.

'Here, boy, over here, pop down by me.'

Beetlebrow walked over and knelt down beside Zello. She smelt a rich stench of peat radiating from the flaky black soil.

'Just pull out anything that doesn't look like it fits,' Zello said. 'Anything you're not sure if it's a weed or a flower, ask old Zello. And if I don't have an answer for a question, then it's not a question worth asking. Right? Get cracking.'

'You reckon the princess'll come by here at all?' Beetlebrow asked.

Zello peered at her face. 'You're not from Essum, are you boy? I can tell by your accent. Where you from?'

'I came from Levep with my friend, Pook, out of love for the Painting.'

'Well, wherever you're from, in this city we have something called respect, and Her Highness needs to be addressed by the proper title.'

Beetlebrow nodded. 'Will Her Highness come by here, then?'

'Not likely.'

Zello held out his palms out towards her. Beetlebrow saw the dry black mud ingrained in the whorls across their callused surfaces.

'There's no dirty hands inside the palace,' Zello said. 'And Her Highness don't like to leave her room at the best of times, not since the divorce. Then again, if Duke Frederick comes to visit, sometimes the little feller likes to go out for a walk.'

'Duke Frederick?'

Zello frowned. 'Don't you foreigners know nothing? Duke Frederick's Her Highness's son, with Prince Tevyan.'

'Oh.'

'Duke Frederick's the Lord of the city of Drayzhed, like every heir to the throne is. Didn't you even know that?'

'No.'

'He's a funny chap, the duke. Whenever his mum ain't around, he gets angry fits, starts kicking people. I've got quite a few bruises on me legs from Duke Frederick. He's a playful little feller.'

Zello chuckled. He shook his head. 'He'll make a great prince one day.'

He glanced at Beetlebrow again.

'Now, that's enough talking, boy,' Zello said. 'You've wasted enough time jawing away. It's time for us to work.'

Beetlebrow looked at the flowerbeds. She saw the buds kept small by winter and the thorny stems of roses. She grabbed at a plant and ripped its stems from the earth. Its pale roots spilled dirt from their tendrils as she threw the plant aside.

31
The south of the city

Beetlebrow watched the morning fading away as she weeded across the flowerbeds. She felt the privet hedge stretching its shadow over her body.

She looked at the patch of earth in front of herself. The blue and yellow flowers were standing alone in the dark soil. She saw the space for these late-blooming plants to thrive.

She glanced left and noticed the miles of weeds across the flowerbeds ringing around the palace.

The bell tolled its deep tone twice.

'That's the morning shift over, is it?' Beetlebrow asked Zello.

'That's right, boy.'

She leapt up to her feet and brushed her hands together. Her palms still felt sore from holding the bridle across the plain.

'Shifts ain't a perfect system,' Zello said, 'but it means lots of people get to work here. If they still wanted to, that is.'

He stared down at the flowerbeds. 'It's lucky there's loyal people like me staying to do the morning and afternoon shifts, otherwise this place'd fall to ruins. There used to be hundreds working here. All of them took a solemn oath to serve Her Highness when they joined her service. Now there're barely fifteen servants left across the whole of the palace. Disloyal the others are. The strong black jaw-line of the Painting showed us a better way.'

He looked at the thorny stems of roses. Beetlebrow saw his gaze becoming distant. She heard a bird twittering in the privet hedge above.

'Well, boy,' Zello quietly said, 'see you tomorrow. If you come back, that is. And I hope you do; Her Highness needs the help.'

'Bye,' Beetlebrow replied, walking away across the grass.

She stepped across the white gravel path.

She spotted Pook standing beside the trunk of a weeping willow by the west side of the palace. Beetlebrow glanced up at the tree. She saw its thick branches were cut down to leafless knuckles.

She stopped under its shadows. She felt the eastward wind pulling at her tunic, and the soreness of her hands. She noticed the oil stains across Pook's robe.

'My day was a complete waste,' Beetlebrow said. 'We should just get out of this city, take the Dalcratty coins and – '

Pook put a finger to her lips.

'I bet people listen all the time here, waiting to report things,' Pook whispered. 'Darvan Kess said we shouldn't even mention we're from the Empire.'

'Well, I don't know what we were thinking, coming to this palace,' Beetlebrow whispered. 'As if we'd learn about the prison here, or the princess'd tell us things.'

Pook nodded. 'I was in the kitchens all morning. It was boiling hot in there. And there was only me and a woman, Josephine. And Josephine's going to work for the prince's palace tomorrow.'

'Everyone's leaving, aren't they? I think they're scared of something.'

'It does mean something good though. Josephine told me. There's spare rooms upstairs in the servants' quarters.'

'Rooms?' Beetlebrow asked. 'How much do they cost?'

'Nothing,' Pook said, her smile rising.

Beetlebrow felt warmth flowering in her face. She smiled back.

'Let's get our wages from the bursar and then head into city,' Pook said. 'We can get in a few hours looking for the prison before it gets dark.'

Beetlebrow was paid three copper coins for her shift; Pook was paid two. They walked out the white building of the palace and crossed the driveway, passing the pair of soldiers guarding the gate.

Beetlebrow looked at the row of white limestone houses in the street outside the palace grounds. Every window was shuttered and every door barred. The walls of the houses barricaded all view of the city beyond.

Beetlebrow glimpsed three women and two men standing outside the gate. On the polished flagstones by their feet, she noticed bundles of fresh yellow lilies clustered against the tight green coils of the privet hedge. The delicate stems of the blooms were tied together with wispy brown strings.

The five people beside the flowers wore grey robes. They were clutching lighted tallow candles in their tight-knuckled hands.

One man was placing his bunch of lilies against the shear wall of privet. Beetlebrow noticed the lines of tears streaming down his fleshless cheeks, their transparent courses drifting down into his shaggy grey beard.

A tall woman, her face lean with hunger, glanced at Beetlebrow and Pook for a moment, and then started stepping towards them.

Beetlebrow's hands tensed down by her waist.

The tall woman's gaze touched upon the soldiers behind the gate before she faced Beetlebrow and Pook again.

'How... how did Her Royal Highness Princess Atalia look?' the tall woman asked. 'Does Her Highness seem well?'

Beetlebrow heard the group of women and men by the flowers draw in breath. She saw white mist rolling across the flagstones between their willowy bodies and covering their feet from sight.

'I haven't seen Her Highness look unhappy for a moment,' she said, 'in all the time I've been working here.'

The tall woman smiled, and glanced back at her group. Beetlebrow saw the women and men grinning at each other, the expression shared between their haggard faces.

'Thank you,' the tall woman said to Beetlebrow.

Pook nodded.

Beetlebrow and Pook stepped beyond the flagstone road, walking out through the wide, clean boulevards and into the darker streets beyond. Beetlebrow smelt the stink of sewage rising among the murky wooden shacks as they headed south through the city and reached the street behind the market.

She spotted the dented metal cup on the ground by the wooden wall. She heard the roar of the crowds buying and selling paints and brushes for silver coins and reproductions of the Painting for gold. The sound bowled through the narrow, dirt-row streets like sea-spray splashing down into rock-pools by a shore.

'This is where we were last,' Pook said, 'so let's start searching from here.'

They passed a lane of burnt-out stone houses. They looked through doorways and windows across the hours of the afternoon, and saw people sleeping in roofless dwellings beside empty jars and paint-saturated brushes.

Beetlebrow looked down at the broken houses of the neighbourhood. She stopped walking.

She saw the sun setting above the slanted rooftops of the neighbourhood, swirling silver streaks of clouds within its dark-orange light.

She thought of all the hundreds of similar passageways there would be in the Essum, and all the thousands of houses lining their twisting routes. *They'll all have to be searched*, she thought. *Every one.*

Her teeth gritted together. She looked at Pook.

'We're not going to find the prison like this, just looking through the streets,' Beetlebrow said. 'It's going to be somewhere where no-one sees it.'

She heard the distant tolling of three bells. 'At least at the palace we have something. We get wages there, a room to sleep in... that's more than most people have. It's more than anything you and me've ever had. Perhaps we don't need to do nothing else.'

Pook stared into her eyes. 'Have you forgotten what we're doing in this city? What we've got to do?'

Beetlebrow glanced around the street. 'But...'

'*By stumbling hearts...*' Pook said.

Beetlebrow looked at her. '*...growth split sleep...*'

'*...and engraved the earnings...*'

'*...two could not keep.*'

Pook smiled. She leant towards Beetlebrow, closed her eyes and puckered her lips.

Beetlebrow pulled her head away. She looked at the surrounding houses. The shutters on their windows were closed.

Pook stepped closer towards Beetlebrow. Their faces were only inches apart. Beetlebrow heard Pook's heartbeat.

'Who's going to mind seeing a boy and a girl kissing?' Pook whispered.

Beetlebrow leant forwards. Her lips pressed against Pook's mouth.

They separated. Beetlebrow glimpsed the late afternoon sun turning peach-coloured above the city.

She spotted a row of four market-stalls. Their salesmen were packing away their wares from the dimming light, resigning into crates and boxes the foods they had failed to sell.

She noticed the tapering cracks across the surrounding grey plaster walls. She watched the women and men drifting by. Their grey robes matched the dusty dirt by their bare feet. Beetlebrow saw their hungry eyes waiting for any rotten fruit to be thrown away.

She and Pook cupped their hands together by a brown mud-brick wall and pooled their eight copper coins between their palms. Beetlebrow saw the three left over from the mule they had sold to the butcher. *Peddar and Ava's mule*, she thought.

'We'd better only buy one loaf,' Pook said. 'We'll need to save our wages.'

'It's hard when we've got so much from before,' Beetlebrow whispered, nodding towards her leather bag.

'If only we knew someone we could trust.'

'But we don't.'

Beetlebrow saw vivid green apples and plump oranges stacked in piles across a stall to her right. She noticed four scuffed red pomegranates in a round wickerwork basket on the table to her left.

She glanced at the salesman standing behind his counter. He was staring at Pook. Beetlebrow looked down at her own body. She glimpsed her grey tunic, and smirked.

She glanced at Pook and nodded towards the fruit-stall.

'What do those signs say?' Beetlebrow asked.

'*Apples and oranges, half dozen for a copper,*' Pook replied. '*Imported pomegranates, five coppers each.*'

'You get some loaves,' Beetlebrow said, handing her the copper coins. 'I'll be around the corner.'

'Around the corner? What you mean?'

Beetlebrow pointed across the street. 'Over there. I'll see you in a minute.'

Pook's lips curved into a smile. 'What are you up to?'

Beetlebrow nodded towards the bread stand. 'Go on.'

Pook's grinned, shook her head and limped away.

Beetlebrow stepped towards the fruit-stall, her eyes fixed on the man standing behind the boxes of apples and oranges. He was still looking at Pook.

The left side of Beetlebrow's tunic brushed across the wickerwork basket. She walked around the corner and stood by a brown mud-brick wall.

She saw Pook stepping towards her. She was clasping a round loaf in her hands.

Beetlebrow held up a pomegranate. Pook grinned. Beetlebrow slipped the red fruit back inside her leather bag.

Pook glanced down at the loaf. 'This cost three coppers.'

'Really? Why's that?'

'Not much grain about, the salesman told me.'

Beetlebrow noticed a stout man stepping up onto wooden box by a smoke-blackened wall below the upper storeys of thin houses looming over the street like weeping willows.

His white goatee twitched as he glanced across the dozens of people crowding across the dirt, their grimy rags held together by rectangular patches.

Beetlebrow saw his right hand feeling along the golden lining of his bright white robe. The wrinkles around the stout man's narrowed eyes tightened. He rolled back on his sandaled heels. The wooden box creaked underneath his feet.

Beetlebrow and Pook walked over and stopped behind the people in the street.

The stout man's solemn expression aimed itself above the crowd. 'Our beneficent and incorruptible Majesty, His Highness Prince Tevyan, our esteemed curator of the original artist's work, has begun his final preparations for tomorrow's Seventh Addition to the Painting.'

Beetlebrow saw the crowd facing towards each other and smiling.

The stout man cleared his throat. The crowd looked at him again. Beetlebrow saw their expressions fading away.

'We are truly fortunate,' the stout man went on, 'to live in an age of progress, when our prince wishes to give so much to his people. And we must not forget what the last Addition illustrated. That strong line of the jaw shows the strength of Essum, and eschews those who wish to further ideas foreign to our city, of avarice and power and money.'

'Dalcratty,' a woman's voice muttered.

Beetlebrow glanced towards the sound, and saw only faces focused on the stout man.

'When I visited the Painting this morning,' he continued, 'as I do every day – as every good citizen does – I began thinking about how any citizen could design the perfect brush or the perfect tint that His Royal Highness Prince Tevyan could use to guide us towards understanding what his ancestor, the unknown artist, started all those centuries ago, before the invaders tried to take away who we were.'

Beetlebrow noticed a white-haired woman in the crowd leaning closer towards the stout man; she appeared as if she were warming herself in front of a fire.

'I grew up, as we all did, in the wake of the Fifth Addition, by High Royal Highness Prince Yohann, over ninety years ago: the shading upon the right ear,' the stout man went on. 'I was in awe of it, as every citizen should be, but I never expected such brilliance as his grand-nephew, His Royal Highness Rashine, showed to us with his Addition. The strong line of the jaw tells us to stay in our communities. The original artist did not intend for us to step away and see what is around us, standing up high to get perspective; no, the Painting wants us to stay humble and to follow what it has decided for us, and what it will decide for us in the future.'

His light-brown eyes remained looking high above the attentive crowd, his gaze flitting left and right.

'Only today I have heard of people drawing focus to themselves,' he continued, 'men dressed as women and women dressed as men, performing unspeakable acts with each other in secret meeting-houses within the very streets of Essum. I do not see the jaw of the Painting so adorned with pride. I do not see such excesses being ascribed to the sacred portrait. Such lives are attempting to take us all away from our duty as citizens. We have no prisons in Essum, because we do not need prisons... those who do not adhere to our values are asked to leave the city.'

Beetlebrow watched the crowd's heads bobbing as they nodded, their expressions and clothes mirroring one another in every detail.

'Excess is the foreign disease, citizens. It is always coming for us, and we must be ever vigilant for its influence. That a neighbour or one of our family members might be overcome by these contaminations cannot be avoided – it is one of the sacrifices we must make to live amongst purity. It is that sharp line of the jaw that shows us this.'

Beetlebrow saw him gesturing his right hand out towards someone at the front of the crowd.

'If you would, please, Gullissa...' the stout man said.

Beetlebrow saw a narrow-shouldered, trembling young woman shuffling towards the wooden box. Two limp plaits of black hair trailed from her thinning scalp and hung down the back of her hessian robe.

The stout man bent over towards Gullissa. He clasped her left hand, stepped down from the box and kept his grasp on her palm as she slowly stepped up onto its wooden surface.

Gullissa glanced across the crowd, her bare feet wobbling underneath her bony legs. Her unfocused gaze began to turn above the people in the street.

Beetlebrow looked at her face, and saw the hollows in her golden-brown cheeks and the deep black bags underneath her wide brown eyes. She guessed Gullissa to be in her early twenties.

The stout man glanced around at the women and men standing in the dirt for a moment, and then let go of Gullissa's hand.

'If you could remove your robe, miss,' he whispered.

Gullissa shrugged her hessian robe away from her sinewy shoulders. The garment dropped down to the ground.

Gullissa wore a white vest and a white loincloth underneath. Her ribs were defined on her chest and her needle-thin arms were covered in red sores. Her waist tapered down towards prominent hip-bones, jutting out left and right above her skeletal thighs.

The stout man faced the crowd. 'Gullissa has dedicated herself to the Painting. She has no use for the pleasures of fine foods or soft beds. She is concerned only with the Painting. She lives in chastity, with her family – people of modest standing, the father a brush-maker – and by the grace of several generous patrons, she visits the Painting several times a day. Gullissa is a true woman of Essum.'

Beetlebrow noticed one white-haired woman in the crowd – her dark eyes focused on Gullissa – had driven the finger-nails of her right hand so deeply into the flesh of her left palm that spots of blood were dripping down into the dirt.

The stout man began clapping, and the crowd's applause thundered between the houses. Beetlebrow glanced at the people around herself. She saw rapt attention on every face.

She looked at Pook, and saw her applauding.

Pook leant towards her. 'Join in.'

Beetlebrow faced Gullissa and started clapping.

Gullissa stepped down from the wooden box. She looked at the ground by her bare feet.

Beetlebrow saw the crowd walking away from the street, the families and groups separating as each person headed out alone into the connecting roads.

The stout man remained standing next to Gullissa, his wide body looming above her stick-like figure, and started whispering into her right ear. Gullissa nodded as she slid her hessian robe back across her shoulders.

Pook stepped close towards Beetlebrow. 'Now, let's go back the servant's quarters. We can find a room there.'

Beetlebrow looked into her eyes. 'A room of our own...'

They hurried through a district of concrete-brick houses as darkness drew over the city. Beetlebrow noticed weeds growing tall as people in the surrounding alleyways. She smelt cooking oil and sickly-sweet perfume. She saw the light of candles shining out from square windows far above her head.

She noticed dozens of silent women standing by the walls. Burning torches, mounted across nearby buildings, were casting their light down at the dirt.

Beetlebrow glanced at the women's faces. Tired and hungry, they appeared to her as still and as silent as the copies of the Painting in the market.

She spotted a line of three men in white robes trickling down the dark centre of the dirt-row street. They were stepping between the puddles in the ground and making comments about each woman in turn.

'Too dark.'

'Too old.'

'The state of you.'

Beetlebrow watched two of the three men turning a corner on the right of the street. A short, thin man remained behind.

Beetlebrow saw him approaching one of the women by the wall. The woman's long black hair draped down over her shoulders and against the skinny belly of her thin grey robe. Her expression was blank. The man's face was shadowed from the light of the torches.

Beetlebrow glimpsed him looking up and down the woman's body.

The man's right hand grabbed the woman's left arm just above the elbow. Beetlebrow shuddered. The man began talking into the woman's ear. The woman started nodding to his words. Beetlebrow knew the man was telling her what he thought she was worth.

She glanced at the other women standing in the light by the wall, their bare feet in the dirt and their cold hands numbed beyond trembling.

From a high window, the cry of a baby rose to a strained, rasping scream. Beetlebrow heard a woman's voice quietly shushing the infant into silence.

Pook nodded towards a shadowed doorway. Beetlebrow spotted Sellessen kneeling in front of a stocky, round-faced man.

He was tying his brown belt around the waist of his white robe. He pressed several copper coins into Sellessen's right hand. Sellessen clasped the metal discs in her palm and smiled up at the man's face.

Beetlebrow looked away. She stared down the dark street towards the west. She felt her eyes pricking.

Pook touched her left shoulder. 'Bee?'

Beetlebrow felt a tear falling from her right eye. It dropped down her cheek.

She turned and faced Pook.

'Oh, Bee...' Pook whispered.

'My mum...,' Beetlebrow said, 'she was like these women. I'd hoped it was different here, for girls, but it's just like everywhere else.'

Pook quickly kissed her lips. Beetlebrow felt a chill coursing across her shaved head.

She glanced down at her tunic. 'Kiss me again.'

She felt the warmth of Pook's lips pressing against her mouth. Pook held onto her hands.

'Let's go find ourselves a room at the palace,' Pook whispered. 'We'll search for the prison again tomorrow, after the morning shift.'

They walked north through the city. Beetlebrow saw that the sky was becoming black, the streets indigo, and faint stars were peeking out above the square buildings of the neighbourhood. The gate of the princess's palace was open. Beetlebrow spotted a soldier's spear leaning against the privet hedge.

She and Pook stepped through the gateway. Beetlebrow felt gravel crunching under her feet. She heard Pook's steps limping by her side.

'This way,' Pook said.

Beetlebrow followed her into the western wing of the palace, up four flights of stairs and into a low-ceilinged corridor beyond. Along the brown walls, she saw the amber light of oil-lamps flickering in arched niches. The marble floor appeared golden in the reflections of their glow.

She noticed Pook walking across towards a doorway on the left. She heard the silence in the corridor. She picked up one of the lamps.

'In here,' Pook said.

Beetlebrow stepped after her.

She watched the light of the lamp showing the bare, grey walls of the square room inside. She noticed the high slit of a window in the top-right corner. She closed the door behind herself, shutting away the golden light in the marble corridor outside.

She put the lamp down on the ground. She heard it clink against the tiles. Her dark-brown eyes met Pook's gaze.

They faced one another as they sat down cross-legged on the floor, their knees touching and their hands held together.

Beetlebrow took the pomegranate out from her leather bag. Her knife slit open its red skin. She and Pook tore the hard covering of the fruit down through its yellow pith and revealed the ruby-red jewels inside.

Beetlebrow dug her left hand into the pomegranate's sticky centre. She saw Pook's lips parting, and the black centres of her eyes becoming wide.

Beetlebrow scooped out several seeds from the fruit with her left index finger. She held the red jewels up towards Pook's mouth. Pook's wet lips slipped over her finger and sucked the pomegranate seeds from its length.

Beetlebrow and Pook took off each other's dowdy clothes in the middle of the little room in the servant's quarters of the princess's palace. Beetlebrow grasped Pook's thighs and looked into her gaze.

32

Princess Atalia

Beetlebrow woke up sitting against a wall. She saw the darkness in the room in the servant's quarters. She smelt the scent of the pomegranate.

She heard Pook sleeping beside her, and a rumbling noise rising approaching through the hush of the night-time city outside.

'Hmm?' Pook mumbled.

Beetlebrow was still. She heard carriages hurtling across the palace grounds.

'What's happening?' Pook whispered.

'I don't know,' Beetlebrow said.

She grabbed her leather bag and jammed their blankets and leather shoes inside.

She heard shouted orders and bootsteps flooding through the corridors of the palace. She clutched Pook's hand and started running through the gloom and towards the door.

'Bee!' Pook hissed.

Beetlebrow stopped. She felt Pook's grasp squeezing against her hand.

'We have to go slower,' Pook said. 'You know I can't walk fast anymore.'

They stepped out of the room, and felt along the smooth walls of the darkened palace, heading down the staircases until they reached the ground floor.

Beetlebrow heard garbled echoes circling around the surrounding corridors.

'Which way do we go?' she whispered to Pook.

'Boy!' Zello called.

Beetlebrow saw his thickset figure running towards her from the corridor to her right. The flame of Zello's candle was wobbling through the blackness; the passageway appeared to Beetlebrow like a dark tunnel around its flickering light.

Zello stopped two paces from Beetlebrow and Pook. 'We need to save Her Highness. The soldiers have taken her away.'

Beetlebrow saw the glow from his candle become swamped by the light of crackling torches. Eight tall soldiers crowded around Zello's chubby body.

The soldiers' featureless golden masks stared down at Beetlebrow and Pook.

'Why're you servants still here?' a rasping voice snapped. 'You should've been smart and taken jobs with the prince.'

Beetlebrow heard carriages distantly speeding away from the palace, their metal wheels scything across the gravel path.

'You're leaving, servants,' the voice sneered. 'We don't want anyone left here. This stupidity with the princess has gone on long enough. Prince Tevyan can't keep giving her money now they're divorced. It'll divide the people's loyalties.'

Beetlebrow saw the soldiers marching away along the corridor to the right, the flames of their torches burning through the blackness, and Zello hurrying after their light.

She glanced at Pook as the orange glow of the torches drained away. She heard the soldier's bootsteps storming into the distance.

Beetlebrow listened to the quietness in the passageway. She felt attention slipping away from her body as darkness enfolded between the walls. She saw Pook sinking inside its black obscurity.

'What do we do?' Beetlebrow whispered.

She heard bootsteps behind her feet. Pook grabbed her right arm. She and Beetlebrow started stepping down the corridor, heading towards the light the soldiers were taking away.

Zello glanced back over his shoulder. Beetlebrow noticed tears shimmering down his cheeks.

She saw the soldiers and Zello stepping out through the broken front door of the palace. She and Pook slowly walked out onto the driveway.

Beetlebrow noticed the orange flickers of torches flashing across the darkness of the grounds.

Two carriages were standing in the driveway, their doors open, and their teams of four white, muscular horses pawing at the white path. Beetlebrow spotted deep parallel lines scored across the gravel by the wheels of the vehicle.

A dozen soldiers, bearing torches, advanced towards Beetlebrow and Pook.

'Into the carriages!' a masked soldier barked. 'You're leaving this palace, servants, and you're not coming back. We're taking you to the docks. We don't care where you go from there.'

Beetlebrow noticed Zello looking up at the row of golden faces. His hands were cringing against his chest.

'Where's Her Highness gone?' Zello asked.

'Somewhere secure,' a tall soldier replied.

'What does that mean?' Pook asked.

'She's in protective custody.'

'Her Highness is in prison?'

Beetlebrow saw the tall soldier's eyes staring down at Pook through the eye-slits in his golden mask.

'You from here?' he slowly asked. 'You don't sound local.'

Beetlebrow glanced at Pook. She saw her hands were lowered, her fingers splayed, as if she were falling and might need to grab onto anything she could to survive.

'These two came here out of love for the Painting,' Zello said.

The tall soldier glanced at him. 'True believers, eh? That's all right then. We don't grow wheat or barley or potatoes here in Essum. Pilgrims to the Painting are our crops.'

'So is Princess Atalia in prison?' Pook asked.

'It's the safest place for her, miss,' the tall soldier replied. He sniffed, and then gestured over his shoulder with his right thumb. 'Now, into the carriages, the three of you. Don't make trouble.'

Beetlebrow stared up at the soldiers. She felt her heart pounding against her chest.

'We need to see Her Highness is safe before we can leave her service,' she said. 'We took a solemn oath to look after her, and we can't break it without her say-so.'

She gulped down breaths. Her skinny chest rose and fell. She saw the row of blank golden faces glaring down at her. Her fingers curled inwards against her chest. Her hands brushed against the bracelet in the pocket of her tunic.

The soldiers glanced at each other.

'The captain's gone with the princess,' one whispered to another. 'I... don't know what we're authorised to do.'

'We only need to see that Her Highness is safe,' Beetlebrow went on. 'We took an oath.'

A thin soldier held up his right hand. 'All right, all right. We took an oath ourselves, to Prince Tevyan. I guess we can't make you break yours to the princess.'

He reached underneath his breastplate, and between his shining bronze gauntlets held out a length of white rag.

'Put this over your eyes,' he said to Beetlebrow.

She glanced at Pook.

'Just the young master,' the thin soldier said. 'Where we're going's no place for a girl.'

Beetlebrow shook her head. 'I'm not going without her.'

'You take what you're given or you'll get nothing.'

Pook looked into her eyes. 'It's all right. I'll wait for you at the docks.'

Beetlebrow slowly nodded. She took the white woollen rag from the soldier, and placed it across her eyes. She smelt the scent of sweat. She saw the light of the torches fading into blackness as she tied the ends of the woollen rag around the back of her shaved head.

She heard a single pair of bootsteps walking towards her. Her fingernails bit down into her palms. She felt the rag squeezing tighter against her forehead as a soldier tugged at its knot.

A hand cupped her left elbow.

'This way,' a soldier said.

'Tell me what you find,' Pook quietly said.

Beetlebrow looked towards the sound of her voice and nodded.

She felt hands grasping her arms, guiding her up three wooden steps and into the cab of the carriage.

She sat down on the firm leather seat inside. She smelt brass polish and varnished wood. She felt her bare feet dangling far from the floor. The door to her right slammed shut. She heard a key click in the lock.

A metal fist banged twice against the wall outside. A whip cracked above her head. Beetlebrow heard the carriage shooting across the gravel path and out onto the flagstone street beyond the palace grounds.

She lifted a hand to the blindfold and prised up an edge below her left eye. She saw the windows inside the cab were blacked out, and no light could enter within. In the darkness, Beetlebrow touched a space on the leather seat where Pook would have sat.

33

Frederick

Beetlebrow felt the carriage bumping across paved and dirt-row streets, skidding around corners and charging down straight roads.

She closed her eyes in the blackness. Her hands clenched together. She listened to the sound of the carriage hurtling through the streets of the city, and held onto the thought of being taken to the prison.

The vehicle halted.

Beetlebrow heard the door to her right swinging open. She smelt fresh air. Gauntleted hands grabbed her arms. They led her down the three steps outside. Beetlebrow felt cold paving-stones underneath her bare feet.

'Forwards,' a deep voice said.

Beetlebrow started walking forwards. She heard two pairs of hobnailed bootsteps following behind her heels.

The sound of muttered voices surrounded her. Beetlebrow felt a flash of torch-flames to her left. For a moment she glimpsed its glow through her blindfold.

She felt herself being ushered into a warm and silent room. She heard a wooden door closing behind her, and a key clanking in a lock ahead. A handle was turned. A metal door was scraped open.

Beetlebrow felt a gauntleted hand prodding her back. She stepped through a doorway. She smelt clammy air, rotten leather and urine. Under her toes, the stone floor felt as smooth as glass.

Her shoulders were held. Hands untied the blindfold. Beetlebrow felt the release against her temples. The coarse woollen cloth fell away from her eyes.

By the flickering light of a torch she saw the grey stone floor ahead. It was covered with spores of green moss. She glimpsed four six-foot-square cages to the left of the aisle, and three to the right. Their rusted iron bars were criss-crossed horizontally and vertically along their frames.

'Forwards,' the deep voice said.

Beetlebrow started heading down the aisle. She heard the two soldiers walking behind her, the sound of their bootsteps striking against the moist floor. Beetlebrow guessed one carried a torch. She saw its light twitching across the iron bars and displaying the solitary men shackled at the centre-point of each cage. The prisoners were chained to the floor by their wrists and ankles, their long beards and wire-thin limbs trailing down towards the blood-stained floors.

Beetlebrow glimpsed milk-white hands covering frightened eyes from the approaching glow of the torch. The fingers of her left hand reached across her tunic. She felt the hard outline of the silver bracelet hidden inside. She remembered lifting it away from the king's hand. Her fingers touched its silver edge. The bracelet felt solid among the iron bars and the chains of the prison, like an island in the middle of the stormy sea.

The torch revealed the cage at the end of the prison. Beetlebrow saw a skinny young woman sitting alone on a stone shelf set against a moss-bearded wall. There was a furry sable stole draped around the woman's narrow shoulders and a pearl choker strapped across her golden-brown neck. Her cheeks were hollow, and her knees were huddled up in front of her chest.

Beetlebrow stopped several paces away from the iron bars of the cage. She glimpsed the woman's unblemished golden-brown skin and her black hair, curled in twisting shapes above her ears.

Beetlebrow heard a dripping sound somewhere in the prison; drops of water tapping down onto stone. She remembered Darvan Kess saying it had been twelve years since Princess Atalia had married Prince Tevyan, when the princess had been eleven and the prince seventeen.

'Princess Atalia?' Beetlebrow whispered.

The woman's dark eyes met her gaze. She leant forwards, her stare focusing on Beetlebrow's face.

Beetlebrow saw the longing in the princess's expression. *She's waiting for someone to unlock the door and take her back to her palace*, Beetlebrow thought, *where she could shut herself inside again.*

Beetlebrow turned around. She saw the two soldiers standing several yards away from her down the aisle, their broad frames spanning the width between the cages.

The torch flickered in the soldier on the right's gloved hand.

Beetlebrow stepped further into the light. She smelt the torch's pitch and tallow burning away.

She looked up at the soldiers' blank golden masks. 'I need five minutes alone to talk to Her Highness.'

The soldier on the left shook his head. 'That's not going to happen.'

Beetlebrow looked at him, and then glanced at the soldier on the right.

'Her Highness is never going to leave this prison, is she?' she whispered.

The expressionless golden masks remained still.

'I've been a servant to Duke Frederick since he was born,' Beetlebrow went on. 'Tomorrow I'll join his servants at Prince Tevyan's palace. I'll be around Duke Frederick every day. The princess knows she'll not see her son again. She'll want to give me a few private words to pass on to Duke Frederick.'

The soldier on the left shook his head. 'It's against protocol to let you be here alone.'

'Please,' Beetlebrow said. 'Please let me... for... for his mother...'

She felt her eyes beginning to sting. She remembered the smell of the bread Elisa had given her. *Two loaves*, Beetlebrow thought. *Elisa gave me two loaves.*

Her thoughts began slipping towards Floodcross. Beetlebrow gritted her teeth. She felt tears slipping down her face. She kept her focus on the flame the soldiers held between the cages.

'Please,' she went on. 'For Frederick.'

The soldiers glanced at each other.

Beetlebrow heard drops of water dropping down onto stone.

'All right, boy,' the soldier on the left said. 'I know it's been hard for you today, but it's there's no need for a feller to cry. There's no need to get upset, lad.'

The soldier on the right held out his torch. 'Five minutes then. And not a moment more.'

Beetlebrow nodded. She stepped forwards, and took the torch from the soldier's gauntleted hand. She looked at his eyes, peering down at her through the slit in his golden mask, and felt the heat of the torch burning above the grasp of her fingers.

'Thank you,' she said.

'We'll be back in five minutes, and then you're going straight to the docks.'

Beetlebrow sniffed. 'I understand.'

She watched the two soldiers walking away from her down the aisle. They opened the metal door. Beetlebrow saw the golden light splashing between the cages for a moment before the door clanged shut again and darkness returned to the prison.

She stood alone in the hush and the gloom between the cages.

She wiped the tears from her cheeks with the back of her right hand. The fingers of her left reached into the pocket of her robe. She felt the edge of the bracelet against her fingers. She pulled out the silver band and held it up above her head. She saw the bracelet gleaming to the light of the torch she carried.

'Messenger...' a parched voice said.

Beetlebrow spotted a pair of frail hands grasping against the iron bars to her left, reaching out from the dark confines of their cage.

Beetlebrow headed towards the sight. She saw the glow of the torch drift towards the prisoner's hands. She heard his shackles rattling as he raised his withered arms across his face.

Beetlebrow lowered the torch, and the prisoner removed his hands from his eyes.

She saw stringy grey hair flowing down either side of his paled, wrinkled face, long white eyebrows and bushy white beard. She glimpsed his stained and tattered leather tunic, and his large, dark-amber eyes focusing on the bracelet in her hand.

'You're a messenger, aren't you?' the prisoner quietly said, his patrician voice slicing through the gloom. 'An imperial messenger? From Stellingkorr?"

'Are you Bussert Maris?' Beetlebrow asked.

He nodded slowly. 'You'll want the passphrase?'

'Yes.'

She watched his pale hands clasping around the iron bars of his cage, and remembered Ray Rez's liver-spotted hands stroking across one another as he had stood alone in the corridor by the light of a whale-oil lamp. She recalled Ray Rez walking away through the darkening passageways of the palace, trying to keep his steps precise and his memories from straying towards what he had left behind in Essum.

'I met Ray Rez in Stellingkorr,' she said. 'He hasn't forgotten you.'

Bussert's dark-amber eyes stared at her face.

'He didn't want me to remind you of him,' Beetlebrow went on. 'He said you'd be better off not thinking about when you lived free.'

Bussert glanced up towards the ceiling.

Beetlebrow saw the wrinkles around his eyes scrunching together; in the darkness she could not tell if he had smiled.

Bussert's gaze levelled. 'Thank you, my girl. Ray always was uncomfortable with sentiment.'

His hands loosened their grip on the iron bars.

Beetlebrow watched the glow of the torch stretching vertical shadows across his scrawny frame. The flame danced and the black lines twitched. Bussert remained still.

'The passphrase,' he went on, 'is thus, *None of the high nor savage creatures of my false sun do I bring*. Saying these words at the gates of Dalcratty will give you entry into the city, and access to King Hassan.'

He glanced down at Beetlebrow's hands. 'Do you not wish to write this down?'

'My girlfriend does the reading and writing.'

'Girlfriend?' Bussert asked.

'Yes.'

Bussert chuckled. Beetlebrow heard his chains clinking together.

'Then there is still some light out there,' Bussert said.

Beetlebrow saw him smile.

'Please, my girl,' Bussert went on, 'if you could say the passphrase back to me.'

'*None of the high nor savage creatures of my false sun do I bring.*'

'Thank you.'

Bussert turned around. Beetlebrow watched him slipping away from the light of the torch and entering the darkness at the back of his cage.

'What's this message about?' she whispered into the blackness.

'Tirrendahl,' Bussert softly replied.

'What do you mean?'

'Tirrendahl. Don't travel through Relleken to get to Dalcratty. Travel through Tirrendahl.'

Beetlebrow glanced to her right. She saw Princess Atalia staring at her from behind her criss-crossing bars. *Pook would say something nice to the princess, to reassure her*, Beetlebrow thought.

She walked over to the princess's cage.

'Duke Frederick is safe,' Beetlebrow said.

She saw a faint smile crossing Princess Atalia's face for a moment, and then the princess looking down at the mossy-stone by her bare feet.

Beetlebrow turned around. She glanced across the prison, taking a last look at the cages, each containing a single, white-haired figure shackled to a bloodstained floor. She did not know if what she had said to the princess was true, but she was certain the princess would never know if it was false.

She walked back down the aisle towards the metal door. She turned the stiff handle and stepped into the darkness of the corridor outside. She felt warm tiles under her heels.

She looked left and saw blackness. She looked right. Beyond the darkness of the corridor was a brown hessian sheet hanging across a glimmering golden wall. Beetlebrow glimpsed a painted head and shoulders portrait of a man.

'You were supposed to wait inside,' a deep voice said.

Beetlebrow felt her shoulders being grabbed by gauntleted hands. The torch fell away from her fingers. Its light became extinguished on the dry tiles in a muted burst of sparks. She felt the woollen rag being tied back over her eyes.

Through the blackness she was yanked along the corridor. She felt the chill of the street against her skin. She was pushed up the wooden steps and back inside the cab of the carriage.

To her right she heard the door slamming shut. The whip cracked. The carriage lurched forwards. Beetlebrow was flung down into the aisle in front of the leather seat.

She sat on the floor of the cab, her back against the wood-panelled wall. She heard the horse's shoes clacking against stones, and the vehicle's metal wheels thundering through the streets for several minutes.

The wheels skidded. The door of the carriage was opened.

Beetlebrow felt hands grabbing her right arm.

'Out!' a voice snarled.

Beetlebrow was pulled out of the carriage and thrown down into the dirt. She landed on her hands and knees. She heard the carriage clattering away across the streets.

She listened to its sounds fading from the neighbourhood.

Beetlebrow smelt the scent of seaweed. She gripped the silver bracelet inside her left fist as she rose to her feet. Tiredness was hobbling her thoughts. Her legs felt leaden.

She took her knife from her robe and cut the knot of the blindfold. Free from its covering, darkness surrounded her naked eyes.

To the east she noticed the white glow of light above the docks. She heard footsteps heading towards her, the left foot slightly limping behind the right. Beetlebrow felt the stiffness in her body soften.

'I got it,' she whispered into the darkness. Her voice sounded loud when it was all alone.

'Bee?' Pook asked.

'I've got the passphrase.'

'Then we can finally leave,' Pook said.

'Only if we can resist the Painting.'

In the blackness Beetlebrow felt the touch of Pook's warm hands against her cold fingers. She pressed the bracelet into Pook's palm and closed her grasp around it.

'You take this,' Beetlebrow said, 'since we've only got one.'

Pook squeezed her left arm.

'The docks,' Beetlebrow whispered.

'You sound tired, Bee. We can stop a while.'

'No. We stopped here and we got lucky, at the palace, and we can't stop again. We've got to keep moving.'

34

Tirrendahl

Beetlebrow and Pook headed through the darkness of the night-time Essum towards the brightness in the east of the city's narrow streets, and stepped between the open gates of the docklands.

Beetlebrow heard bells ringing and numbers being called. She saw square miles of torch-lit wooden boardwalk laid out alongside the shimmering blackness of the sea. She noticed longshoremen carrying barrels, hessian sacks and crates past piles of oyster shells, stacks of lobster-pots and rows of pedlars selling steaming broths for copper coins.

Squares of yellow light were streaming from windows of wooden huts at the edges of the docks. Men in long robes were sitting at trestle tables piled high with coins and brass scales. In front of their barricade of shining metal, Beetlebrow saw lines of weary-faced sailors waiting to collect their pay.

She glanced across the ships lined up beside the boardwalk. Below their prows, men were calling out prices for ochre, poppy-oil and pearls; by the men's feet, sea gulls and gannets were fighting over fish-heads and whitebait.

Beetlebrow spotted a scowling, bulky man standing alone on the pier by the gangplank of a dark, single-masted ship.

She saw a wooden table beside him. An oil-lamp was set in its middle. Beetlebrow noticed three dice, the spiralling peel of several oranges and an empty set of brass scales set inside its sphere of yellow light.

'Him,' she said to Pook

They stepped across the boardwalk towards the bulky man. He turned his gaze away from the glow of the docks and looked towards their approach.

Beetlebrow and Pook stopped in front of his table.

'Are you the captain?' Pook asked.

'That I am, young miss,' he replied, peering at her face. 'You looking for your old man or something?'

'We want to buy two passages to Tirrendahl,' Pook said.

The captain frowned. He shook his head. 'Don't mess me about. I've had a long day already. Get out of here, kids.'

'Please. We've got to get to Tirrendahl.'

The captain leant down towards Pook, 'Are you trying to get me killed?' he whispered. 'I don't know what you've heard, but I don't take nobody to no Dalcratty territories. Our route's to Drayzhed and back, just like everybody else here. So go home, the pair of you. Get out of here.'

Beetlebrow glanced at Pook. Pook shared her gaze. Beetlebrow watched her slowly reaching inside her robe and bringing out her four Stellingkorr gold coins.

She looked at the captain again, and saw his eyes widen. He glanced out across the boardwalk, and then faced Pook again.

Pook handed him the coins. The captain's stumpy, blue-tattooed fingers tightened around the money.

'Tirrendahl, you say?' he whispered. 'Get aboard then. Quickly now.'

Beetlebrow and Pook walked up the gangplank. Beetlebrow heard it rattling under their feet. She smelt whale-oil and pine-tar as they stepped onto the wooden deck. She heard ropes tensing like bow-strings above her head, and saw sailors running in and out of the illumination of the single oil-lamp by the mast.

The captain stepped up the gangplank. 'New course. East. Step lively, men.'

With its sail unfurled and its barrels tied down, the ship started slipping away from the lights in the darkness of Essum.

Beetlebrow watched the captain walking out across the deck, his rolling gait isolating his body from the undulating motion of the waves.

He began looking between the gold coins in his hand and the trail of ships bearing north-east towards Drayzhed. Beetlebrow saw him glance at her for a moment, and then douse the flame of the oil-lamp. She heard the bones of the ship creaking as the vessel turned east.

Beetlebrow and Pook sat down in a shadowed corner behind two barrels. Beetlebrow heard Pook's breaths become deep and low. She listened to the sailors' bare feet pattering across the deck. She kept her eyes open while Pook slept in her arms.

She heard the sea hissing as the prow of the ship slit along the surface of its skin, and her eyes began to close. She heard the vessel bobbing and soaring across the waves.

She saw an image of golden double-doors in front of a white palace in Dalcratty. They opened in front of her like a pair of jewelled wings.

She and Pook were standing in the hall inside. A forest of round pillars lined its white marble floor. They supported a stone ceiling three storeys high. Beetlebrow noticed, in the gloom at the end of the hall, several dozens of yards in the distance, a thin pale man sitting on a chair.

She saw Pook walking towards him, her bare feet gliding between the rows of pillars. Beetlebrow began stepping after her. She felt her body remaining still. She glanced downwards, and noticed silver bracelets chained around her ankles. They were securing her legs to the ground.

She looked ahead. She saw Pook's slim figure diminishing across the marble hall.

Towering waves of gold coins, dozens of yards high, entered from the left and right of the pillars. Their gleaming banks crested, and then swept downwards and flooded across the floor.

Beetlebrow watched Pook walking between the drifts of golden coins. Pook glanced back over her shoulder at Beetlebrow. Her eyes were bright. Pook's mouth widened into a smile as the metal pieces washed over her feet like the lapping surf along a lonely beach.

Beetlebrow stretched out her arms. She noticed the knife in the palm of her right hand and a fig and a pomegranate in her left.

She saw the gold coins surging around Pook's waist. Pook's smile remained focused on Beetlebrow as the metal waves swept over her shoulders, and then as her body was covered underneath their shimmering waves.

Beetlebrow heard a grinding noise. She looked back over her right shoulder. The double-doors were closing against the light of the sun. She heard the golden wings slamming shut. Blackness filled her sight. She heard a key turning in a lock outside.

She woke up sweating in the light before dawn. She felt Pook's slim body in her arms. Beetlebrow tightened her grasp around her shoulders. She listened to Pook's sleeping breaths and the sound of the ship shouldering eastwards through the waves.

Beetlebrow and Pook stood by the port-side railings of the ship in the cloudy grey glow of the new day. In the overcast afternoon they watched the mist-wreathed land emerging from the flat water of the eastern horizon.

Beetlebrow observed the ship making a drifting approach towards the white-clouded edge of the eastern continent. Seagulls were gliding about in the gloom above, shrieking as they circled the deck.

Beetlebrow looked at the shore. It was roughly a hundred yards away.

The captain stepped towards her and Pook. He cleared his throat. 'We ain't going to risk getting no closer to Tirrendahl. Dalcratty's got an army camp a mile east of town. Essum'd have my head if they found out

I came here, and Dalcratty'd do the same if I tried to make land. So I'm not going to chance it, even with the money you've given me.'

'Why's there an army base here?' Pook asked.

'The Empire's building a new port,' the captain replied, glancing towards the shore. 'Well, rebuilding the old one, from ancient days. Don't know why. The port of Relleken's on Dalcratty's doorstep, and it's only a day's sail to the south.'

He tied two knotted hessian ropes to the deck and dropped their ends over the railings. 'Fifty yards from here, you'll be able to wade to shore.'

Beetlebrow heard the ropes splashing down into the water below.

'And watch yourself east of Tirrendahl, travellers, if that's where you're going,' the captain went on. 'None of my business I'm sure – especially with what you've paid me – but this time of year, the deer around this place get drunk on the rotten fruits, the apples and figs, and they're skidding about, running into things.'

Pook glanced at Beetlebrow. Beetlebrow saw her eyes glinting.

'What?' Beetlebrow mouthed.

Pook smiled, looked towards the eastern shore, and then clambered over the railings and scaled down into the water.

Beetlebrow slipped her leather bag across her right shoulder and grabbed onto the remaining rope. She mounted the railings, wrapped the hessian line three times around her right wrist and descended, hand beneath freezing hand, down the slippery side of the barnacle-covered hull.

She felt the cold touch of the sea against her heels. Her fingers tightened their grasp around the rope. The sharp scent of salt rushed up her nose. She felt goose-pimples rising along her arms.

She lowered herself down until only her head remained above the water, and then she let go of the rope. She began swimming east, following Pook's bobbing head towards the shore.

Beetlebrow watched the lights of Tirrendahl growing nearer. She heard the ship turning back out to sea.

She felt seaweed brushing against her legs. She looked forwards again. She listened to the water swishing away from her hands whenever her fingers broke through its surface.

She felt hard sand beneath the soles of her shoes. She saw Pook walking towards the shore, the tepid waves of the shallows swirling around her thighs.

Pook's long black hair was slickly glistening. She was looking towards Tirrendahl as she tied the strands of her hair at the nape of her neck with her black headscarf.

The headscarf Peddar gave her, Beetlebrow thought, *just over a week ago.*

She started wading out onto the stony beach. Waves were pushing white trails of foam across the shore. To Beetlebrow, they looked like fingers pointing the way east.

She heard the smooth stones clacking together under her shoes as she left the shallows behind and walked out onto the beach. She felt her sodden clothes weighing down her steps.

She spat out a mouthful of saltwater. She noticed scaffolds being built around the timber frames of Tirrendahl. She heard hammers striking and saws rasping. Silhouetted men bearing wheelbarrows and brick-hods were stalking through the mist.

Beetlebrow stopped beside Pook. She saw her gazing into the darkness north of town.

'Dalcratty's only two or three days' walk away,' Beetlebrow said.

Pook glanced at her and smirked.

'What is it?' Beetlebrow asked.

'I'll show you.'

They walked through the quiet northern edge of Tirrendahl and into a field behind its illuminated streets. Beetlebrow saw the stone remains of a ruined palace in the ankle-high grass, its arched doorways and low walls standing up straight from the ground. Beyond the field, she noticed several rangy trees hanging their empty branches over a patch of bare earth devoid of leaves and fruit.

'*By stumbling hearts growth split sleep,*' Pook whispered, '*and engraved the earnings two could not keep.*'

Beetlebrow stopped. Pook faced her.

'I always thought it was "*hearts*", like the heart in your chest,' Pook said, 'But I think it's "*harts*". The name for a male deer. It's spelled different.'

She started walking under a grey stone arch curved like the vertebrae of a spine. Beetlebrow's steps felt light as she followed behind her lead. She recalled Gregory saying the wheat could not be taken across the Central Sea. She spotted a symbol of two roses set in the middle of the arch. She glanced back towards the west and saw the distant ship sailing away in the moonlight.

She looked forwards again, and spotted Pook stepping past the archway and heading towards the sinewy folds of a fig tree. Beetlebrow felt a breeze pushing against her body. She thought she could smell the approach of spring. She felt bare earth underneath her feet.

Pook stepped up onto the roots of the fig, reached above her head with her left hand and touched the bark. Beetlebrow saw her fingers drifting across its wrinkled surface.

Pook glanced back at her. Her lips parted, and Beetlebrow saw her smile flashing through the gloom.

'There're carved letters here,' Pook said. '*AR* and *HR*. Ancissus Rashem and Hassan Rashem. The cousins, the kings, they engraved their names here, on this fig tree.'

Pook looked upwards, and Beetlebrow followed her gaze. The leafless limbs of the skeletal tree were blackly set against the smoky clouds of the starless sky. Where the trunk separated, half-way up the height of the fig, two platforms of wooden planks circled around the bark.

'*Growth split sleep*,' Pook said. 'The cousins must have slept in this tree-house. I guessed they stayed in Tirrendahl, as teenagers, before Ancissus left the eastern continent and crossed the Central Sea on his way to Stellingkorr, all those dozens of years ago.'

Pook stepped back from the roots of the tree. 'This is it. The wheat's buried here, I'm sure of it.'

Beetlebrow felt a shiver running down her back.

She watched Pook pick up a stick and jab it into the soil. It sunk down two inches into the dirt before it struck something beneath the surface.

Pook pulled the stick out of the ground. 'It'll be in urns, like burial urns. *The earnings two could not keep.*'

Beetlebrow looked across the bare earth below the trees. 'There must be dozens of urns under here.'

'Maybe hundreds,' Pook said. 'All this wealth here, and nothing can grow anymore.'

Beetlebrow heard footsteps approaching her from the west. She turned around. She saw the dark figure of a short, stout man stalking towards her.

'Stop!' Pook shouted.

Beetlebrow heard her voice echoing across the field. She stared at the shadowed man as she took out her thin knife from her robe.

He leapt forward. His right arm swung at her face.

Beetlebrow felt his knuckles striking her right cheek. Pain burst open in her jaw. White light swirled in front of her eyes. The knife fell from her hand.

She slumped backwards. She felt earth pressing against her shoulder-blades.

She opened her eyes. She saw Alder's sweating, black-bearded face grinning down at her.

'I've got you, Beetlebrow,' her brother snarled.

35
Alder

Beetlebrow felt Alder's stubby fingers worming across the nape of her neck.

'Up, up!' he hissed, grabbing her shoulders and hauling her to her feet.

She glimpsed Pook walking towards her from several yards away.

'Let her go!' Pook shouted.

'She's not your concern,' Alder growled at Pook.

His fingers started sliding across the back of Beetlebrow's scalp. 'What happened to your hair?' Alder asked. 'Are you trying to be a boy? You and your friend, you're not unnatural, are you?'

He grabbed the shoulders of her tunic and began pulling her away from the field of trees. Beetlebrow felt her feet stumbling across the ground. Her blurry sight was threaded through with spots of white light. She felt cobblestones underneath her thin shoes.

'I followed you from the docks in Essum and got on the boat,' Alder sneered. 'I wouldn't've guessed, when I caught you, I'd find you playing around in the dirt like a child. Perhaps I should've guessed you'd be doing something stupid.'

'Get away from her!' Pook screamed.

Beetlebrow saw the curved stone arch in front of her path. She felt Alder's hands grasping onto the back of her head. He shoved her face forwards. Beetlebrow's nose smashed against the stone surface. Pain seared across her head. She felt blood dripping down from her nostrils.

She staggered backwards. She tried to keep her eyes open. She fell down onto her knees. She rushed her hands out towards the ground. She felt the round cobblestones under the loose grip of her fingers.

'This is what you get,' Alder said. 'This is what you deserve.'

Beetlebrow felt his skinny left arm slipping around the front of her neck and pulling her upwards again. His grasp squeezed against her throat. Beetlebrow rose to her feet. She felt Alder's bony chest pressing against the back of her head. She glimpsed the gleam of the horn-handled knife in her brother's right hand.

She saw Pook running towards her through the gloom. Alder's right fist swung out, and struck Pook's cheek. She fell backwards onto the cobblestones.

Beetlebrow stretched out her empty hands towards her. She felt Alder's left arm gripping tighter against her neck, binding its clasp against her wind-pipe. Beetlebrow's hands lowered. She felt weak underneath her brother's strangling hold.

She saw Pook lying on the cobblestones.

'I told you to leave,' Alder spat at Pook. 'You've no-one to blame but yourself for getting hurt.'

Pook kept a glaring gaze on his face as she rose to her feet and wiped blood from her mouth with the back of her left hand.

'Let her go,' Pook said.

'You'll stay down if you know what's good for you,' Alder replied.

He looked at Beetlebrow again and squeezed his arm against her neck.

'You just don't learn, do you?' he growled into her right ear. 'I knew you'd keep trying to take this message to Dalcratty. I knew you gave up the bracelet too easy. But this childishness ends here. I'm taking you back to Floodcross, where you belong.'

Beetlebrow felt warm blood streaming down from her nose and slipping down onto her cold, closed lips. She saw Pook striding towards her.

'No further!' Alder shouted at her.

Pook stopped a few feet away from him and stared at his face. 'Let her go.'

'I'm sorry I hit you, girl,' Alder said. 'That's not me, to hit a girl. It's not who I am. You just got me riled up, that's all. You don't seem like a bad person, but you weren't paying attention to me.'

Beetlebrow opened her mouth. She caught a sip of air. She felt hot, copper-tasting blood seeping down onto her tongue. She closed her mouth again.

'Don't you stupid girls understand this message'll only hurt our people?' Alder snapped, spit flaring out from between his teeth. 'It'll mean the House of Rashem'll get stronger. It'll mean more red and browns on the streets of Stellingkorr, more violence, more work for less money, less food, less control for our people. We know the message is about some big shipment of wheat, and we know it's going to be given to the southern empires to keep them at bay, or it's going to be a bribe to Essum so they'll re-open the old trade route to Tirrendahl, but whatever it is, the benefit won't be going to the likes of us.'

'Where's Gregory?' Pook asked. 'We'll only talk to him.'

'Me and Gregory had an argument,' Alder replied. 'Gregory's gone.'

'Gone?'

'No, he ain't dead,' Alder said, squeezing the grasp of his arm around Beetlebrow's throat. 'I'm not evil like this one here. Gregory's slunk back to Dalcratty.'

Beetlebrow croaked, 'We'll only talk to Gre –'.

'Shut your mouth!' Alder shouted.

Pook took a step towards him.

Alder faced Pook again. 'You – whatever your name is – you can leave. Head back west to your mummy and daddy, and leave me to deal with my sister.'

'We're not going to do what you say,' Pook said.

'Well, I didn't come here to say anything; I came here to take Beetlebrow home. I ain't a big talker like Gregory – I do things when I want to do them. Talking's a stalling tactic, like those coins this one threw at me. I had a good time with that cash, but it don't make things equal, not after what she did. And this all started with money, didn't it, Beetlebrow?'

She felt his mouth pressing close against her right cheek, and his beard pricking against her skin.

'You stealing Mum's life savings and being too scared to face me and Joe again afterwards, this is how this all began, isn't it?' Alder said. 'With those gold and silver coins Mum had saved over the years, Joe might've had a chance, he wouldn't've been forced to rob that trader, and he wouldn't've been locked away.'

Beetlebrow felt his hands loosening their grasp on her shoulders. She turned around, her feet stepping backwards.

She saw the slight figure of Pook standing behind Alder's stocky frame. Pook's left hand was wrapped around his right shoulder. She was holding the shining silver bracelet against his neck.

'You feel my knife at your throat?' Pook said.

'Yes, you little whore,' Alder replied.

'Drop your blade,' Pook said.

Beetlebrow heard Alder's horn-handled knife hit the cobblestones.

'Crouch down low,' Pook said.

Alder's eyes flicked left and right.

Pook pressed the bracelet closer against his throat. 'Crouch. Down.'

Beetlebrow saw Alder slowly kneeling down in front of her.

Pook kept the bracelet against Alder's neck as she circled around and stood in front of him.

Beetlebrow reached up her left hand to her neck. She felt the tenderness of her throat, and then she looked at Pook, containing Alder inside the threat of the bracelet's edge.

'Close your eyes,' Pook whispered to Alder.

His heavy eyelids squeezed shut.

'I'll tell you when you can open them again,' Pook slowly said.

She glanced at Beetlebrow. Their gazes met.

Pook faced Alder, kneeling on the cobblestones, his eyes closed and his hands held behind his back.

'Don't move,' Pook hissed. 'I've still got this knife. Me and Bee are going. Don't try to follow us. Go back west, go south, but don't try to follow us.'

She stared at Alder as she stepped backwards,

Beetlebrow saw Alder's eyes flash open. He looked at Pook. His attention turned to the bracelet in her grasp. He raised his right hand to his neck and felt the indent in his flesh.

'Liar!' Alder yelled at Pook.

He grabbed his horn-handled knife from the ground, rose to his feet and started limping across the cobblestones, his heavy-lidded eyes focused on Pook.

Beetlebrow saw her hurrying towards the fig tree. She glimpsed the thin, rusted knife laying beside its roots.

Alder was staring at Pook as he hurried past Beetlebrow.

Beetlebrow's left foot shot out. She felt her brother's right ankle hooking under her heel. Alder yelped. He tripped forwards with the knife in his right hand. His arms stretched out in front of himself. His right fist hit the ground. It buckled back against his chest.

Alder's face struck a cobblestone. Beetlebrow heard his teeth shattering.

Pook hurried back towards her. Beetlebrow looked away from Alder and stared into the wide black centres of Pook's brown eyes.

'Can you walk?' Pook whispered.

Beetlebrow blinked hard. She felt a warm trickle of blood dripping down from her nose.

Pook wiped it away with her left hand. Beetlebrow felt the touch of her fingers against her tender skin.

'Emma,' Alder slowly said.

Beetlebrow glanced at her brother.

She saw him looking back at her over his right shoulder, his head raised up several inches from the cobblestones while his body remained flat on the ground.

His eyes were half-closed, and his black beard sodden with scarlet blood. Beetlebrow saw his mouth as an open, glistening, gummy maw.

'Pleashh...' Alder slurred. 'Pleashhh help me, Emma.'

Beetlebrow watched his right hand reaching up towards her. She remembered his fingers slipping into Lana's robe, and taking all the money their mother had earned in the night.

She glanced at Pook. 'The army base,' Beetlebrow said. 'No one can follow us in there.'

She took Pook's arm in her grasp and started lurching away eastwards across the cobblestones. Beetlebrow's body felt tired. Her feet felt strong. She and Pook hurried across the field of bare earth and out into the white mist beyond.

Beetlebrow felt grass brushing against her ankles. She glanced towards the west. She saw only fog in her wake. She looked at Pook.

'I'm sorry,' Beetlebrow softly said. 'About Alder. I had to put up with him for so long. You shouldn't have to too.'

Pook stepped close towards her. 'My home wasn't any good either.'

Beetlebrow gazed into her eyes.

'What do you want to call me?' Beetlebrow quietly asked.

Pook smiled. 'You're my Bee, and I'm your Pook.'

Beetlebrow smiled back. She faced towards the light in the east.

'Are you sure about this, going into an army camp?' Pook asked.

'We don't know who else is out here, trying to stop us,' Beetlebrow replied. 'It might not just be Alder, there might be others.'

'But what about the message?' Pook asked. 'What Alder said... ?'

Beetlebrow looked at her.

'My brother might be right,' Beetlebrow said.

Pook glanced towards the light of the army camp, and then faced her again.

'So what do we do?' Pook asked. 'We don't know what these royals are going to do with the wheat, but I reckon they won't be giving it to the people who need it.'

'If we go into the army camp, and show them the bracelet, I bet they'll help us get into Dalcratty. Once we're inside the city, then we just need to find the local rebels.'

Pook nodded. 'I think that's the only way to make sure it gets to the people, like Gregory said back in Kosair.'

She squeezed Beetlebrow's left hand. Beetlebrow looked towards the east. She saw the pale illumination of the army camp. She felt its light drawing her through the darkness of the fields.

36

The army camp

Beetlebrow smelt the stench of pig manure and wood-smoke spilling across the gloom. She felt the grass of the field getting patchier. The earth became rutted and muddy underneath her feet. She heard throaty shouts, distant laughter and axes splitting logs.

She noticed fluttering gold and white banners displaying the double-rose insignia of Dalcratty. She felt the wet soil pulling her leather shoes down into its sticky grasp. She saw Pook looking forwards as they stepped into the camp.

Beetlebrow felt light flashing on her face. She saw low fires surrounding her body, and she felt entwined within their illuminations.

Hundreds of triangular tents, the colour of ox-blood, were piercing up from the red-brown mud of the field. They appeared to Beetlebrow like thorns mounted on the stem of a rose.

She felt a pang of pain across her face. Her cold fingers touched her swollen nose. She felt its soreness joining her aching feet, the cuts along her knuckles, and the strain in her hands from the bridle.

She glanced at Pook, and saw her bruised shin and split lower lip. *But we survived*, Beetlebrow thought, *we survived all this*.

She spotted soldiers swaggering along paths of planks laid across the mud between the tents. Their tunics were red and slats of tan-leather armour covered their shoulders and arms.

Beetlebrow noticed a group of soldiers heading towards her.

'The bracelet,' she whispered to Pook.

Beetlebrow noticed a grey-bearded soldier staring at her. She felt her breaths quickening. The soldiers were only a few yards away.

'Hello there, girls, want to earn a bit of money?' the grey-bearded soldier asked.

Pook held out the bracelet. 'We're imperial messengers. This is our proof.'

Beetlebrow saw the glinting reflection of the edge of the silver band shivering between Pook's fingers.

'Sarge!' one of the soldiers called out.

'What?' a voice growled from the right.

Beetlebrow noticed a pot-bellied soldier ambling towards her. He had the three white stripes of a sergeant on the right shoulder of his red tunic. His black hair was curly on top and its shaved sides were speckled with silver. There were wrinkled purple bags below his eyes.

He stopped in front of Beetlebrow and Pook. Beetlebrow saw the sweat-marks circling around his arm-pits, and the muddy splashes across the bulge of his round stomach.

The sergeant glanced at the bracelet in Pook's hand and then faced the band of soldiers.

'Back to your tents,' he said, his voice a low murmur.

Beetlebrow watched the soldiers dispersing back among the wooden paths of the camp.

A single soldier remained. The sergeant stared down at his wiry frame. Beetlebrow saw his chubby face in profile, the light of the fire illuminating the coarse pockmarks across his cheeks.

'But Sarge,' the soldier said, 'you know we haven't enough girls for all the men here.'

He glanced at Pook and then faced the sergeant again. 'And... my socks need darning.'

The sergeant wiped the sole of his muddy right boot across the top of the soldier's left sandal.

'You've got dirt on your shoes,' the sergeant said. 'Go clean 'em.'

Beetlebrow watched the wiry soldier walking away again between the tents.

The sergeant faced Pook again. He nodded towards the bracelet. Beetlebrow saw the silver band shining thinly above the red-brown mud.

'You're imperial messengers, then?' the sergeant asked.

'We've travelled from Stellingkorr,' Pook said. 'We've got a message for King Hassan.'

Beetlebrow spotted a space between two tents, where she could escape into the darkness taking Pook by the hand.

The sergeant dipped his head towards the bracelet. His chubby mouth smeared into a grin. 'This is an honour. You'll be given all the help we can spare.'

He glanced at Beetlebrow, and tapped his nose. 'You need bandages, boy?'

'I'm a girl,' Beetlebrow replied.

The sergeant shrugged. 'All right then, but do you need patching up? It's a nasty-looking cut you've got on your nose. You got bruises on your cheek too. Getting you some bandages'd be the least I could do for an imperial messenger.'

Beetlebrow's hands tightened into fists down by her waist. 'No. We just need help getting to Dalcratty. Please.'

The sergeant nodded. 'As you wish. I'll need to talk with the officers first, and see if we can spare the men to escort you into the city.'

He glanced to his right. Beetlebrow followed his gaze. She noticed a square white tent standing several feet taller than the others. She saw the hundreds of camp-fires spread out across the miles of the field, and felt her feet sinking down into the mud.

'What are your names, messengers?' the sergeant asked. 'You may call me Sergeant Karem.'

'This is Bee, I'm Pook.'

Karem nodded. He raised two fingers to his mouth. Beetlebrow heard his shrill whistle striking through the air.

She spotted five figures in red and brown emerging from the right of the camp.

Pook's right shoulder bumped against Beetlebrow's left as the five soldiers encircled them in a perimeter a body's length wide. Beetlebrow glared up at their shadowed faces.

'Stay here,' Karem said to Beetlebrow and Pook.

He looked at the five soldiers, and his expression hardened into a scowl.

'These two are imperial messengers,' he growled. 'They carry the correspondence of one king of the empire to another. If any harm comes to them, you'll swing for it.'

The soldiers saluted.

Beetlebrow watched Karem's pot-bellied figure walking towards the square tent. She glanced at Pook, and saw her gaze darting across the surrounding ring of soldiers.

'Pook,' Beetlebrow said.

Pook's brown eyes settled on her face. She looked at Beetlebrow for a moment, and then leant towards her ear.

'We might have made a mistake,' Pook whispered, her voice small and quiet. 'We should've just gone to Dalcratty by ourselves.'

Beetlebrow placed her trembling right hand in Pook's left. She felt Pook grasping onto her palm.

'We're nearly there now,' Beetlebrow said. 'Just a little longer with them.'

She heard a roar of male voices to her right.

A loose circle of soldiers was crowding around a pair of teenage boys. There was a fire flickering at the heart of the circle of men. Beetlebrow saw the sweat on the boys' hairless chests shining with reflections of its blazing light. The two boys were leaping up and kicking black-booted feet at each other's bloodied shins. One struck the other on the stomach with his heel. Beetlebrow heard the crowd's deep, brief cheer.

She noticed Karem waddling back towards her across the mud. There was a knife strapped on the left of his black belt and a sword on his right.

Karem glanced at the circle of soldiers. He limply raised a hand against his forehead. The soldiers returned the salute and marched away.

'Well, messengers,' Karem said, 'it looks like I volunteered myself. I'll be escorting you to Dalcratty. The officers think we should keep this quiet, so it'll just be me and a driver. But you're now under the protection of His Divinity, King Hassan the Seventh, and you're safe. Your work is nearly over.'

Beetlebrow saw the chainmail on his right hand glinting as he gestured eastwards through the camp.

'This way,' Karem said. 'We've a cart allotted to us.'

He turned on his heels and started walking away along a path of planks.

Beetlebrow glanced around at the camp. The tents and fires appeared to be surrounding her body.

She noticed Pook stepping after Karem. Beetlebrow followed.

She heard the planks rattling under the tread of her feet. She glanced at the tents to her left and right. She glimpsed soldiers polishing boots, smoking pipes, cooking over fires and hanging up shirts on lines. She noticed one or two looking at Pook, their eyes chasing her slim figure.

Beetlebrow glanced at her. She saw Pook looking east. Beetlebrow looked ahead. She watched Karem becoming a dark-grey silhouette in the white mist beyond the tents.

The line of planks ended. Beetlebrow felt a chill across her body as she left the warmth of camp-fires behind.

She spotted two ragged teenage girls, their faces pale with hunger, walking out slowly from behind a heap of broken wooden pallets. They headed towards Karem and pulled down their dirty grey robes to display their breasts.

Karem frowned. 'Get out of here, mud-rats,' he muttered. 'No business for you today.'

Beetlebrow watched the girls' starving forms retreating back to a pile of broken wooden pieces and cracked jars.

Karem began walking towards a horse-drawn cart on the right of the mud-path.

Beetlebrow noticed a hooded figure sitting on the driver's seat. He was grasping the reins of the two grey horses standing in front of the vehicle.

'We should arrive at the gates of the city sometime tomorrow morning, messengers,' Karem said, climbing onto the seat beside the driver. 'If we don't get held up.'

Beetlebrow clambered up onto the vehicle. She felt exhaustion hanging on her body as she turned around.

She saw Pook standing alone on the muddy ground. Beetlebrow reached down her left hand towards her. She felt pain throbbing across her face. Beetlebrow's palm opened. Her fingers spread out.

She felt Pook touching her hand. Their fingers clasped together.

Beetlebrow saw Pook's large brown eyes look up at her face. She pulled her up into the cart and together they sat down on its wooden floor.

Beetlebrow put her left arm around Pook's shoulders. She felt her body shivering under the grasp of her hands.

The driver flicked the reins. The cart jerked forwards. Beetlebrow glanced at the misty, south-eastern path ahead of the horses. The rutted earth in front of the vehicle appeared to her as if it had been torn open by a giant plough.

She felt Pook squeezing her right hand tighter.

'We'll deliver the message soon,' Pook whispered.

'Yes, don't you worry, messengers,' Karem said, grinning back at them. 'We'll be in Dalcratty in no time'

Pook faced Beetlebrow. Beetlebrow looked into her eyes. She felt the cart rattling forwards, and she kept her left arm grasped around Pook's shoulders.

37
Dalcratty

'Bee...' Pook whispered.

Beetlebrow awoke in darkness. She felt the cart shaking its clattering rhythm across her ribs, and light drops of rain landing across the shoulders of her tunic. The blackness of the sky above, embedded with faint stars, was being interrupted by the faint yellow light of dawn in the east.

Beetlebrow rubbed her tired eyes. Her cheeks felt numb. Her nose was stinging with pain. By the glow of an oil-lamp she noticed Karem's chubby frame sitting beside the hooded driver at the front of the cart. The two were rocking left and right to the motion of the vehicle.

'We're nearly there,' Pook said. 'It's almost dawn.'

Beetlebrow saw her face by her side. Pook was illuminated in the fringes of light from the oil-lamp; her black hair merging with the darkness, her cinnamon skin shaded in shadows, and her pensive eyes reflecting the glow of the flame.

Beetlebrow heard the metal wheels of the cart leaving the dirt-road behind. Fires were roaring from a square gate at the end of the flagstone road ahead. Beetlebrow saw a stone wall surrounding its light. The blank grey surface of the wall was several storeys high. It stretched out across the eastern horizon.

This is Dalcratty, Beetlebrow thought. She felt the idea of the city and the sight of it become one.

She saw the orange light of the oil-lamp stretching to the left and right of the cart. Wooden shacks were slumped either side of the square flagstones of the road; their miles of houses lining the walls of the city appeared like shallow foothills humbling themselves below the peak of a mountain. Beetlebrow imagined the people who lived in these houses stepping out of their doors each day and seeing Dalcratty looming over their neighbourhood.

'There's smoke above the city,' Pook said.

Beetlebrow looked upwards. She saw thin grey twirls rising beyond the saw-tooth battlements of the stone wall.

Karem shook his head. 'Don't you worry, messengers. They're just trouble-makers, these rebels. They're trying to cause a fuss over nothing.'

'It looks like the whole city's alight,' Pook said.

'Little fires travel far,' Karem replied, 'but only when there ain't nothing else.'

His right index finger gestured left towards the northern edge of the wall. Beetlebrow spotted a square-topped shape cutting out a rectangle of blackness from the stars above the city.

'See how far the tower of the royal palace is from the smoke?' Karem said. 'These rioters can't reach anything important. It's just their own neighbourhoods who'll suffer.'

'That's far enough!' a man's voice ahead barked. 'You're beyond your jurisdiction, soldiers!'

The hooded driver yanked at the reins. Beetlebrow felt the cart becoming still.

'Soldiers, state your business!'

Beetlebrow guessed the light of the gate to be ten yards away from the front of the cart.

She saw Karem's chubby body standing up from his seat. He became silhouetted against the square of flaming light. He lifted his right hand to his mouth.

'Sergeant Karem reporting, sir!' Karem shouted. 'I've two imperial messengers here.'

Beetlebrow heard the echoes of his deep voice trailing away across the darkness.

Karem lowered his right hand back down to his side. Beetlebrow noticed his fingers twisting around the hilt of his sword.

She reached her left hand down underneath her grey tunic and into the pocket of her robe. The woollen fabric felt flat against her fingers. She remembered her thin, rusted knife falling from her hand and landing in the field of dirt underneath the fig tree outside Tirrendahl.

She felt down deeper inside the pocket, and touched something metallic and smooth. She brought it out and held it in her left hand. It was the single copper coin her mother had earned, all those days ago. Beetlebrow remembered Alder grudgingly placing it into her palm.

'Approach, messengers!' a hoarse voice ahead called.

Beetlebrow saw Karem looking back at her.

'Best you get down now, messengers,' he quietly said. 'I can't get no closer to the city. Not in uniform anyway. You know something's gone wrong with a city if it lets red and browns inside its walls. But don't worry. You'll be safe in the hands of the city police from now on. They'll look after messengers like you.'

Beetlebrow's fingers ran over the gold and silver coins and two blankets inside her leather bag. She saw her fast breaths making white clouds in front of her face. She slipped the bag across her right shoulder and stepped down from the cart.

She stood in the road. She heard the rain splashing around her. She felt its puddles seeping into her shoes.

She reached out her hands up towards the slim, shadowed figure of Pook. Pook took them in her grasp and slid down from the vehicle. Beetlebrow saw her wincing as her left foot touched the flagstones.

'To the gate, messengers,' a voice said.

Beetlebrow heard bootsteps chasing behind her heels.

She and Pook started walking towards the square of light. Beetlebrow saw the black, vertical metal bars of the square gate a few yards ahead of her feet.

She felt the warmth of the flames on her face. She noticed dozens of policemen standing behind the bars, their blue tunics, silver armoured shoulders and pointed silver helmets illuminated by the torches blazing in their mailed fists.

'Passphrase, messengers!' a voice called.

'*None of the high nor savage creatures of my false sun do I bring,*' Beetlebrow said.

She heard chains rattling to her left and right and wheels ratcheting above her head. She watched the long iron spikes at the base of the gate dragging themselves out of the holes they had bitten down into the flagstones.

'We'll escort you to His Divinity King Hassan,' a deep voice said.

Beetlebrow saw the gate clanking to a stop several yards above the ground.

Blue and silver uniforms surrounded her body. Chain-mailed hands grasped her arms. She felt the leather bag being lifted away from her right shoulder.

'You'll get this back after you've seen His Divinity, the king,' the voice said. 'Forwards, messengers.'

Beetlebrow and Pook felt walked shoulder-to-shoulder through the mouth of the gate. Beetlebrow felt icy raindrops dropping onto her tunic.

She glimpsed the blocky shapes of buildings rising into the dull yellow glow of the sky. She felt cobblestones underneath her shoes. To the north was the tower of the royal palace, and it looked to Beetlebrow like an eagle in its eyrie bearing down on the dark streets of Dalcratty.

'There're still some rioters in Hartriss Street,' one policeman muttered to another. 'We'll take the other route to the palace, by the Arrendath district.'

Beetlebrow saw four policemen marching abreast several yards in front of her path. By the light of their burning torches, she was shown the four-storey houses to the left and right of the street.

She glanced back over her right shoulder as she and Pook walked onwards. Beetlebrow noticed, several yards back along the cobblestones, a second line of flames following her through the gloom.

She glimpsed Pook in the patchy light of the torches; Beetlebrow glanced across her cheekbones, her darting brown eyes and her slim hands, fidgeting with the sleeves of her grey robe.

'We've only a few minutes before daybreak,' Pook whispered.

'At least we've got the advantage here,' Beetlebrow replied. 'They don't think we wanna escape.'

She noticed an alley between the stone buildings to her right. She glanced between its slender walls. She heard Pook's slow footsteps by her side, and looked forwards again.

'To the left,' Pook whispered.

Beetlebrow glanced left. The light of the torches was drifting across the grey stone surface of a narrow house joined side-by-side to its identical neighbours. She spotted a vertical slice of darkness roughly seven feet up its surface.

'These windows, we can get through them,' Pook whispered. 'These men can't.'

Beetlebrow watched the glow of the flames leaving the first grey house behind and slipping across the second in the row.

She saw a line of blackness seven feet up its grey wall. Beetlebrow held her breath. She lowered her hands down to her waist. She loosened her fingers. She watched the light of the torches flowing beyond the second house and drifting across the third.

'Go,' whispered Pook.

Beetlebrow ran through the darkness towards the second house. She stepped against its wall, turned around and pressed her back against its stones.

She heard Pook heading towards her. Beetlebrow lay her left palm on top of her right. She felt Pook grabbing onto her shoulders and her soft leather shoes stepping into her hands.

She heard Pook climbing up beyond her grasp and heading towards the slender window. Beetlebrow turned around. She reached out her hands into the darkness above her head.

She felt Pook's fingers clasping onto her wrists. Pook began pulling her upwards. Beetlebrow felt her shoes leave the cobblestones behind.

Warm torch-light splashed across the back of her neck. Beetlebrow glimpsed a black shadow of her skinny frame being cast across the grey surface of the wall.

'What you doing?' a soldier shouted.

Beetlebrow heard bootsteps running towards her across the cobblestones. She felt Pook's grasp tightening around her wrists.

A gauntleted hand grabbed onto the back of Beetlebrow's tunic. She felt the heat of torches swamping across her body.

'Get down from there!' the soldier shouted.

The gauntleted hand yanked at Beetlebrow's tunic. She felt the garment tearing open at the back. Pook pulled her up towards the window. Beetlebrow felt her tunic being ripped away from over her grey robe, and heard her copper coin clinking down onto the cobblestones.

'Come back, messengers!'

Beetlebrow's shoulders scraped between the stone edges of the slender window as she squeezed through its frame.

Her stiff legs scurried into the blackness of the room beyond. She felt a rickety wooden table wobbling underneath her thin leather shoes. She smelt congealed fat and fragrant herbs.

'Messengers!' a soldier called.

'Find a door,' Pook whispered to Beetlebrow.

Beetlebrow leapt down onto the darkness of the ground and barrelled forwards along the floor-tiles. Her frantic hands felt across a stone wall. She found an oak door secured by metal hinges. She heard Pook stepping towards her.

Beetlebrow felt a cold iron handle in the clasp of her fingers. She pressed it downwards. She heard the door rattling against its frame. Beetlebrow yanked the handle down again. She heard the door shudder.

She felt Pook's hand touching her left shoulder. Beetlebrow let go of the handle. She heard Pook's hands feeling across the surface of the door, and then a bolt being withdrawn.

Beetlebrow turned the handle again. She felt the door springing inwards to her touch. She grabbed Pook's left hand. Together they hurried through the blackness of the corridor beyond the doorway.

Beetlebrow saw light around the edges of the square, shuttered window at the end of the passageway. She smelt fresh air. She shoved open the shutters.

She saw the yellow glow of dawn rising above the red-brown dirt of the street outside. Between the smoking remains of whitewashed houses, a dozen men were lying on the ground in bloodied blue and silver uniforms. Their bodies were threaded between several dozen men in shredded and torn black robes sprawled out across the dirt, their bodies impaled with arrows and spears.

Beetlebrow and Pook climbed out of the window. Beetlebrow spotted a tall, lean man stepping around a whitewashed corner to the left. He was wearing a black robe. She remembered the rebels wearing similar clothes in Stellingkorr. She and Pook hurried after him.

The lean man hobbled around the corner. Beetlebrow and Pook followed.

Beetlebrow spotted him hurrying between the low roofs and shallow puddles of the narrow backstreet beyond. She glimpsed Pook taking the bracelet out of her robe.

Beetlebrow looked at the lean man. 'Hey!'

He sped up as he glanced back over his right shoulder.

Beetlebrow saw his dark eyes staring out from between his thick black beard and shaved head. His cheeks were swollen with bruises and the lower right side of his ragged black robe was gleaming with blood.

Beetlebrow noticed him looking at the bracelet in Pook's hand. His pace slowed to a walk.

'We've got the message from Stellingkorr,' Pook said. 'The one for the king.'

'Come with me. Jackals are hunting the streets for rioters.'

'Jackals?'

'Police. Come on, through here.'

Beetlebrow and Pook followed him down a narrow alleyway between grey, mud-brick walls. He ducked underneath the broken planks of a wooden fence. Beetlebrow noticed spots of scarlet trailing in his wake.

The lean man opened a pinewood door in a whitewashed wall. Pook bent down to step through the doorway after him. Beetlebrow followed, her cropped hair brushing against the top of the frame.

Beetlebrow and Pook trailed the lean man's steps down a creaking staircase and through a shadowed doorway. Beetlebrow smelt a damp scent in the walls. She and Pook entered the room beyond.

Beetlebrow saw the splintered plaster walls inside by the shadowy light of three tallow candles. Eight black-clad, heavily-bearded men were lying on the dirt floor beneath a canopy of withered roof-beams. Bloodied hessian rags were tied across their faces and bodies. Beetlebrow saw their muddy hands clutching their bruised faces and seeping wounds.

'We couldn't fight any longer, Gregory,' the lean man said, shutting the door behind himself and sliding its bolt against the frame. 'We'd kill one jackal and three more'd arrive.'

Beetlebrow spotted the bushy-haired, gangly figure of Gregory sitting against the beige plaster wall to the left of the room. His right eye was bandaged over, and across his dark-brown chest were purple bruises outlined in livid yellow smears.

Beetlebrow saw his left eye stare up at her.

'We can give you the message,' Pook said. 'And tell you where the wheat is.'

Gregory blinked. 'The message? I asked for the message in Kosair. How come you didn't tell me before?'

'We still believed what we'd heard in the palace back then,' Pook replied. 'We thought the Empire was going to give the wheat to the starving people. We know that ain't true now.'

'So what's the message, then?'

'*By stumbling harts...*' Beetlebrow said, and then glanced at Gregory. 'Harts like a deer.'

Gregory nodded.

'*Growth split sleep...*' Pook said.

'*And engraved the earnings...*'

'*Two could not keep.*'

Gregory looked down at the floor. His eyes flicked left and right and his lips moved silently, and then he glanced up at Beetlebrow and Pook again.

'But what's this nonsense mean?' he asked. 'There's no point telling me the message if it's just some rhyme about deer and engraving and stuff. Have you decoded it? Do you understand what it's trying to say?'

'Pook worked it out,' Beetlebrow replied.

'There's ruins of a palace outside Tirrendahl where Ancissus Rashem and Hassan Rashem stayed as teenagers,' Pook said. 'The fruit-trees in its garden used to drop apples and figs. These'd rot on the ground, and get fermented. The deer would eat them, and get drunk. That's what "*by stumbling harts*" means.'

Gregory nodded. 'All right.'

'"*Growth split sleep*" is about the two sides of the tree-house Ancissus and Hassan slept on, where they were separated by the width of the tree. "*Engraved the earnings*" means Ancissus's and Hassan's carved initials on the bark, as well as the urns of wheat buried below the orchard. And "*two could not keep*" means this wheat was for Ancissus, and he had to leave Hassan behind to rule in Stellingkorr.'

Gregory looked at the lean man. 'You hear all this, Haroon?'

Haroon glanced at Beetlebrow and Pook, and then looked at Gregory again. 'I hear.'

'These kids have had to carry around all these fancy word-games and weird sayings in their heads for weeks,' Gregory went on. '*This* is why we need the time of kings and queens to end, so we don't have to put up with any more of this kind of madness in our lives.'

He looked at Beetlebrow and Pook again, and then held his right hand around his bruised ribs as he slowly rose to his feet. 'Can you take us there, where the wheat is buried?'

'Yes,' Pook said.

'I'll round up all the men and wagons we have left.'

38
Below the fig tree

Beetlebrow and Pook lay in blackness underneath their grey blankets on the back of a wagon. Beetlebrow forced her drowsy eyes to stay open against the fullness of the night. She clutched Pook's left hand and listened to her sleep. She closed her eyes against the darkness and squeezed her palm within her fingers.

She felt the wagon stopping. Knuckles rapped twice against its side.

Beetlebrow shook Pook's shoulders. Her eyes opened. Beetlebrow helped her to step down onto the ground. Together they looked out west across the night. The stars above were obscured by clouds, as if the sky were painted over by a swathe of tar.

Beetlebrow heard the wind hissing through the grass. She saw isolated spots of light in the west illuminating the half-built structures of Tirrendahl. She heard dozens of vehicles rumbling towards her from the east.

Beetlebrow and Pook started walking towards the light of Tirrendahl. Beetlebrow felt soft grass brushing against her ankles. She smelt the salty scent of the sea. She looked back over her shoulder. She glimpsed the army camp as a blurry ember of light in the distance.

She felt bare earth underneath her shoes. She looked upwards. She saw the fig tree dividing the white stars between its leafless limbs.

She raised two fingers to her mouth and gave a high whistle. She heard the sound falling away across the darkness.

Quiet footsteps approached her from all directions.

A square of orange light appeared below the fig tree. Beetlebrow looked at the oil-lamp. Three of its four glass sides had been blackened. She glimpsed Pook's tired face in its muted radiance.

Gregory stiffly stepped into the light. He glanced at Beetlebrow and Pook.

'It's here,' Pook said.

Gregory nodded, and looked out across the darkness. 'Let's get to work.'

Men in black robes entered the orange light below the trees. They stopped at the boundaries of its glow. Beetlebrow saw the spades and shovels glinting in their hands.

'You should all split into two groups,' Pook said. 'One digging downwards and one breaking through the topsoil to see how many burial sites there are. They'll probably be all across the field.'

Beetlebrow saw the men remaining still.

She noticed a line of shovels lying on the earth to her left. She walked over, picked two up and gave one to Pook.

Beetlebrow and Pook stabbed the shovels into the ground. Beetlebrow placed her left foot on its blade and pushed the shovel through the topsoil. She felt it hitting something hard below the surface. She heard a few men stepping forwards, and then glimpsed dozens of others joining her and Pook as they dug down into the earth.

They cut through the ground until a bulbous, man-sized terracotta urn was revealed beneath the dirt.

The men quietly tied ropes around the round body of the urn and began hauling it out of the ground. Beetlebrow saw the light of the lamp shining across its terracotta surface. She noticed the iron collar around its neck.

'I reckon there's a ton-and-a-half of grain in this,' a man said.

Gregory was leaning cross-armed upon the wooden handle of a pristine shovel. 'Pile it neatly in one of the wagons. There's going to be many more.'

A man whispered from the darkness to the left, 'We've counted seventy-three plots across the field. And I'm sure the urns'll probably be several deep.'

Beetlebrow wiped sweat from her forehead. She noticed a heavily-bearded man glance at her.

'It's tiring this, isn't it?' he said.

'If you want to have a rest, have a rest,' Beetlebrow replied.

Pook looked at him. 'We'll be carrying on though, because there's work to do.'

Beetlebrow heard laughter rustling across the darkness as she pressed her shovel down through the yielding ground.

Across the hours they gutted the earth below the rangy trees. The men placed ladders against the steep sides of the hole and threaded ropes through pulleys around the naked boughs of the fig.

Beetlebrow watched the hundreds of bulky terracotta urns being carried into the blackness where wagons silently lay.

She looked at Pook. Her eyes were closed, and her right foot was perched on the blade of her shovel.

Beetlebrow took her left arm. She helped Pook up a ladder, and together they climbed out onto the bare earth above the hole. Beetlebrow handed her a water-pouch and looked up at the fig tree. She heard the ropes straining as their hessian fibres twisted around its branches.

She spotted Gregory walking towards her, the blade of his shovel shining in his hands.

'You know, you could've got a lot of money from the royals for delivering this message,' Gregory said. 'Enough money to live in luxury for the rest of your lives, eating and drinking anything you wanted to eat and drink. You could've got land, prestige, maybe even married yourself some lords.'

Pook glanced at Beetlebrow, and their eyes met.

'No, really, you'd've been heroes,' Gregory went on. 'You'd've been famous across the empire.'

Pook faced him. 'If we'd taken the message to the royals, we'd be rich, but people in the city'd still be hungry. And we don't want that.'

'And you can't think of anything new if you're starving,' Beetlebrow added. 'All you think about is food, and you don't have time for nothing else. And me and Pook, we want people to be well-fed, because we want things to change.'

She heard a soft pair of footsteps to her left. A tall girl entered the glow of the lamps. Beetlebrow looked at her narrow face, long grey robe, and large dark eyes. The girl's straight, black hair trailed down her waist.

'Gracelynn, head down to the shore and whistle twice,' Gregory said to the girl. 'When you hear a ship signalling back, return here.'

Gracelynn turned around. Beetlebrow heard her footsteps hurrying away into the blackness.

'A ship?' Pook asked Gregory.

He nodded. 'We've several ships, in fact. Lent to us by... our benefactor. We'll take the urns by wagon down into Tirrendahl as if they're building supplies. From there we'll take them by sea, south-east along the coast to Relleken. It's a bigger port there, and things are easier to smuggle through the southern gate of Dalcratty than they are here. From the south we can deliver the wheat through the suburbs, house by house, person by person.'

Beetlebrow noticed the final urn being hauled out of the ground and placed on the back of the last wagon.

A second lamp was placed in a space between the myriad holes in the field. Beetlebrow saw Pook and Gregory's faces illuminated in its orange light.

'What're you two going to do now?' Gregory asked Pook. 'Go back to Stellingkorr?'

'No,' Beetlebrow said.

Pook glanced at her, and then faced Gregory.

'There's nothing for us back there,' Pook said.

'And it's all new for us here,' Beetlebrow added. 'The Empire started in this city. We can help make it end here too.'

She heard a rumbling noise several yards away to her right. Through the darkness she glimpsed dozens of oxen-drawn wagons, each laden with terracotta urns, heading across the fields towards Tirrendahl.

She faced Gregory again. 'If you're helping the city, like you say you are, we want to be part of it,' she said. 'And if you're not, then me and Pook'll find a way to help the city on our own.'

'We are helping the people, I promise you,' Gregory replied.

He glanced at the departing wagons for a moment, and then looked at Beetlebrow and Pook again. 'We do need your help right now, in fact,' he went on. 'The two of you, for something specific.'

'Yes?' Pook asked.

'I've heard you broke into the palace in Stellingkorr. Is that right?'

'That's right.'

'We tried to do the same here, and didn't succeed. The royals left the bodies of our comrades hanging from the walls, to try to shame us with our failure. We need you to break the palace in the north of Dalcratty and keep the police distracted, so we'll have some breathing room while our forces sabotage some key military sites across the city.'

'I bet me and Pook can find a way into the palace,' Beetlebrow said.

Gregory smiled. 'I bet you can too. All right, I'll tell you the details tomorrow.'

He picked up one of the oil-lamps from the ground and stepped away.

Beetlebrow and Pook remained standing by the fig in the light of the second lamp.

Beetlebrow watched Gregory walking towards the last remaining wagon, about five yards away from the fig tree, and clambering up the stack of urns on its back. She kept her staring gaze upon him as he raised his shovel above his head.

'It's going to take a lot more than destroying some military sites to get rid of the House of Rashem,' she whispered to Pook.

Gregory began addressing the dozens of black-clad men gathered below the wagon. Beetlebrow heard him talking about revolution, and the future.

'What do you mean?' Pook whispered to her.

'They're thinking too small,' Beetlebrow replied. 'They want us to get inside the palace and make some noise? We've got to move faster than that if we want the royals gone. King Hassan deserves to be killed, for all the evil and starvation he's caused. And if we can sneak into this palace, we'll have the best chance to get to him, and to do it ourselves.'

Gregory climbed down from the wagon. Beetlebrow heard a whip-crack as the oxen hauled the wagon in the direction of Tirrendahl.

'Whatever's going to happen in Dalcratty,' she said, keeping her focus on Gregory, 'it's not going to be with that lot leading the way. We can slip through places where men can't. And we can kill the king.'

She looked at Pook. Between the darkness of the trees and the earth, Beetlebrow saw her face illuminated by the orange light of the oil-lamp on the ground.

'Could we do something so difficult, something so... huge?' Pook asked. 'You and me?'

Beetlebrow gazed into her brown eyes. She saw Pook's wearied expression.

'You and me can do anything,' Beetlebrow said.

Pook's lips parted. Her wide smile broke through her tiredness. Beetlebrow saw her fear and excitement. The sight appeared to Beetlebrow as bright as the moon.

She heard the last wagon heading into the darkness, its wheels gouging furrows down into the muddy ground, and the black-clad men beginning to follow, their boots trudging across the soil.

Beetlebrow and Pook stepped out from underneath the empty branches of the fig tree and started walking west, towards the lights of the shore.

THE END